Rave Reviews
for Ela

HALF-MOON RA

"This novel is exciting. … immensely."

—*Harriet's Book Reviews*

TO MEET AGAIN

"Elaine Barbieri certainly knows how to capture the reader's attention. Utterly delightful characters, tender romance, and plenty of harrowing adventures make for a splendid western."

—*Romantic Times*

NIGHT RAVEN

"A fast-paced page-turner, *Night Raven* will keep you up all night until you get to the satisfying end."

—*Romantic Times*

HAWK

"Ms. Barbieri never disappoints and readers will treasure *Hawk* as another in a long line of memorable reads from a grande dame of the genre."

—*Romantic Times*

EAGLE

"The situation is explosive! Ms. Barbieri knows how to pull you through an emotional knothole. Her characters are terrific!"

—*The Belles & Beaux of Romance*

WISHES ON THE WIND

". . . skillful . . . vivifying . . . !"

—*Publishers Weekly*

WINGS OF A DOVE

". . . will bring out every hope and dream you could have . . . run to the nearest bookstore and find this five-star book!"

—*Bell, Book and Candle*

BATTLE OF THE SEXES

"*I* own the Rocky W, Cal." Pru's jaw was tight. "I want you to remember that."

"Do you want me to remember, too, that you didn't even know if you had a herd when I got here?"

Pru did not respond, but her expression remained the same. More angry than he knew he had a right to be, he snapped, "I can fire these fellas as easy as I hired them, if that's what you want."

"That isn't what I want."

"What do you want, then?"

The question hung on the air between them.

Cal eyed Pru's slender figure. He silently wondered if she had any idea what she wanted, because he was beginning to get a pretty clear idea of what *he* wanted.

"All right, you win."

There it was again—*you win*. He didn't want to win. He just wanted her.

Other books by Elaine Barbieri:

HALF-MOON RANCH: RENEGADE MOON
TO MEET AGAIN
THE WILD ONE (SECRET FIRES)
LOVE'S FIERY JEWEL
NIGHT RAVEN
AMBER TREASURE
HAWK
WISHES ON THE WIND
WINGS OF A DOVE
EAGLE
AMBER FIRE
TARNISHED ANGEL
CAPTIVE ECSTASY
DANCE OF THE FLAME

The *Dangerous Virtues* series:

HONESTY
PURITY
CHASTITY

Texas Star

Elaine Barbieri

LEISURE BOOKS  NEW YORK CITY

To my family,
the source of all of the joy and love in my heart.
You are the sunshine of my life.

A LEISURE BOOK®

January 2004

Published by

Dorchester Publishing Co., Inc.
200 Madison Avenue
New York, NY 10016

ISBN 0-8439-5179-6

The name "Leisure Books" and the stylized "L" with design are trademarks of Dorchester Publishing Co., Inc.

Printed in the United States of America.

Visit us on the web at www.dorchesterpub.com.

TEXAS STAR

Prologue

New Orleans, 1850

Jeanette Borneau's stylish afternoon gown contrasted sharply with the shabby New Orleans hotel room in which she stood, her face streaked with tears. She stared at the dashing Texan a few feet away, incredulity holding her motionless as Buck Star snapped his traveling bag shut, turned toward her and said, "You can't tell me you weren't expecting this to happen sooner or later, darlin'. We both knew it couldn't last forever."

"I don't know what you mean." Her flawless complexion pale, her voice a hoarse whisper, Jeanette forced herself to continue, "I love you. You said you loved me. I thought you meant those words."

"I did mean them . . . for a while."

Buck scanned her face with blue eyes that had glowed with passion while she had lain in his arms. She remembered the first time she saw him, when their glances met and she had known in an instant she would love him. She recalled the ecstasy of their lovemaking, a glory that had grown greater and more powerful with each touch. But there was neither passion nor emotion shining in his eyes as he continued with an offhand smile, "Listen, darlin', I'm not saying we didn't have a fine time together. Hell, no other woman ever pleased me more than you did."

"Are you afraid of my husband?" Jeanette took a shuddering breath. Her delicate features twitched as she hastened to reassure him, "Antoine's an old man. He's no match for you even if he should try to stop us."

"Stop us—from what?"

"That's what I came to tell you. I'm leaving Antoine and going back to Texas with you—so I can be your wife, so we can always be together."

"You're already married, remember?"

"I'll petition the church to have the marriage annulled!"

"You have an eight-year-old daughter."

"Celeste can stay behind with Antoine. She'll be better off with him anyway."

Surprised that the concession did not please him, Jeanette continued in a rush, "I never loved Antoine! I was sixteen and desperate; he was wealthy and he wanted me. I wouldn't have married him if there was any other way. I didn't love any of the other men I've been with in the time since, either. You're the only man I've *ever* loved—only you! We can be happy together. We *will* be happy together."

Buck frowned. "Look, the truth is, I had a visit from your husband this morning." At Jeanette's gasp, he added, "He's a nice old man, you know. He was real civil about everything. He's ready to forgive and forget just like he did all the other times you found a fella who caught your eye. His only condition is that I leave New Orleans right now and never look back."

"But—"

"He was real generous, too, paying for the new stock I'm having shipped in for the ranch, plus all my expenses here, with a little bit extra besides. The way things worked out, I'm going back to Texas practically a rich man."

Jeanette clutched a nearby chair for support. "But I love you."

"It's just your pride, darlin'. Your pride's hurting because I'm ending things before you're ready. You'll get over it."

"That isn't true!"

"You'll forget I ever existed when the next good-looking young fella comes your way. In the mean-time, your husband's home, waiting for you."

"I love *you*. I couldn't bear to lie in Antoine's arms or anyone else's but yours ever again!"

Buck swung his case off the bed and shrugged. "Whatever you say, but the stage is leaving for Texas in an hour. I'm going to be on it."

"Take me with you, Buck, please!" Throwing herself against him, Jeanette pleaded, "Let me show you how much I love you. Let me prove to you what a good wife I can be."

"Jeanette, honey . . ." Buck paused. His voice deepened. "The thing is, I've already got me a wife and family back in Texas, and I'm going home to them."

Stunned, Jeanette remained motionless as Buck pried her clutching fingers from his shirt. She was unable to speak when he then tipped his hat and said, "Thanks for everything, ma'am, but I'm saying goodbye."

Numb, she watched as he drew open the door and strode out of sight.

Celeste Borneau's petulant screams echoed through the opulent Charters Street mansion as she broke free of Madalane's restraining grip and scrambled down the hallway toward her mother's room. Screaming louder when her mother's devoted nanny grasped her arm again, she shouted, "Get away from me! Leave me alone or I'll tell my mama to fire you! She'll send you back to walk the streets of that island you came from, and she'll let you rot there!"

The handsome Negress squeezed Celeste's arm almost painfully tight as she said, "Your mama is upset. She does not wish to be disturbed."

"I don't care!"

Struggling free again, Celeste ran toward the doorway at the end of the hall and burst through, then halted at the sight of her mother lying on the bed, gasping for breath. Celeste paid no notice to Madalane when the silent nanny left her side to pick up the glass that had fallen from Jeanette's hand, sniffed it, then stood back with restrained emotion. Instead, annoyed that her mother did not greet her warmly, Celeste ran to the bed and was about to shout her demands when her mother grasped her hand in a painful grip.

". . . can't go on, Celeste." Jeanette stared up at her, struggling to breathe. "He destroyed me . . . left me with nothing."

Her eyes bulging with the effort to speak, Jeanette clutched Celeste's hand more tightly and gasped, "He *never* loved me . . . just made a fool of me. I hate him! You must make him pay, Celeste. You must promise me . . ."

Becoming frightened at her mother's gasping demand, Celeste attempted to withdraw her hand. She didn't want her mother to be sick now. She wanted her mother to take her to buy the new hat she had promised her. She wanted—

Her mother's biting grip cut into Celeste's thoughts as she demanded more harshly, "You must . . . promise me . . . someday to make him pay."

Nodding, Celeste snatched back her hand as a strange rattle sounded in her mother's throat.

Suddenly furious that her mother would dare disappoint her, Celeste shouted, "Get up! Get up now!"

She was screeching and stamping her feet at her mother's refusal to respond when Madalane dragged her away.

* * *

Her stubborn tantrum still raging an hour later, Celeste screamed at the locked door of her room. She didn't like being locked in. She would not stand for it! She would cry and howl until her father came for her as he always did. Her mother often ignored her for the pretty fellows who gathered around her. She broke her word without a thought when one of them whispered in her ear, but she wouldn't get away with it this time. Celeste would tell her father. He would be angry, and he would make her mother buy her a new hat, and more.

That thought inspiring her to wail anew, Celeste looked up at the sound of a key in the lock. Her cries died in her throat when Madalane entered, her expression grim.

"You must prepare yourself to accept difficult news, Celeste." The Negress took a stabilizing breath. "Your mother is no longer with us. She died by her own hand."

Momentarily motionless, Celeste then raised her chin. She didn't care. Her father would take care of her. He would buy her anything she wanted.

Madalane continued, "Your father was overwhelmed with grief when he learned of your mother's death. His heart was weak. It stopped beating." She paused again. "Monsieur Borneau is also dead."

With furious tears suddenly falling, Celeste shrieked, "No! You lie! Mama isn't gone. She's sleeping—and Papa would never leave me!"

Her tirade was halted by Madalane's stinging slap. Shocked into silence, Celeste listened as the devoted servant rasped, "Your tears are useless! You cry because you think you are alone, but you are not. I will care for you just as I cared for your mother—but I tell you now . . ."

Grasping Celeste's shoulders, Madalane leaned down to stare into her eyes as she hissed, "Your mother's faithless lover is responsible for her death. *He* is the one who stole her will to live. *He* is the one who killed your father. *He* is the man who took from you everything you had."

Madalane shook away the last of Celeste's tears with dark eyes burning. She grated, "Listen to me. Remember the pledge you made to your dying mother, for I now make this pledge to you:

"Together, we will honor the promise you made.

"Together, we will achieve her vengeance."

Chapter One

Wyoming, 1869

The snow had started falling slowly, with small flakes swathing the valley below in a hazy mist. Heavily laden clouds had obscured the peaks of the Bighorn Mountains in clear warning that the previous night's blizzard had merely been a preview of what would follow; yet with a stranded herd foremost in mind, Caldwell Star realized belatedly that he had misjudged the pace of the storm.

He was now paying the price.

Ducking his head against the biting wind blasting him with icy pellets of snow, Cal pulled his hat down lower on his forehead, hunched his shoulders against the powerful gusts, and pressed his struggling mount steadily forward. The trail to the upper pasture had been steep and rough, full of cutbacks and rocks, but despite the difficult terrain, he hadn't expected to find so many heifers stranded by the overnight storm. It had taken him longer than anticipated to move them to a point of safety. With daylight rapidly fading, he was beginning to wonder if he should have searched out a point of safety for himself, too.

Cal negotiated the last steep drop from the ridge, then sighed with relief, his breath emerging from his lips in a frozen puff as the outline of the Bluestone Ranch came into view. His mount secured in the barn a short time later, he pushed open the bunkhouse door to the raised brows of wranglers comfortably sprawled around a fireplace where a roaring fire blazed.

Stripping off his stiff clothing and brushing the ice from his beard, he prepared himself for an onslaught that wasn't long in coming.

"Hey, there, Cal, ain't you never going to be able to read the signs of a Wyoming winter?"

"What happened out there, Texas boy? The storm did all but shout how fast it was coming."

"Seems like you're getting fond of freezing up your vital parts."

Then the inevitable, "Wasn't it cold enough out there for you?"

Cal's stiff face creased into a reluctant half smile at their well-meaning gibes. He did not bother to reply. He had ridden hard and searched long for a place where the nightmares of his past wouldn't follow. In these mountains, as dissimilar to the natural terrain of Texas as he could possibly imagine, he had found a tentative peace unattainable to him elsewhere. A few pointed reminders about his lack of attention to a dangerous situation was a small price to pay.

Cal stripped down to his short clothes and pulled on dry clothing with a shiver that elicited a few chuckles. A mustached wrangler nodded toward the table behind him and said, "You almost missed that letter you got waiting for you over there. From the looks of the envelope, it did some fancy traveling before it found you, too."

Cal's half smile faded. Hesitating briefly, he picked up the envelope and ripped it open. He read the simple printed message it contained:

Have you forgotten Bonnie?
It's time to go home.

The unsigned note left him shaken.

He heard Bonnie's sweet laughter—saw her smiling face.

Haunting images he had hoped were buried forever flashed vividly across his mind.

Suddenly furious, Cal crushed the letter in his fist and strode toward the fireplace. He halted beside it and stared for long moments into the hungry flames licking steadily upward.

Slowly, with great deliberation, he tossed the letter into the blaze.

Chapter Two

Lowell, Texas, 1869

Cal's expression was emotionless as he urged his mount past a heavy growth of twisted mesquite, spiny yucca, and prickly pear cactus. He observed the diverse landscape with marked ambivalence. The hill-country terrain was one of contrasts, where harsh granite outcrops were spotted with tall, lush grasses, where fine oaks stood proudly in sun-drenched pastures, and where heavily laden pecan trees grew along meandering riverbeds.

Home—where the heart is.

The thought jolted him.

Cal lifted his hat from his head and ran a large, callused hand through his unruly, sun-streaked hair. His sharply chiseled features determined, his newly clean-shaven jaw firm, and his broad shoulders erect, he refused to fall into the trap of reminiscence. Instead, he scanned the passing terrain with a hard-won maturity reflected not only in his imposing, muscular stature, but also in his rock-hard demeanor. He regarded the world with a keen, honey-colored gaze, observing much while commenting little.

The morning sun climbed toward its apex as a turn in the road brought the outline of Lowell into view, and Cal's gaze hardened. Minutes later he wound his way through the early-morning traffic of supply wagons, shoppers, occasional horsemen, and a stagecoach loading passengers on the main street, alert to the changes the years had wrought.

The changes were few. Main Street was still the only commercial street in town. False-fronted buildings housed the necessary businesses: the general store, bank, hotel, restaurant, barbershop, livery stable, telegraph and stagecoach offices. Most prominent of all and sporting the most obvious change in appearance was the newly enlarged and elaborately painted Last Chance Saloon and Dancehall—a fancy name for the establishment that he was certain still guaranteed Sheriff Carter's one-room jail its weekly quota of customers. He saw that Miss Ida's fancy house was still located around the corner from the saloon from which it drew most of its customers, and that the residential district a respectable distance from the commercial section of town now sported a few more modest homes.

Spotting a familiar storefront, Cal turned his horse toward the hitching post. He was unable to suppress a fleeting smile as he dismounted and glanced at the fading script on the window.

Squeaky door hinges announced his arrival in the office without need of a bell. He heard the bustle of movement from the rear room a few seconds before a buxom, middle-aged woman, her gray hair confined in a tight bun, pushed her way through the curtained doorway. Stopping short, she exclaimed, "Bless my soul—can that be you, Caldwell Star?"

Grinning, Cal grunted aloud as he was swept into a spontaneous hug and squeezed enthusiastically against Doc Maggie's ample proportions. He felt a momentary thickening in his throat that was dispelled the moment she stood back and said, "Hell's bells, you've been away too long—and damned if you didn't grow up to be a handsome fella! I bet you drive all the ladies crazy."

"I'm thinking you're a bit prejudiced, Doc, seeing you brought me into this world."

"That I did, and I'm proud of it, too." Without waiting for a response, Doc Maggie continued, "When did you get home, boy? We've all missed you around here."

"I just rode into town and you're the first person I stopped to see."

"The first?" Doc's broad smile faltered. "Then you haven't been out to the Texas Star yet?"

Cal's smile also dimmed. "No."

The full power of Doc's smile returned. "I'm mighty flattered. Sit down, boy, so we can get reacquainted." She paused to add with characteristic candor, "I'm glad you came back. I'm thinking your pa could use a bit of family on that ranch right now."

As candid as she, he responded, "I'm thinking he didn't feel that way when I left—him or Taylor."

"Your brother's gone from the Texas Star, too, you know."

Cal frowned.

"Your pa was fixing to get married again, and Taylor told him right out he didn't like the idea, being your ma was only dead a few months. Of course, that didn't make no difference to Buck. He wouldn't listen to anybody, much less his fifteen-year-old son. All I can figure is that Taylor started getting under his skin afterwards, because it wasn't any time at all after the wedding before your pa sent him off packing to some military school back East."

Cal paused to calculate, then said, "That had to be at least eight years ago."

"Nine. Taylor graduated from the school—he sent me a letter when he did—but he never came back home. He just went off on his own, and he's been making his own way ever since."

Cal nodded, his stomach tight.

"Taylor wrote to me a couple of times afterwards." Doc Maggie shrugged. "He didn't say much, except that he was doing fine. To tell you the truth, I expected that boy would do well wherever he was. He always was a real bright young fella."

Cal nodded again.

"I don't think he kept in contact with your pa,

though." Doc Maggie searched Cal's gaze. "You neither, I expect."

Cal's silence confirmed her speculation.

"I was wishing I could tell Taylor something about you when I wrote back to him at that post office box, but there was nothing to tell. Nobody seemed to know where you were."

Cal's brief smile had a bitter edge. "After Bonnie, I didn't think anybody much cared."

"Cal . . ." Remembered pain flashed across her face before Doc Maggie changed the subject abruptly and asked, "Tell me what you've been doing with yourself besides growing big and handsome."

"Doc—"

"No wife? No little Cal running around somewhere?"

"No."

"I'll have to see what I can do about that."

Intensely sober, Cal replied, "That isn't why I came home."

Suddenly as sober as he, Doc Maggie replied, "Why did you come home then, Cal?"

Cal searched the dear woman's face. Her apple cheeks were bright and rosy and her gaze direct as he responded, "I received a letter . . ."

Doc Maggie's gaze didn't flicker.

"It mentioned Bonnie."

"Bonnie?" Her eyes spontaneously filled. "What did it say?"

Cal did not have a chance to reply before the door

burst open and a frantic young fellow burst in to gasp, "It's Jenny, Doc. The baby's coming and it's coming fast. You'd better hurry!"

Frustration registering in her expression, Doc Maggie turned to Cal with regret. "This is Ethan McCall, Jenny Ritter's husband. You remember Jenny, the shy little girl with all the freckles. She never did have very good timing." She shook her head. "I have to go, but I want to finish this conversation. There are some things you need to know."

At Cal's questioning glance, she replied, "You'll understand soon enough after you get home."

"Hurry up, Doc!"

"All right." Turning back toward Cal as she grabbed her bag, Doc Maggie directed, "Come back so we can talk, you hear?"

Cal stared after the departing doctor as she disappeared through the doorway.

. . . *some things you need to know* . . .

A familiar frustration tightened his gut as he stepped back out onto the street. What he needed right now was a drink, and he was going to get one.

"Hey, ain't you Caldwell Star?"

Cal was seated at a corner table in the poorly lit saloon, a bottle in front of him and his glass refilled for the second time. He looked up at the bearded fellow swaying unsteadily beside him. Eyes narrowed, he attempted to identify him.

"It's me, Roddy Boyd! I worked for your pa for a while when you was a kid—remember?"

Roddy Boyd. How could he forget? His pa had kicked the cowboy off the ranch for stealing.

"You sure growed up some." Roddy shook his head with a laugh. "You was so puny, I figured you'd never be more than a runt."

Cal did not smile. "I was twelve years old."

"Yeah, and you wasn't much older than that when your pa run you off like he run me off."

Beginning to bristle, Cal replied, "I'm not interested in rehashing old times."

"You ain't, huh?" Roddy's face reddened. He snapped, "Well, I guess I wouldn't be either if I had to look back on the things you're remembering."

Cal struggled to hold his temper. The fellow was drunk. He was also a thieving scum who wasn't worth dirtying his hands on—but that didn't make him feel any less like making him eat his words.

Roddy glanced up when a swaggering wrangler pushed his way through the swinging doors. Roddy sneered at Cal, "See that fella over there? Now, *he's* somebody worth talking to."

Roddy staggered back to the bar as Cal watched, his jaw tight.

Memories returned full bore:

At twelve years of age, Cal had considered his father whipcord tough and all a man could ever want to be. At the age of thirteen, however, he discovered his idol had feet of clay.

He remembered his shock the first time he was approached by one of Buck's women on Lowell's main street. It wasn't the last. With the wisdom of youth, he had consoled himself, however, that his mother, Emma Star—the woman he eventually came to realize Buck loved as much as he was able—never suspected Buck's infidelities.

He was still uncertain if Taylor, three years younger than he, had been similarly approached. He suspected he had, but Bonnie had been eleven years his junior—only a baby—too young to become aware of their father's failings. He had been determined to protect the innocence that had shone in Bonnie's sparkling gaze by keeping the truth about their father from her as long as he was able.

In retrospect, Cal realized he had believed his father's infidelities were the greatest threat to their family—until the unexpected death of his mother when she was thirty-six.

Surprisingly, Buck had been as devastated as his children by Emma's death, but his manner of grieving differed greatly. Spending most of his time drinking in town during the weeks that followed, Buck surrendered seven-year-old Bonnie totally to Cal's care. It was to Cal's endless regret that he had not been up to the task.

Only a month after the funeral, Cal had discovered Bonnie crying in the corner of her room. Not able to bear her tears, Cal left a protesting Taylor at home to finish his chores while he took Bonnie into town to buy her favorite peppermint sticks at Mr. Bower's store. He remembered she was smiling when they emerged with the candy—but then he saw Buck staggering toward them, laughing uproariously with his arm around one of the women from Miss Ida's fancy house.

Cal panicked. Sending Bonnie off to visit her friend at the other end of town so she wouldn't see Buck, he had then faced his father down.

His memory grew blurred at that point. He could not quite remember exactly when Millie Ackerman came running down the street, calling for help—or exactly when his father and he reached the well into which Bonnie had fallen. All he could clearly recall was that his father blamed him for Bonnie's death; that Taylor, as distraught as he, also blamed him for the accident; and that, worst of all, he blamed himself.

Overwhelmed by guilt and grief, Cal was unable to face Bonnie's funeral. He rode off in the dark hours before dawn without saying goodbye, determined never to return.

That resolution was reaffirmed a year later when he met a former Texas Star wrangler on the trail and learned that barely six months after his mother's death, his father had married a widow young enough to be his daughter.

Cal had forcibly ejected thoughts of the Texas Star ranch from his mind in the time since, yet the mysterious, unsigned note received on that wintry Wyoming evening had revived painful memories he was unable to ignore. He was uncertain when he'd finally accepted the reality that his long years of absence from home had merely been a period of marking time until the day when he would return to face the past—and Bonnie's grave.

Yet other questions now nagged relentlessly at his peace of mind.

Who had sent him the letter?

And why?

Cal's wandering thoughts were interrupted by a burst of laughter from the bar. He looked up as the swaggering wrangler who had entered a few minutes earlier continued loudly, "That fool woman don't know a damned thing about ranching! She inherited that place from an old geezer who ran it into the ground before he kicked the bucket. I don't know what she was thinking when she came out here—her being a skinny, dyed-in-the-wool widow from back East who don't have a man and figures she don't need one. She was green as grass and ripe for the picking when she hired me, and I'm only too happy to give her what she has coming."

The fellow continued, "And the next thing I'm going to do is teach that little brat she dotes on how to respect his elders."

Unable to think with the commotion the wrangler and his drunken cronies were stirring, Cal tossed down his drink and was about to stand when he was stopped in his tracks by a startling female apparition in black that swept furiously through the saloon's swinging doors. The woman, tall and thin—a widow from the top of her heavily veiled hat to the tips of her high-buttoned shoes—was obviously ready for battle as she boldly approached the loud-mouthed wrangler. Butting up to him as close as the broad brim of her hat allowed, she glared through the black veiling for a silent moment, then snapped, *"You're fired!"*

The brief silence that followed was broken by a chorus of laughter that accompanied the widow back out through the swinging doors—but Cal wasn't laughing. He wasn't even amused.

Shooting a contemptuous glance toward the bar as he passed, Cal emerged out on the street and turned toward the hitching post where his mount was tied. He had taken only a few steps when he felt a sharp sting strike his backside. He took a few more steps and felt another stinging strike on his back. He halted and frowned down at the pebbles that had struck him, then scanned the street. He concluded that they had been kicked up by a passing wagon and was about to continue on his way, when with a sharp, popping sound, his hat was knocked forward over his eyes.

Setting his hat back squarely on his brow, Cal scrutinized the street with a scowl. His gaze halted on a little boy partially concealed behind a barrel outside the general store across the street—a boy no more than five years old, who was holding a slingshot still aimed in his direction.

Cal gritted his teeth and started toward the boy. He had taken no more than a few steps when the widow he had seen in the saloon emerged from the store, swept the boy up into the wagon with her, and snapped the horse into motion. His anger surged up a notch when the boy glanced smugly back at him as they departed, then tucked his head against his mother's shoulder as they drove out of sight.

The brat who didn't respect his elders . . .

Turning back toward his horse, Cal could not suppress the lingering thought that perhaps the saloon blowhard had a valid point after all.

Barely in control of her anger and anxious to leave Lowell far behind her, Prudence Reynolds slapped the wagon reins against her horse's back. The fluttering of her heavily veiled hat annoyed her as the wagon began moving more rapidly along the rutted trail and she pulled it off, then tossed it atop the packages behind her with a grunt of satisfaction.

The rush of air that bathed her dark, tightly bound hair somehow lessened her soaring frustration as she glanced down at her son seated beside her. His brown eyes were wide with excitement and his smooth cheeks flushed as he urged unexpectedly, "Make the wagon go faster, Mama!"

Pru flicked the reins and spurred the horse to a gallop with a sudden impulse to please him. Jeremy's delighted shout, "Yahoo!" was still echoing in her ears when the joy of the moment was halted by an unexpected bump in the road that almost jarred them from their seats.

Pru pulled back hard on the reins, regretting her lapse of judgment. They were traveling at a more reasonable speed when Jeremy complained, "We're going too slow."

"Better safe than sorry, Jeremy." Pru inwardly winced at the bromide she had uttered. Not only did she now look the perfect widow—an appearance she had never anticipated at the age of twenty-three—but she was beginning to *think* like one.

She paused to amend, "The road's too rough here. If it smooths out a little, I'll turn Blackie loose again and let him run."

Jeremy's responsive smile soothed her anxiety as Pru turned her attention back to the road while attempting to contain the anger that still singed her.

Damn that Jack Grate! How she had ever hired that obnoxious brute to work on her ranch was a mystery to her!

Pru corrected that thought. No, there was no mystery about it. He had been *recommended.*

Pru took a stabilizing breath. It had been difficult for Bruce and her when they discovered shortly after they were married that he was desperately ill. It had been heartbreaking to hear the doctor say, only a few days after her son was born, that her husband's time was limited. It had been devastating to learn, after her husband finally passed, that due to a stipulation in his father's will, the proceeds of his estate—all she had to live on—reverted back under the control of a supposedly trustworthy solicitor. It had been demoralizing to have been forced to appeal to that niggardly, condescending member of the bar for every cent she needed. It had been humiliating conforming to a stipulation in her conservative father-in-law's will stating that "family widows must wear suitable widow's garb for a period of no less than five years in order to benefit from family funds." Yet she had been totally unprepared when she was called to the solicitor's office and informed that the entire proceeds of the Reynolds estate had been "lost" in a bad investment, that not only were Jeremy and she penniless, but they must vacate their home within thirty days.

Her panic had been temporarily incapacitating.

With no other recourse available to her, she had decided to use her limited funds to travel to the Texas ranch she had inherited from a distant uncle. The expense had not even left her enough money to replace her widow's weeds for more suitable clothing.

She had been desperate when she finally arrived in Lowell a few months earlier and viewed her inheritance for the first time. The Rocky W's horrendous state of disrepair had left her at a total loss—which had led her to the mistake of appealing to Lowell's only lawyer, William Leeds, for advice.

Leeds's advice: She should hire a ranch hand to help her straighten things out. The fellow he recommended was Jack Grate.

It did not take her long to ascertain that Grate was lazy, slovenly, and discourteous. She had learned only moments earlier, however, that Grate was a thief as well, that he had run up charges on her accounts for items never used at the ranch—charges in amounts she would not be able to pay in a dozen years!

"Are you all right, Mama?"

Pru glanced down at her son's concerned expression. Jeremy was too young for the confusing role of man-of-the-house in which he saw himself. She owed it to him to lighten that burden. She was trying, yet seeming to settle more deeply into failure with each passing day.

Jeremy was waiting for her reply. Determined to see his smile return, Pru replied with a positive attitude she did not feel, "I'm fine—especially now that we won't be seeing Mr. Grate around our place anymore."

"I never liked him, Mama." Jeremy's gaze was too wise for his limited years. "He always looked like he was laughing at us, and he made me mad."

"He won't be laughing at us anymore, dear."

Appearing unconvinced by her optimistic facade, Jeremy responded encouragingly, "You don't have to worry, either. I'll take over his chores and we'll be fine, just the two of us."

"Yes, just the two of us."

Her throat suddenly tight, Pru directed her attention back to the road ahead. A ranch house that was no more than a shack, a barn that was a tumbling-down wreck, ranch stock depleted by rustlers and just plain neglect. Yes, they'd be all right with just the two of them.

Cal glanced up at the sun as it made a slow arc toward the horizon. Mid-afternoon, and the Texas Star ranch house would soon come into view. He had been traveling on Texas Star soil for the past hour, a terrain with which he was painfully familiar.

He had ridden past the sign marking the northern boundary of the ranch, remembering the day he had accompanied his pa to that spot to nail the marker into place. He had followed the curving bend of the stream where ranch stock watered easily in the spring. He had glanced at the pecan trees, remembering carefree jaunts as a child to gather the fallen fruit under his mother's watchful eye. He had glimpsed an abandoned holding corral, recalling the time Taylor and he had first worked alone to gather calves for branding.

His reminiscences had turned into gradual disbelief, however, as he had ridden deeper into Texas Star property and viewed its startling deterioration. Run-down fencing, damaged windmills, fouled water holes—and most alarming of all, the neglected appearance of surprisingly small, scattered herds.

The Texas Star ranch house came into view, and Cal's stomach twisted tighter. The house that had been his mother's pride and joy was badly in need of paint. The porch where she had spent countless twilight hours when the day's work was done now sagged badly, the screened door hung on lopsided hinges, and the small garden she had carefully tended lay barren and dry. The outbuildings, barn, and corrals were similarly neglected, contributing to a further appearance of decline.

Yet Cal was unprepared for the greatest shock of all when he reined up beside the front porch and

Buck Star stepped into view. He did not immediately respond when his father welcomed him by saying coldly, "Well, what do you know . . . my oldest son has returned." Buck continued with a sarcastic twist of his lips, "You are Caldwell Star, aren't you? I can't rightly say I'm sure, it's been so long since I saw you last."

Cal stared at his father. Buck's voice was the same, deep and strong with familiar mockery, but that was where the resemblance to the robust man he remembered ended. Hair that had once been thick and dark was startlingly thin and gray. Harsh lines, gaunt hollows, and dark circles marked his formerly handsome features, and his clothes hung limply on his emaciated frame. Yet the pale blue eyes assessing him had not changed. They were still sharp and accusing.

"What's the matter, Cal? Cat got your tongue?" Buck waited for a reply that did not come, then asked flatly, "What brought you back after all this time? If you're in trouble, I can't help you, and if you need money . . . well, I guess you can see there's none to be had."

Regaining his composure, Cal dismounted and asked abruptly, "What happened here, Pa?"

"What happened here?" The angry lines in Buck's face tightened. "Do you think you have a right to ask that question?"

"Ma would never have let the ranch get—"

"Your ma's dead."

Irate heat flushed his face at his father's response,

and Cal grated, "Yeah, I know. And it looks like her memory died with her."

"Is that what you came back for, to lecture me about your ma? Well, that's not going to work." Buck's bony hands tightened into fists. "Just remember, you're the one who left the Texas Star and your ma's memory behind when you took off."

"I never forgot Ma."

"Or Bonnie . . . I suppose you never forgot Bonnie, neither." Buck sneered. "Hell, as far as you're concerned, your mother and sister might just as well never have existed."

"That's what you want to believe."

"Is it?" His chest beginning to heave with agitation, Buck spat, "What else did you expect me to say? Did you expect me to welcome you with open arms?" He gave a harsh laugh. "If you did, you were wrong. You ran off like a coward in the night! My son . . . *a coward*."

Cal chose to remain silent, refusing to respond with the names his father deserved to be called.

"Got nothing to say for yourself, even after all these years? Well, I've got plenty to say, things I've been waiting a long time to get off my chest." Appearing to swell with expanding ire, Buck grated, "I haven't forgotten how your sister died. I never will. You let me down! Your ma always said you were the dependable one. I thought I could trust Bonnie in your care."

"That's all water under the bridge."

"Your ma was wrong, wasn't she?"

"I said—"

"You got Bonnie killed, then you ran off, proving just how wrong your ma could be . . . and just how wrong a man could be about his own son."

"Oh, is that right, Pa? What about how wrong a fella could be about his own father—seeing him with his arm around one of the town whores before his wife was cold in her grave."

"Don't try to switch the blame onto me! You're the one who was supposed to be watching your sister. You were eighteen years old—old enough to know that my sweet little girl might not realize the danger when she was trying to get that bucket out of the well."

"Pa—"

"It's your fault Bonnie's dead, whether you want to admit it or not!" Buck took a shuddering breath. "And I've been wanting to tell you that for nine years."

Taking long moments to recuperate from his father's searing words, Cal replied, "Is that why you sent me the letter?"

"What letter?"

Cal studied his father's expression more closely as he replied, "The letter about Bonnie."

"Don't flatter yourself!" Buck was beginning to shake. "I never picked up a pen to write your name—not once in all the years you were gone. As far as I was concerned, if you didn't want no part of the Texas Star, the Texas Star didn't want no part of you."

"All right. You said what you wanted to say, so I guess I know now where we stand."

"If you'd have stayed around instead of running off, you would've known a long time ago where *I* stood."

Cal turned toward his horse and mounted.

"So you're running off again, just like the last time."

Turning back toward his father, Cal responded, "No, I'm not running off—not like last time."

"Meaning?"

"Meaning I've got things to do, and you can depend on it—I'll be back."

"Yeah, I'll depend on it. Cal, the *dependable* one."

His jaw locking tight at his father's final, cutting gibe, Cal spurred his mount into motion.

Buck took a shaky breath, uncertain of his reaction to the sight of Cal's departing figure. He had been waiting for this day. It had been a long time in coming—and it had left him somehow winded.

Buck frowned as Cal disappeared from sight. Strange . . . he had somehow forgotten how much Cal looked like his mother with those tawny eyes and that hair streaked with color from the sun. Cal hadn't smiled during their exchange—there had been no reason for it—but he remembered that Cal had his mother's smile, too. It was Emma's smile that had first drawn him to her, the way it lit up her face and made him feel all good inside.

Suddenly aware that he was trembling, Buck slid his palm down over his eyes. It wouldn't do no good to think about Emma. She—

The sound of a step behind him turned Buck toward the woman who pushed open the porch door and walked to his side. Looking up at him with eyes as blue as the summer sky, she whispered, "Buck, I'm so sorry it went badly with Cal."

Buck looked at his lovely young wife. Unlike him, who seemed to be aging years with every passing day, she was even more beautiful than the first day he saw her.

She slid her arm through his and whispered in a voice that was soft and gentle, "Don't get yourself upset over him. Just as you said, he ran away before, and he's run off again. He's not worth fretting over. Forget him."

"He said he'd be back."

"Do you believe him?"

"I don't know." Buck shook his head. "I never knew Cal to say anything he didn't mean."

"Yes . . . he's the *dependable* one."

Buck did not respond.

"Forget him, darling. Put him out of your mind. We don't need him. We're doing just fine without him."

"Yes, but—"

"It's getting late—time for supper. Let's go inside."

Buck nodded. He didn't want to argue with her. Hell, she was young and lovely—and she loved him in spite of everything. How did he ever get so lucky?

That question lingering in his mind, Buck walked back into the house with his wife, the beautiful Celeste Borneau Star.

Chapter Three

The Texas Star ranch house had disappeared from sight, but Cal's angry exchange with his father was still fresh in his mind. It had been nine years since he'd been faced with outspoken blame for Bonnie's death, yet the pain was as fresh as it had been that first day. He remembered the ragged fear he'd known when Millie Ackerman came running up, crying out Bonnie's name; his incredulity when he saw her small body lying at the bottom of the well; then his devastating, mind-numbing despair when he realized he was too late to save her.

Cal breathed deeply against his acute sense of loss. The time had now come for the task he dreaded.

Drawing back on his mount's reins when he reached a familiar, sunny knoll, Cal dismounted and approached the small, fenced-in graveyard where his mother had been laid to rest. He stopped, motionless with incredulity, when he saw the two gravestones standing side by side. The small plots were overgrown, so neglected that the names chiseled on the stones were obscured by weeds and vines.

Somehow, as many times as he had envisioned this moment, he hadn't expected to find Bonnie's and his mother's graves lying forgotten and untended—dismissed from memory as if those two loving people had never existed.

Cal crouched down and yanked furiously at the weeds. Breathless minutes later, he stood back to look at the neatly cleared graves and attempted to draw his emotions under control. He was mature now and far wiser than that boy of eighteen had been; he had known the past contained hard truths that would be difficult to confront. He admitted them to himself. He had failed his mother when he failed Bonnie; he had dishonored them both by running away; there was no place he could run or hide where those failures would not haunt him. He also knew that the unsigned letter he had received on that snowy Wyoming evening had merely been the catalyst which forced him to admit he could never go forward until he went back.

His gaze fixed on the lonely graves as bittersweet memories ran rampant across his mind; Cal raised his chin with determination. He wouldn't fail them again. He was home now. He'd stay until the Texas Star was back on its feet, until it was again the ranch his mother had been so proud of . . . until he was certain that the land where these two loving people took their final rest would always belong to their family.

Cal looked up at a Texas sky streaked with the pink and gold of the setting sun. It was getting late. It was time to return to Lowell to ask some questions that needed answers—but he'd be back.

Cal smiled at the two sturdy stones, remembering the ready smiles of the two buried there. His throat tight, he tipped his hat in loving respect.

Yes, he'd be back. That was a promise.

The pained bawling from the barn grew louder. Pru knew she had to do something.

"Mama, Lulu's crying. She needs to be milked."

"I know, dear." Pru gave a stiff smile in reaction to Jeremy's concern. She knew only too well that Lulu's sacks were full and needed to be emptied. She had put the chore off as long as she could.

"It's not hard to do, Mama. I watched Jack do it a few times. You just have to pull and the milk comes out."

"Yes, dear, of course."

Pru picked up the pail by the kitchen door and walked out into the yard with Jeremy at her heels. Milking the cow was a simple chore, and the first of many she would be faced with in Jack Grate's absence—the first of many she was sorely ignorant about.

Aware that Jeremy was close behind her, Pru held her head high. She hadn't wanted to buy a milk cow. She hadn't thought it was necessary when she already owned so many cows roaming around somewhere on Rocky W land. She had held out until the previous week when Jack had finally convinced her. Lulu was a prize milker, he'd said, who would eliminate any concerns they would ever have about getting fresh milk; Lulu was being offered to them at a bargain price, and a ranch was really no ranch at all, he'd added, unless there was a good milk cow in the barn. As ignorant as she was about ranch affairs, she had never considered that Jack might've had an ulterior motive in mind—that he might have had a scheme to make money on the deal. Instead, she had finally relented, telling herself that although she couldn't afford it, she'd just add the expense to the tab all the ranchers seemed to run up with the bank until they managed to sell off some stock. She hadn't realized at that time how high her tabs around town already were.

They'd had the cow no more than a week—a cow she didn't know how to milk. She also had a horse she didn't know how to care for, chickens scrabbling at her back door for the feed she'd forgotten to spread, a rooster that attacked her heels every time she walked across the yard, and last but not least, a scrawny herd somewhere on her property that was supposed to be the Rocky W's lifeline, a herd that seemed to grow smaller with every passing day.

Oh, yes, Jeremy and she would be fine with just the two of them.

Pru entered the barn, then stopped in her tracks

when Lulu turned toward her with a wary eye.

"You have to put the stool by her back legs, Mama—but be careful. She kicks."

Great.

Pru situated the stool and sat down.

"Now you have to pull on her . . . you know, on those things hanging down there. The milk will come right out."

Pru reached tentatively for the engorged teats. She gritted her teeth and pulled.

Nothing.

She tried again.

The same result.

"I don't think you're doing it right, Mama."

Really.

She pulled again, then gasped as the pail disappeared with a loud moo and a swift kick from the angry cow.

Jeremy's smile was weak. "I told you she kicks."

"Maybe you should try milking her, Jeremy." Pru strained for a smile as Jeremy retrieved the pail. "Lulu doesn't seem to like me, and you get along with her just fine."

"I can't, Mama." Jeremy's expression was acutely sober. "Jack said I wouldn't have the touch. He said all females, including Lulu, like fellas with big hands, especially if they know how to use them."

Pru bristled. If she ever saw that Jack Grate again . . .

"Mama?"

Smiling as Jeremy replaced the pail, Pru responded, "Well, whether Lulu likes my touch or not, I'm sure she'll be grateful to be relieved of her milk. I'll manage," she mumbled, ". . . small hands and all."

Gasping when the pail flew out from underneath the agitated animal again, Pru felt perspiration rising on her brow. How hard could it be to milk a cow?

She gritted her teeth, the answer to that question eluding her.

The trail had rapidly darkened after Cal left Texas Star land. His stomach growled loudly, reminding him that the supper hour had passed. It would be dark before he reached Lowell, and a suddenly overcast sky would not make traveling easy.

Cal reviewed the recent few hours with a frown. What had he been expecting when he saw his father again? Had he thought his father would welcome him into the house and ask him to stay for supper as if the past nine years had never transpired?

He should have known that would never happen.

What he hadn't expected, however, was the immediate, spontaneous resumption of the same hostilities that had driven him away. Nor had he expected the startling changes in his father and in the Texas Star.

In retrospect, he realized that the ranch's deterioration was evident in more ways than had been apparent on first sight. The lack of activity in the ranch yard was noteworthy . . . and more than a little strange. There had been no hired hands or horses in sight anywhere. As a matter of fact, Buck had appeared to be the only person on the premises.

He wondered where his father's young wife was. If she had been in the house, why hadn't she come out to see who her husband was talking to?

A loud bawling interrupted his thoughts, and Cal frowned. The sound had grown continually louder as he neared the Rocky W until it was now an unmistakable wail. A cow that needed milking made a sound all its own; no self-respecting rancher would ignore it. He wondered if there was something wrong with Old Man Simmons—if the aging rancher had finally gone completely deaf or feeble. Simmons was a crazy old coot who had never married, but he'd always been kind to the Star boys. He remembered Simmons had given Taylor a puppy when his dog had a litter. Taylor was eight years old then, and he had been thrilled. Ma showed her appreciation by sending Simmons one of her pecan pies. Cal recalled delivering the pie to the old man and feeling that the fellow had been more touched by Ma's thoughtfulness than he wanted to admit.

The bawling grew louder, and Cal's frown darkened. Old Man Simmons must be pretty old by now. He wondered how the old fella was handling things, if he was still able to get around easily. It wasn't like him to ignore—

The sound of a gunshot startled Cal from his thoughts. It had come from the direction of the Rocky W ranch house.

Turning his mount without a second's hesitation, Cal raced toward it.

"You missed him, Mama!"

Pru picked herself up from the ground and dusted off her backside, then reached for the heavy shotgun beside her as another loud bawl came from the barn. She had almost welcomed the sight of the chicken hawk that Jeremy had spotted—a diversion that had allowed her to put aside for a moment her pitiful failure to get even a drop of milk out of Lulu. But the truth was, that same chicken hawk had already gotten some of her best hens, and the way things were going on the ranch, she was going to need every hen she had left.

She had grabbed the loaded shotgun Jack kept in the barn and had run outside. Her lack of experience with firearms had not fazed her. After all, she had reasoned, how hard could it be to point a gun at something and shoot it? But nobody had ever told her that a shotgun had a kick that might knock her flat on her backside if she wasn't expecting it, or that she'd need an eye like an eagle to hit that hawk as it swooped past.

She had missed the hawk, but she had scared it off, all right.

Proud of even that meager success, she turned toward the barn, but the thundering of approaching hooves stopped her in her tracks. She looked back just as a horseman burst into the yard and drew his mount to a sliding halt.

Pru grabbed Jeremy's arm and pushed him behind her. The rider steadied his snorting horse as he looked at her, then glanced toward the barn, where Lulu continued bawling.

Pru's throat went dry. The fellow appeared to tower over her with shoulders that seemed incredibly broad, muscular arms that held his mount in strict control, and long legs that hugged his horse's sides with obvious power. His features were strong and sharply cut, and the brim of his hat was pulled down low on his forehead over penetrating gold eyes that seemed to stare right through her.

A quiver rolled down her spine.

Determined not to be intimidated, Pru raised her gun toward him.

Damned if it wasn't *the widow*, again!

Cal stared down at the woman as she pointed her shotgun in his direction. Up closer, she was tall and skinny, all right, just like the saloon loudmouth had said. At least she looked that way in the baggy black dress she was wearing. She didn't look so bad without that black hat, though. Her face was small featured and pleasant enough—at least he supposed it would be pleasant if she wasn't frowning—but her finger was on the trigger of a gun, and he'd seen her in action in the saloon. She had a temper that made her toss caution to the wind. He wasn't about to be her temper's next victim.

"You're making a mistake pointing that gun at me, ma'am." The bellowing from the barn sounded again as Cal continued, "I heard that cow bawling while I was traveling past and I figured something had to be wrong with Old Man Simmons if he wasn't taking care of it. Then I heard a shot."

"I fired at a hawk." She added, "Mr. Simmons died a while back. I own the ranch now."

"Oh." He nodded. "I knew it wasn't like the old fella to leave an animal in so much misery."

"I beg your pardon!" The widow's eyes went wide with affront—startling clear gray eyes that contrasted vividly with the midnight color of her hair. "Are you implying—"

"Ma'am, I'm only saying that cow needs milking."

"I know he needs milking!"

"She."

"She what?"

"*She* needs milking."

The widow's face flushed. "I resent your implication that I'm insensitive to that animal's distress."

"I didn't say that. I figure you're just careless."

"For your information, I tried to milk her." The widow raised her chin. "She won't cooperate."

. . . green as grass . . .

"She won't give up any milk."

. . . who don't have a man and figures she don't need one . . .

"She tried to kick me."

If he had any sense, he'd ride out of the yard and not look back. Instead, Cal repeated, "Ma'am, that animal needs to be milked."

The widow opened her mouth to respond, only

to be forestalled by the boy who stepped out from behind her and shouted at him, "We don't need any advice from you!"

"Jeremy!"

"I don't like him, Mama. Tell him to leave."

"I'll handle this, Jeremy."

The slingshot kid. Cal flicked a stern glance at the boy, then said, "That'll be fine with me, ma'am. If you'll just lower that shotgun, I'll be glad to leave. It appears I made a mistake turning this way after all."

The widow lowered her gun cautiously. "You're free to leave any time you want, of course."

The cow bawled more piteously than before, forcing Cal to add, "A word of warning before I go: if that cow hardens up on you and gets a fever, she'll be a mighty sick animal."

"My mama doesn't need you to tell her anything! She'll milk that cow just fine when she gets the knack of it."

When she gets the knack of it.

Cal inwardly groaned.

The cow was still bawling.

Against his better judgment, he dismounted.

The widow's gun snapped back up. "What are you doing?"

"I'm going to milk that cow."

"I told you, my mama doesn't need—"

"Jeremy . . ."

Cal started toward the barn. The widow followed, protesting, "This is unnecessary. I have a hired man who'll milk Lulu when he returns. He's due back any time now."

The boy started, "But Jack—"

At a sharp glance from his mother, the boy cast his eyes toward the ground.

Cal entered the barn and frowned at the wary cow's distended sacks. Lulu turned toward him as he adjusted the stool and positioned the bucket. He said soothingly, "You're going to be fine now, Lulu."

Milk streamed from the animal's teats at his touch, and Cal breathed a sigh of relief. From all appearances, he had arrived in time.

The widow and her son stood behind him as the rhythmic pinging of milk striking the pail echoed in the silent barn.

Speaking up, Jeremy offered peevishly, "It's his hands, Mama. Like Jack said, all females like fellas with big hands, especially if they know how to use them."

Cal heard the widow gasp.

Standing up minutes later, Cal handed her the filled bucket. He could not resist. "Yes, ma'am, it's all in the hands."

The widow's pert nose twitched as she replied, still refusing to smile, "I suppose I should thank you, but I didn't really need your help. Jack would have taken care of Lulu when he returned."

"Mama, he knows Jack's not coming back." The boy persisted, "He was in the saloon when you fired him."

"Oh."

"Just tell him to go away. We don't need him around here, Mama. We don't need anybody."

"Jeremy . . ."

Cal started toward his horse. He'd had enough of both of them.

"Just a moment, Mr . . ." The widow paused until Cal turned reluctantly back toward her. "I don't know your name."

"It's Star. Cal Star."

Not bothering to offer her own name in return, the widow said, "I want to pay you for your services, Mr. Star."

"No, thanks."

"I'd feel better if I paid you."

"I said, no."

"I insist. I dislike unsettled accounts."

"Don't want to be obliged to me, ma'am?" Annoyed by her determined condescension, Cal heard himself say, "Don't worry, I won't hold you to it. It wouldn't be worth the trouble."

The widow's clear skin flushed and her lips twitched. She was angry. She was also a stiff-necked, unyielding, *dyed-in-the-wool widow* who had deserved the setdown he had given her. He should've turned around and ridden off as soon as he saw her.

Not deigning to respond, the widow turned back toward the house in a huff, and Cal mounted up. He had ridden only a few yards when with a familiar popping sound his hat was knocked forward over his eyes.

Pushing back his hat, teeth gritted, Cal turned to

glimpse the boy's pointed glance as he slipped his slingshot back into his pocket and ran to catch up with his mother.

Cal stared after them.

Damned right. It wouldn't be worth the trouble.

"Buck, dear, you're not eating."

Her clear blue eyes focused intently on her husband's face, her faultless features composed in a mask of concern, Celeste waited for Buck to reply. He was seated across the supper table from her in the dining room where the ranch hands had formerly joined them for meals at the end of the day—a situation that she had brought to an abrupt halt after marrying Buck. She had adamantly discouraged any kind of personal relationship with the hired help. They were an ignorant bunch, too rowdy and coarse for her civilized, New Orleans temperament, and she'd wanted no part of them.

Besides, she'd wanted Buck all to herself.

Celeste unconsciously compared the man her husband was now to the man he had been when she'd married him. He had been bold, confident, maturely handsome.

Now he was just . . . old.

That pleased her.

Celeste waited, looking at her husband with spurious devotion as he hesitated in response. She struggled to conceal her contempt. He was such a fool. Like all men, he allowed himself to be ruled by a part of his anatomy too distant from his brain for sensible decisions. A woman had only to appeal to that weakness, to smile adoringly with her relentless seductiveness, and the victory was hers.

Buck had not even been a challenge. His wife had been dead only a few months when Celeste came to Lowell, but it hadn't been difficult to capture his attention. He hadn't recognized her as his former lover's daughter, of course. He'd only seen her once when she was a child, and since she had inherited her fine features and blond coloring from her father's side, she had known there would be no problem there.

A familiar inner rage stirred as the difficult years following her parents' deaths flashed across Celeste's mind with sudden vivid clarity. Eight years old and deeply indulged, she had not easily grasped the fact that it was necessary to sell even her father's elaborate New Orleans residence to cover the huge debts he had incurred while attempting to keep his young wife satisfied. Celeste had protested vehemently when the last of her inheritance was gone. With no other options open to them, Madalane and she had moved to the New Orleans slums, where Madalane had supported them with the meager income her knowledge of island potions afforded. Celeste had refused to accept the reality that the luxuries to which she had become accustomed were a thing of the past—but that reality soon made itself clear.

Celeste looked up as Madalane entered the room and nodded at her, then placed a tray of biscuits in front of Buck. Reality, with a little help from Madalane, had taught her to use her beauty to advantage as she grew older. At the age of thirteen, she was the preferred courtesan in Miss Ruby's elite New Orleans bordello. She had enjoyed her power over the wealthy men who frequented the establishment, while detesting them with equal intensity.

The clients of Miss Ruby had been so predictable. Celeste's youthful beauty had made them her virtual slaves. They had worshiped her "innocence." They had felt honored to initiate her into the rites of lovemaking, then to enjoy the "expertise" they had taught her. Dupes that they had been, they had not suspected for a moment that she was already well versed in the carnal arts by the time she reached Miss Ruby's, and that it had been *she* who really did the teaching.

She had abhorred those men—every one of them—but remaining foremost in her silent antipathy had been the man whose abandonment of her mother had placed her there.

She was sixteen when she first met and enchanted Henri DuClair, a wealthy merchant much older than she. Totally alone after the death of his wife of many years, he had come to Miss Ruby's so lonely and hungry for love that he had asked Celeste to be his wife. She agreed to marry him, seeing in his proposal the opportunity to regain the wealth and position which had been stolen from her as a child.

She had not anticipated, however, the difficult price she would be made to pay.

The possessive touch of Henri DuClair's eager, shaky hands had nauseated her more with each passing day. The scent of his aging body as she shared his marital bed had grown to be more than she could bear. Her life would have been intolerable if not for the long line of youthful lovers who secretly consoled her. With her mother's example firmly fixed in mind, however, she had used them well without making the mistake of trusting any one of them.

Then had come that fateful day.

Strangely, she had reacted with stoic silence when she read in a New Orleans newspaper a brief account of a wealthy, phenomenally successful Texan who was visiting the city. The likeness accompanying the article had set her heart pounding.

The man's name was Buck Star.

She recalled with utmost clarity the moment when she called Madalane to her side. Holding the faithful servant's dark-eyed gaze with her own, she had said simply, "It's time to move on."

No one questioned Henri's unexpected death a few days later.

Unfettered, she had then investigated Buck Star's situation more thoroughly. She had learned of the success that had followed his heartless encounter with her mother years earlier. His ranch had grown successful, the family *his wife* had given him had flourished, and their future was bright. Her wrath soaring, she had compared it with her beautiful mother's premature death and her own years of deprivation and degradation, then with her future, which was dependent on a surprisingly inadequate sum inherited from her aged husband. All were situations which would never have come to pass if Buck Star had never entered her mother's life.

Hatred had renewed her vow. She had silently sworn to destroy Buck Star a step at a time, to decimate every facet of his life until he was bankrupt in all quarters, with nothing left to live for. It wouldn't matter how long it took. Unlike him, she was young. She had plenty of time.

Celeste smiled more sweetly at Buck as his hesitation in responding became prolonged. He had been so easy. She had wrapped him around her little finger the moment they met. Still handsome and virile then, he had been anxious to bed her—but she hadn't been fool enough to make her mother's mistake of becoming his mistress. Coyly tormenting him, she had refused him her body until he offered marriage.

Celeste's smile briefly faltered. His son Taylor had been a temporary problem, but she had settled it by having him shipped off to an Eastern school. She had made sure Buck maintained his distance from Taylor, and, after graduating, Taylor had not returned.

She had dismissed any concern about Buck's older son, Cal, since he had already left the homestead by the time she appeared on the scene. Her only failure in the time since had been Buck's surprising resistance to writing a will. She had been frustrated by his refusal. She had wanted him to take the ultimate step of excluding his sons from inheritance. She had felt she was close to achieving that goal when Cal appeared unexpectedly. She was finding it difficult to ascertain what Buck was thinking now—and she didn't like it.

Celeste's thoughts were interrupted as Buck finally responded, "I guess I'm too riled to eat tonight."

Celeste covered Buck's heavily veined hand with her smooth palm and urged, "But Madalane prepared some of her special biscuits."

"Looks like seeing my son again stole my appetite. You can tell Madalane to take the biscuits out to the fellas in the bunkhouse. They'll be happy to get them."

"She made them especially for you."

"Sorry, darlin'."

Her expression a masterpiece of concern, Celeste suggested, "Maybe you should go back to see Doc Maggie and have her look at you again. Maybe she can give you a tonic."

"No more tonics."

"Buck—"

"Celeste . . . darlin' . . . let it go. I'll start feeling better in my own time, but for now I'm going to sit outside on the porch and close my eyes for a while . . . so I can think."

"Anything you say, dear."

Madalane appeared silently in the dining room entrance the moment the porch door closed behind

Buck. The woman's ability to anticipate her was irritating, and Celeste snapped, "Don't sneak up on me, Madalane. I don't like it."

"If your husband needs a tonic, I could mix one for him."

Glancing toward the porch to make sure she wouldn't be overheard, Celeste hissed, "My husband has had all he can stand of your 'help' for a while. Remember, I'm not finished with him yet."

"You're right, of course. So much more must be settled before your mother will rest peacefully in her grave."

Reacting sharply to the Negress's subtle reminder, Celeste snapped, "I don't need you to tell me what I must do, Madalane. I'm not a child anymore."

"No, you are a woman, but you will never be the woman you are meant to be unless you—"

"Madalane . . ."

"I'll throw the biscuits away."

Celeste frowned and asked abruptly, "*All* of them?"

At Madalane's nod, Celeste responded, "And if I had chosen to eat one of the biscuits tonight?"

"You would not. You are too smart for that."

Yes, she was.

Celeste raised her hand to the upward sweep of her pale hair and drew herself slowly to her feet. She knew she was beautiful, that the simple blue gown tailored so precisely to her feminine proportions matched the silver blue of her eyes and complemented her flawless complexion. She knew her beauty contrasted vividly with Buck's rapid physical decline—and that the realization plagued his male vanity almost as much as his continuing failure to perform his marital duties affected his pride.

Her satisfaction at witnessing Buck's silent mental distress made past memories almost bearable.

As for the return of Cal Star, the angry exchange between father and son had been reassuring. She'd make sure Buck did not relent in his attitude, and his son would eventually leave.

Celeste turned toward Madalane and said with a gaze of mock anxiety, "I'm going outside to be with my husband now. You know how worried I am about him. We have so much to talk about. The poor old fellow is increasingly dependent on my advice, you know. He *needs* me."

She headed toward the door. She didn't have to look back to know Madalane's response was a dark smile.

Chapter Four

"What's going on here, Doc?"

Cal looked at Doc Maggie's round, sober face. He had awakened early after a restless night in Lowell's only hotel, a run-down establishment with beds much the worse for wear and walls as thin as paper. A lively amorous couple in the next room had kept him awake for the first portion of the night until he was certain their bed would either collapse from the strain or come crashing through the wall at any moment. Their heavy snoring had interrupted his sleep in the hours following.

He had awakened with the sun and taken his breakfast in the town's only restaurant, with one eye on the storefront office behind which Doc Maggie had established residence after the death of her husband. He had been on his feet and out the door the moment he saw movement there.

Cautious in response to his question, Doc Maggie said, "You asked what's going on here, but that question covers a lot of territory. Care to narrow it down a little for me?"

"I saw Pa yesterday. Hell, I hardly recognized him! What's wrong with him?"

"He looks bad, doesn't he?"

"For starters."

"I can't rightly say I know what's ailing him."

Taken aback, Cal shook his head. "Is that all you've got to say?"

"Listen here, Cal." Motioning him to a chair with a frown, Doc waited for him to be seated before she continued. "I've done everything I can to put my finger on what's ailing your pa, but I've had no success. You can tell by looking at him that he's failing, but I'll be damned if I know what started his decline. His hair went gray almost overnight, he's lost his natural ruddy color, and he's had a steady weight loss that's affected his muscle tone and his stamina. There's no doubt he's sick, but I can't put a name to the complaint that's causing it. He's told me about bouts of nausea and vomiting that come on him without warning, but so far, I haven't been able to prescribe anything that'll stop the cycle once it starts." She paused. "That's the negative. The positive is that I've checked his heart and his lungs every time he's come in here, and they seem all right, so far. His circulation seems all right, too, and as far as I can see, his physical condition hasn't had any permanent effect on his memory or mental capacity. He's as sharp as he's ever been."

Cal nodded.

She asked abruptly, "What did he say when you saw you?"

"What do you think he said?"

"That bad, huh?"

Cal didn't bother to respond.

"That's why you spent the night in town instead of at the Texas Star."

"The only way I'll be spending any time on the Texas Star is if I decide to use my saddle as a pillow and camp."

"I'm sorry, Cal." Doc Maggie touched his hand reassuringly. "There never was any way of telling which way your pa was going to jump."

Determined to have a few questions answered, Cal persisted. "The Texas Star is in bad shape, Doc, and there wasn't a ranch hand in sight when I rode in. Pa always had a loyal bunch working for him. Where are they?"

Doc hesitated, then responded by asking, "Did you meet your pa's new wife?"

"No. What's she got to do with it?"

"The hands started leaving, one by one, after your Pa got married again."

"Why?"

"Who knows? Some say Celeste isn't too friendly. Some say that servant of hers made the men uncomfortable somehow. All I know is that your pa gave up seeing most of his old friends and began spending less and less time in town after he married her—reasonable, I expect, seeing as how he was newly married to a woman as young and pretty as she is."

"Yeah." Cal nodded. "Pa always did have an eye for the ladies."

"And a roving eye, if you don't mind my saying so." Doc frowned. "I know that's no news to you, even if your ma never knew. But the thing is, as far as I can tell, your pa stopped his roving ways after he married Celeste."

Bitter resentment held Cal briefly silent before he asked, "What kind of woman is that new wife of his?"

Doc hesitated before answering, "I'm thinking you should make that judgment for yourself."

"Come on, Doc." Cal gave a harsh laugh. "Pa practically threw me off the place. I might never get that chance the way things look right now, and I'd like to know."

Doc sat back in her chair. "She's young, about your age, and she's a beauty. She's got fancy ways, with her coming from New Orleans society—to hear her tell it, anyway."

"What brought her to Lowell?"

"She was a widow. She says she was looking for somewhere to set down roots. It seems somebody in New Orleans told her about Lowell, saying it was a place that welcomed all newcomers, or something like that."

Cal made a scoffing sound.

"I know, but your pa took it all in like gospel with her looking at him with those big blue eyes."

"Do I hear some disbelief in your tone, Doc?"

"If you do, there's no basis in fact for it. Every time Celeste has come in here, she's been real pleasant with me. She seems worried about Buck's physical condition, too." Doc shook her head. "Maybe that's what gets me wondering. Without a hair out of place or a wrinkle in her dress, looking fresh as a daisy like she's ready to go to a New Orleans soiree or something, she tells me she's so worried about him that she hasn't been able to eat or sleep."

"Doc—"

"You asked me, Cal, and I'm telling you. Something just don't ring true—but I'd be the last to say it to your pa. Look, I don't mean to turn you one way or another about her, but the truth is, she's got your pa jumping through hoops, and he don't even know it."

"About the ranch hands—"

"There's only three of them left."

"Three!"

"With all the problems at the ranch these last few years, that's the least of his worries."

"Problems?"

"Sick cattle. Buck had to slaughter a big part of his herd and buy new stock a while back. Then there was watering problems on the ranch and a rash of accidents with the ranch hands. The biggest difficulty lately has been with rustling."

"Rustling?"

"It's been pretty bad. Your pa's ranch, the Rocky W, and the Crazy K have been getting the worst of it."

The Rocky W . . .

"And Sheriff Carter can't seem to get a handle on it."

Cal took a breath. Whatever he had been expecting when he came home, it wasn't this.

"What's Pa been doing about it?"

"Nothing much."

"That isn't like Pa."

"Your pa isn't what he used to be."

Cal asked, "Which ranch hands are left?"

"Mitch, Big John, and Randy."

"They always were fine fellas."

"I know. I wish there was more to tell you, but like I said, nobody sees much of your pa anymore."

Cal stood up abruptly. "I appreciate your help, Doc."

She asked, "What are you going to do?"

"First off, I'm going to visit Sheriff Carter to see what he's got to say."

"And?"

"If you're asking me whether I'll be staying awhile, I figure I don't have any choice. I've got a lot of regrets, Doc. I know some things are past fixing, but some things aren't, and I'm going to do the best I can."

"Where will you be staying if you're not welcome at the Texas Star?"

"I'll figure it out."

"Any way I can help, just let me know." Tears sprang unexpectedly to Doc Maggie's eyes. "Your ma was a good woman and a good friend, Cal. I miss her . . . and I figure you're family."

With the sobering thought that those were the only kind words his return was likely to inspire, Cal walked out the door.

Her fair skin slick with sweat and her breathing rapid, Celeste groaned with pleasure. She clutched her lover's strong, lean body closer as he pounded himself inside her.

"Harder . . ." Wrapping her legs around his back, she gasped, "Come on, Derek, more . . . harder!"

He thrust more deeply, rocking the rough cot with pure, bestial power, and her raging libido soared. This was the way she liked it, hard and hot—with animalistic fervor. The sentiments Buck whispered with sex nauseated her, but Derek's scorching heat renewed her. It temporarily erased the memory of Buck's soft, flagging male organ and the embarrassed apologies that ultimately followed.

Celeste met her lover's thrusts with corresponding heat, pumping, grunting, gyrating; then calling out as his yawping ejaculation brought her the release she sought. Gasping in the aftermath, she pushed her lover's sweating body off her to more easily catch her breath.

A smile touched Celeste's lips as she opened her eyes and looked at the man lying beside her. He was young and well muscled, his features coarse and his body hairy. She liked that. He had a gross male appeal that satisfied her carnal needs without stimulating sentimentality. She knew instinctively that his body would age quickly, but that caused her no concern. He would be used up, out of her life, and forgotten by then. In the meantime, he served her purpose.

"How'd you like that, sweetheart? That made you feel hot, didn't it?"

Derek's crass inquiry was to be expected. Like most men, he expected praise for his performance, whether it was praiseworthy or not. Indulging him because it suited her, she replied in his vernacular, "Yes, it made me feel hot. You never disappoint me."

Gripping her arm when she attempted to get up, he frowned unexpectedly. "Where are you going?"

"I have to get back." She glanced at the morning sun shining brightly outside the window. "Buck rode out early with the men, but I don't know how long he'll last. I need to be there when he returns."

"Forget him. We're just about finished with him anyway."

"That's where you're wrong. There's a lot more money to be made for both of us before this is all over."

"Yeah, he is an old fool, ain't he? Me and the boys run off his cattle and sell it, and he gets himself in deeper debt by buying more, just so we can do it all over again. Celeste, honey, he's going to make both of us rich if he keeps it up."

"Just as long as we play it smart." Slipping her arm free of his grip, Celeste drew herself gracefully to a standing position and looked back at Derek. It had been pure luck to be waiting for Buck outside the barbershop in Lowell when Derek first made his appearance in town, and to hear a cowpoke say he recognized Derek as a fellow wanted for rustling in the territory north of Texas. The rest had been easy. Derek had wanted what she had to offer. He'd had no trouble finding the men he needed to do the job, and their association had been profitable in many ways.

Celeste allowed Derek a long, extended look at her nakedness, aware of the power over him that it granted her as she reached for her clothes and said, "Actually, that's why I came—to warn you that Buck's older son, Cal, is back in the area. You need to stay away from Texas Star cattle until he leaves again."

"I'm not afraid of him!"

"I didn't say you were. I just don't want to give him a reason to stay—or a reason for Buck to expect help from him."

Derek stood and picked up his clothes. "What do you care about the Texas Star anyway? You should be pretty well set with your share of the rustling money, even if it never made much sense to me why you'd be arranging to have cattle robbed off your own ranch."

"But it's not *my* ranch yet, is it, Derek?" Dressed, Celeste tucked a few straying stands of hair back into place. She had no desire to explain that the rustling of Texas Star cattle was only a small part of her well-planned scheme. She walked up close to him and whispered, "And just in case I might not like to wait around until it is *my* ranch, I'm making sure I've gotten all I can out of it. That makes sense to you, doesn't it?"

Derek sneered, "Celeste, honey, you're a crafty bitch after my own heart."

Her responsive smile well practiced, Celeste did not bother to tell him how wrong he was. She wasn't after his heart—or any other man's. She was only after his body, and the good he could do her while she was using it.

Celeste rubbed herself against Derek's male heat and whispered, "Just remember to hit the other ranches for a while so the rustling on the Texas Star won't look suspicious. That'll be better for you anyway, since you don't share those profits with me."

"Yeah, but me and the boys don't have the guarantees that you give when we rustle Texas Star cattle—like making sure the ranch hands will be at the far end of the spread when we get there so we can just drive them beeves off like they was our own."

About to turn away, Celeste was halted when Derek gripped her buttocks and pulled her tight against him to say with a suddenly tight expression, "You don't have to worry about nothing, sweetheart, just as long as you remember who's satisfying you."

"That's you, Derek, because it certainly isn't my husband." With a perfunctory kiss, Celeste freed herself and sauntered to the door. It didn't matter that she and Derek had their clandestine meetings in a dilapidated, abandoned cabin fit only for pigs. She knew no one would ever see them there. At the same time, the deplorable condition of their meeting place somehow so thoroughly incited her lust that she could barely wait until she closed the sagging door behind her before throwing herself into his arms.

Derek watched from the doorway as Celeste walked to the stand of trees where her buggy was secreted. Her carnal needs satisfied, however, she was thinking clearly enough to silently seethe at his parting remark.

You don't have to worry about nothing just as long as you remember who's satisfying you.

Like most men, the fool actually seemed to believe having a male organ gave him the right to dictate her choices.

No, she didn't like threats, or Derek's assumption that he had the right to make them.

Celeste snapped the buggy into motion. It would give her great pleasure to prove to Derek who was really in control when she was ready.

She had much to look forward to.

Still fuming from her encounter with the insulting Mr. Cal Star the previous evening, Pru slapped her wagon reins against the horse's back and sighed with relief as Lowell came into view. The morning sun was rising in the cloudless sky, reminding her she had limited time to take care of an important task.

Lulu would soon be bellowing.

Pru had tried milking the cow again when morning arrived and Lulu's sacks had refilled. She'd had marginal success in relieving her, but she didn't fool herself that the animal's sacks were sufficiently emptied. As she had climbed into the wagon for yet another trip to town, she had admitted to herself that she had acted hastily in firing Jack Grate. The man was a sneak and a thief, but he had taken care of some important tasks at the ranch that she wasn't presently prepared to handle. During the long, sleepless night past, she had also admitted to herself that she was partially to blame that Grate had taken advantage of her. Her ignorance about ranch affairs was at fault. What she needed was good advice—which she obviously had not been given by the town solicitor—and she needed it quickly.

Pru drew up her wagon at the hitching post in front of Doc Maggie's office door and swung Jeremy down onto the street beside her. She had discovered, however belatedly and to her surprise, that Lowell had a woman doctor. She had bonded immediately with the smiling, motherly woman, who was also a widow and seemed to understand better than most the problems she faced. Having come to that conclusion, Pru knew there was only one place to go for the advice she needed.

Pru entered Doc Maggie's office with a tentative smile. She explained her problem, then listened as Doc responded. When Doc was finished, Pru reacted with stunned spontaneity, "You can't be serious!"

But she was.

Out on the board sidewalk with Doc Maggie's advice still echoing in her mind, Pru was somehow unable to move. She glanced at the sheriff's office across the street, then swallowed tightly as Cal Star emerged. There was no mistaking his tall, muscular stature. Nor could she mistake the way he walked, with long, confident strides and his hat pulled down low on his forehead to shade those alert, honey-colored eyes. She watched as he acknowledged with perfunctory nods the occasional surprised greetings of passersby, exuding an aura of power and purpose that was indisputable.

Apparently in deep thought, he walked nearer, and Pru took a calming breath.

"I want to go home, Mama."

"Not now, Jeremy."

She steeled herself and waited.

Deep in thought, Cal walked briskly along Lowell's main street. He responded politely, but without inviting conversation, to the greetings of Adeline Mitchell and Edith Moore, town busybodies who would soon make his return general knowledge. He nodded to Jake Colt and Barney Wiggs, local men who appeared to have more time on their hands than he remembered. He acknowledged automatically other familiar faces along the way, his mind preoccupied by the conversation he'd just had with Sheriff Carter.

The lawman had been cautious when they spoke. He had confirmed Doc Maggie's statement that the ranches surrounding Lowell had suffered greatly from rustling and had admitted he was ineffective against it. He had related that the rustlers seemed well informed as to the location of small herds that could be taken and disposed of easily. That fact had led him to believe the men were residing locally or had contacts in the community. As Doc Maggie had stated, Carter said all the ranches in the area had suffered, but the Texas Star had been most heavily hit, with the Crazy K and the Rocky W close behind.

Sheriff Carter's jowled face had sagged when Cal mentioned his father. The sheriff had told him everybody knew the Texas Star was in trouble financially. He had said he supposed it was being hit the hardest because it was still the largest ranch in the area and because Buck didn't have enough ranch hands to guard his herd. He had finished by saying bluntly that he supposed the rustlers also figured the Texas Star was a good target because, from the looks of Buck, he wouldn't last much longer.

That flat statement had taken the breath out of Cal. Strangely, even during his discussion with Doc Maggie about his father's health, the thought that his father was dying hadn't fully registered.

He thought of his brother, not for the first time since returning to Texas soil. It seemed strange thinking back now and remembering how close Taylor and he had been while growing up, especially since all he had been able to remember in recent years were the accusations Taylor had flung at him after Bonnie was killed. Taylor hadn't bothered to come home after Pa sent him away, but whether Taylor cared or not anymore about what was happening on the Texas Star, he deserved to be informed. It was his right.

Cal needed to somehow find out where his brother was, so he could contact him, but first he needed—

His thoughts were jarred to a halt.

There she was again.

His step faltering briefly, Cal stared at the widow where she stood on the sidewalk ahead, much like a stationary black crow awaiting his approach. The slingshot kid stood beside her.

His eye fixed on the livery stable at the end of the street, Cal was about to stride past with a civil nod when the widow addressed him.

"I'd like to speak to you for a moment, Mr. Star."

He halted beside her, close enough for her pleasing scent to tease his senses, and to make the unexpected discovery that her proportions were delicate rather than thin, and that her eyes were a luminous gray.

But her voice still held that irritating note, and he responded bluntly, "Really? I would've thought the last thing you'd want would be to talk to me."

As blunt as he, she replied, "I would've thought the same thing, but that was yesterday and circumstances have changed. I'm looking for a hired man, and you were recommended to me."

He was too annoyed for niceties.

"You're telling me some fool recommended me as a hired man?"

"Yes."

"Who?"

"Doc Maggie."

Cal turned sharply toward Doc Maggie's window. He was almost sure he saw a shadow flicker there before disappearing.

"Doc Maggie was mistaken. I don't do that kind of work."

"Would you prefer the title 'foreman'?"

"Foreman . . . with no other hands on the ranch but me."

"That's right."

"Is this a joke?"

"No."

Cal's eyes narrowed into an assessing squint. "Lulu's in trouble again, isn't she?"

"She probably will be by the time I get back."

"Are you trying to hold that animal's welfare over my head?"

"Her welfare is the reason I came back to town so early this morning."

"You came all the way back to town because of a cow . . ."

Showing the first sign of impatience, the widow snapped, "You heard the way she bellows. What would you do?"

"I'd find somebody to help me out—but that somebody isn't me."

"Doc Maggie said you'd be in the area for a limited time and you'll be needing a place to stay. She said you might be willing to accept room and board for a few necessary chores until I can find a permanent person to hire."

"Doc Maggie said that, huh?"

"She also said you're thoroughly trustworthy and dependable."

Yeah, *dependable*.

He noted the lines of stress that formed between the widow's brows as she added with obvious difficulty, "I suppose you could say I'm in a desperate situation."

"You ought to sell that cow."

"That wouldn't help my immediate problem."

"But it would help mine."

The widow sighed. The unexpected vulnerability of the sigh reverberated somewhere inside him as she said, "All right. I guess this was a bad idea after all. I'm sorry I bothered you."

He thought he saw the widow's lips wobble as she gripped her son's hand. He sensed by the defiant way she immediately raised her chin that his refusal was another in a long line of frustrating setbacks to which she was unwilling to surrender.

He was still considering that thought when he heard himself say, "All right, I'll take the job."

"Oh." She took a surprised breath. "You know I can't pay you other than with room and board."

"You said that already."

"You understand the job is temporary, that as soon as I find someone to replace you, you'll have to leave."

"Look, do you want my help or not?"

The boy burst out, "Don't hire him, Mama! I'll learn how to milk the cow. I promise I will."

"Jeremy . . ."

Beginning to have regrets, Cal repeated, "Do you want my help or not?"

"I offered you the job. It's yours." The widow's lips twitched as she added, "Jeremy and I are going home now. I'd appreciate your following as soon as you're able."

The widow climbed into her wagon, and Cal continued on toward the livery stable with the growing feeling that he had made a big mistake.

"He's pretty sick, ma'am. I'll fetch Doc Maggie."

"No, you won't!" Celeste commanded, startling Big John and Randy as they entered the house carrying an unconscious Buck between them. "I'll tell you if I think that's necessary. Take him into the bedroom."

Irritated, Celeste watched as the two men disappeared into the hallway. Buck, stubborn fool that he was, had insisted on accompanying the ranch hands as they rode out to round up calves for branding. She had known he wasn't up to it, but she hadn't expected he would be carried home only a few short minutes after she returned from her tryst with Derek.

She didn't like surprises.

Turning toward Madalane as the Negress appeared at her side, Celeste whispered, "See what you've done! We can't afford to have anything happen to him yet, especially now that his son has shown up."

"Do you doubt my skill?"

"He's unconscious, isn't he?"

Anger flared in Madalane's eyes.

"Ma'am, he's asking for you."

Turning at the sound of Randy's voice, Celeste responded with an effort at civility, "I think it might be best if you do go for Doc Maggie after all. I told my husband he was taking on more than he could handle by riding out this morning. I almost expected this, but it would be better if the doctor checked him to be sure."

Celeste did not miss the looks the two ranch hands exchanged as she dismissed them and started toward the bedroom. They didn't like her, but that was all right, because she didn't like them either. As soon as she was able, she'd get rid of both of them, just like she'd gotten rid of the others.

Affixing a suitable expression on her face, Celeste entered the bedroom. Buck's eyes fluttered open as she rushed to his side and demanded, "Why are you so stubborn, Buck? I told you not to ride out with the men this morning. I told you to wait until you were feeling better."

"I'm fine, Celeste, don't worry." Buck's face was chalk white and his voice weak as he insisted, "The boys shouldn't have brought me back. I'll be fine in a few minutes."

Celeste grasped his hand. The touch of his skin revolted her. It felt like old paper, dry and lifeless.

She steeled herself against her revulsion as she whispered, "I've sent for Doc Maggie. She'll be here soon. She'll give you a tonic."

"I told you, no tonics."

His expression suddenly contrite, Buck rasped, "I'm sorry about all this, Celeste . . . more sorry than you'll ever know."

"About what, darling?"

He took a shaky breath. "That you thought you married a healthy fella with a lot of good years ahead of him . . . and got stuck with a sick old man."

"Buck, don't say that!"

"It's true."

"But I love you, Buck."

He took a clipped breath. "I don't know why you do."

"Because you're my husband. You'll get better. I know you will."

"I don't think anybody believes that, not even you."

"Don't talk like that."

Buck stared at her, his pale eyes intent as he whispered, "I've made a lot of mistakes, Celeste, but I want you to know I have no regrets when I look at you."

"Oh, Buck . . ."

Celeste buried her face against Buck's chest and clutched him close. His bony arm slipped around her as a thought rang across her mind.

Buck had no regrets when he looked at her. She'd just have to try a little harder.

* * *

"All you need is a little rest."

Doc Maggie smiled encouragingly at Buck as she tucked away her stethoscope and snapped her bag shut. She concealed her annoyance as she glanced at Celeste, who stood a few steps away. She had ridden to the Texas Star as fast as her buggy could carry her after Randy came to town. She hadn't been sure how Buck would be when she arrived, and after examining him, she still wasn't sure. She needed a few private words with her patient, which Celeste never seemed to allow. She didn't know what Celeste was afraid of. Nor could she imagine why Buck stood for it.

"Why do you suppose my husband collapsed, Doctor?"

Doc Maggie studied Celeste's concerned expression, noting that her cheeks were just damp enough for proof of recent tears.

"He's weak. He's not well enough for the hard work he was trying to do."

Celeste looked pointedly at Buck. "I told you the same thing, dear."

"That doesn't mean, of course, that Buck shouldn't work with the men at all."

"What are you saying, then?"

"He needs to take it slow—ride out if he likes, but come back before he gets exhausted."

"That's easy for you to say, but my husband doesn't know when to stop once he starts working."

"Celeste . . . take it easy." Buck reached for her

hand. "Doc's just saying I'm not an invalid, yet."

"An invalid!" Celeste was aghast. "I never said you were an invalid!"

Doc Maggie interrupted forcefully, aware she was stretching the truth when she said, "Buck's not an invalid, and there's no indication he soon will be." She faced Celeste abruptly. "If you don't mind, I'd like to speak to my patient alone for a few minutes."

"I'm Buck's wife." Celeste's annoyance was obvious. "There's nothing you can say to him that I shouldn't hear."

Buck interjected, "Please, Celeste . . . just a few minutes."

Celeste flushed, then nodded reluctantly and left the room. Doc waited only until the door closed behind her before turning to Buck with a frown.

"You're a stubborn old fool, Buck Star!"

With a hint of a smile, Buck said, "I figure you're about to tell me what you really think now."

"Damned right! You're a sick man, Buck. I'm not saying you're dying, but I'm telling you I'm not sure which way this sickness of yours is going. I'm also saying, if there ever was a time when you needed help, it's now."

"What exactly are you telling me, Doc?"

"I'm saying you've got a lot of things to straighten out in your life."

"I know where this is heading."

"Do you? Just to make things clear—I'm saying your son is back in town, and he's grown up to be one helluva man. I'm saying you need help around here, and you're a fool if you don't accept the help he's willing to give you."

"I don't want to talk about it."

"He came back to set things straight between you!"

"There's no way to set things straight. Bonnie's dead."

"There's no way you can bring her back, but that doesn't mean you have to lose your two sons, too."

"Bonnie wouldn't be dead if Cal hadn't let me down, and Taylor made his own choice."

"They were young. They both made mistakes. I know damned well you've made many of them in your life."

"But I never made a mistake that caused anybody's death."

"Maybe you were just lucky, because I know you never gave it a thought while you were having your way."

"How do you know what I was thinking?"

"Come on, Buck. We've known each other most of our lives."

"That doesn't mean you can read my mind."

"No, but I can come close to it. And I'm telling you, it's time for you to patch things up with your son."

"No, it isn't."

"He's not going to wait around forever. When the widow Reynolds gets herself a permanent fella to work at her place, he'll probably ride off."

Buck's pale eyes narrowed. "Is that where he is, working on the Rocky W?"

"What did you expect him to do, come begging to work here?"

"I don't want him begging, and I don't want him working here."

"You're a liar."

"I told you, you can't read my mind, Doc."

"Like I said, I can come close to it. I—"

"I think it's time for you to leave, doctor." Interrupting boldly, Celeste pushed the door open. Her expression was stiff. "I'm sure you have other patients waiting for you."

"I'm not finished talking to this patient."

"Yes, you are." Celeste moved to Buck's bedside and took his hand. "Isn't she, dear?"

Buck's glance moved between them. Doc Maggie knew what was coming before he said, "I'm tired, Doc. If you don't mind, I'd like to rest for a while."

She had him jumping through hoops, all right.

"All right, but I'll be back." Doc continued unabashedly, "You won't need to send for me, neither. I like checking on my patients unawares, so's I can make sure they're doing what they're supposed to do."

"That won't be necessary." Celeste's smile was rigid. "I can take care of my husband just fine."

"No doubt." Doc's smile was equally fixed. "But I'll be back anyway."

Doc's smile faded as she left the room. *You can depend on it, Celeste*, she added with silent determination.

Chapter Five

Cal followed the widow's wagon into the Rocky W ranch yard to the sound of Lulu's bellows. The widow stepped down onto the ground and swung her son down beside her, then glanced at the barn with a distressed expression that said it all.

Minutes later, the sound of Lulu's milk striking the pail was again echoing in the silent barn.

When the sensation of two sets of eyes boring into his back was more than he could bear, Cal stopped milking and turned abruptly toward the widow and her son.

"All right, who wants to be first?"

No response.

Cal's glance moved between them. He said flatly, "Let's get something straight. I don't expect to waste my time while I'm here milking a cow. One of you will have to take over."

"No, sir!" the boy said belligerently. "Jack said my

mama and me don't have the hands for it. He said—"

"I know what Jack said." Cal cut the boy short. "He was wrong."

The boy continued undeterred, "But you said it was all in the—"

"Never mind what I said." Cal continued briskly, "Milking a cow is easy. Anybody can learn to do it."

The widow looked at him pointedly. "Of course. How difficult could it be?"

What she had left unsaid was . . . *if he could do it.*

Cal stared at her, then stood up abruptly.

The widow's eyes widened. "What are you doing?"

"I'm going to let you finish up here."

"Now?"

Cal waited for the widow to take his place on the stool without bothering to reply. He watched as she reached tentatively for Lulu's teats, then pulled.

Lulu turned toward her sharply, and the widow frowned, "See? She doesn't like me."

"She just doesn't like the way you're pulling on her."

"I did what you were doing."

"No, you didn't."

The widow's lips twitched. "Then perhaps you should explain what I'm doing wrong."

Cal strained for patience. "You're jerking down on her teats. You need to work them with a rhythmic, squeezing motion."

The widow tried again, and Lulu mooed in protest.

"I told you, she doesn't like me!"

"You didn't listen to what I said."

"I heard every word." The widow's light eyes drilled into his. ". . . a rhythmic, squeezing motion."

"That isn't what you were doing."

"It was."

"Try it again."

The widow complied. She glared up at him when Lulu protested more loudly.

"It's useless. She wants you to milk her."

Determined not to let her weasel out of it, Cal crouched down behind the widow. His chest against her back, he reached around her and clasped his hands over hers.

"What are you doing?"

"You're going to milk this cow, and I'm going to show you how. Are you ready?"

"This is unnecessary. I can't see how—"

Cal clamped the widow's hands over Lulu's teats. He ignored the widow's muffled protest as he squeezed with a downward motion, rhythmically alternating the pressure of his hands until the milk was again flowing freely.

He heard the widow sigh with relief as the streams struck the pail. He was adjusting his position, settling his arms more comfortably around her when she said unexpectedly, "I can do it without your help now."

Cal released her.

The streams grew pathetically thin, then stopped

entirely and the boy exclaimed, "See, I told you! Mama doesn't know how to squeeze those things. Jack said females like a man to do it because a man knows how to use his hands."

The widow turned toward Cal. There was a pink tinge to her cheeks as she said, "If you'll show me again, I'm sure I can learn."

Cal clasped his hands over hers with reluctant admiration and said, "Give yourself a chance to get the hang of it this time."

Lulu's milk was again flowing freely when Cal gradually released his grip. The streams continued unabated.

Still crouched behind the widow, Cal observed her silently, becoming gradually conscious of her fragile shoulderblades working against his chest and the sweet scent of her hair as it brushed his chin. He was frowning when the streams stopped and she looked back at him with concern.

She appeared unconscious of the sudden proximity of her lips to his as she asked, "What have I done wrong, now?"

Cal forced himself to stand, his frown remaining. "Nothing. You're done."

"Oh."

The widow stood up as well. With the brimming pail in hand, she said, "I knew I could do it."

Yeah, right.

Aware that she had deliberately avoided thanking him, Cal watched the female sway of her narrow hips with disturbing fascination as she walked out the barn doorway without another word, her dour-faced son beside her.

He shook his head. He had been too long without a woman.

Struck with another thought, he called out after her, "Begging your pardon, *ma'am*."

The widow looked back at him.

"I figure I should know your name if I'm going to be working here."

The widow blinked, then said, "Of course. It's Prudence Reynolds."

Prudence. That suited her.

"My son's name is Jeremy."

That name he knew.

Cal emerged from the barn seconds later and looked around the Rocky W. It was in even worse condition than it had appeared at first glance. He couldn't be sure how long Simmons had been dead before the widow took over the ranch, but he was sure the old man would never have allowed it to get in this condition if he'd had a choice. It occurred to him that the Texas Star and the Rocky W ranches bordered each other, and they both had suffered badly from deterioration and rustling.

Coincidence? He wondered.

Cal turned toward the house as the widow emerged carrying a pillow, blanket, and dazzlingly white bed linens. The boy trudged determinedly at her heels as she halted within a few feet of him.

"I've brought you bed linens, but I'm not certain

where you'll choose to sleep." She glanced at a dilapidated building some distance from the barn. "I understand the bunkhouse was quite comfortable at one time, but I don't think you'd find it suitable right now. Frankly, it hasn't been in use for some time. Jack preferred the barn. He said the loft did nicely."

"Jack didn't care where he slept, Mama." Jeremy's brows knotted into a frown. "He said one place was as good as another as long as you had a bottle of red-eye or a good woman to keep you company."

Silence.

Red-faced, the widow asked, "Where would you like me to leave these linens?"

"I'll take them. The loft will do fine."

She surrendered the linens, then instructed in an authoritative tone, "When you're done, you may come into the house and we'll discuss the chores I expect you to do in order to earn your keep."

"The chores you expect me to do . . ."

Cal threw the bed linens on a pile of hay inside the barn door. He could almost feel the widow cringe as her precious linens hit the ground.

Taking meager satisfaction in that, Cal stated flatly, "I think we'd better go inside and get things straightened out right now."

He followed her as she turned toward the house.

Madalane watched as Doc Maggie started her buggy into motion and departed the ranch yard. The Negress glanced back at the room where Celeste remained behind with her husband. She had heard the conversation that had transpired between the doctor and Celeste after the doctor examined Buck. She had glowed with triumph when Celeste had so sweetly exercised her power over her husband, causing the doctor to be dismissed.

Yet Madalane knew that the doctor would not give up easily. That woman wanted Buck to accept his son again so Cal could take control of the ranch and restore it to what it had once been. What the doctor did not know, however, was that it was too late for the ranch . . . just as it was too late for Buck Star.

Madalane smiled. She had never been more proud of the woman Celeste had become than she was at that moment. She wished her dear Jeanette could see her daughter now, so she could fully savor the downfall of her handsome, deceitful lover. She would be so pleased.

Madalane's satisfaction abounded. Her knowledge of island potions had been vast when her dear Jeanette came under her care so many years ago. She had used that knowledge to advantage all her life, and had supported both Jeanette and Celeste with it when times became difficult in New Orleans. Yet her skill had never served her better than it did now.

Madalane drew herself up to her full height. She had been an orphan found wandering the island streets before coming to New Orleans as a servant many years earlier. She did not know her true age, but age did not matter. The long hair she wore tightly bound with a colorful scarf was only touched with gray, the fine features that proclaimed her mixed heritage were still clear-cut, her chocolate-colored skin was only slightly marked with lines of age, and her tall, well-proportioned figure was still womanly enough to tempt a man's desire. With an amalgam of experiences behind her and many productive years ahead, she seemed ageless. It would not be long before Celeste and she returned to their beloved New Orleans to resume the good life, richer than they had ever been, and free to indulge their slightest whims.

The joy of the moment briefly dimmed. Perhaps then, when all was settled at last, she would no longer see her dear Jeanette's tear-streaked face in her dreams. Perhaps then, she would see Jeanette smile.

As for the woman doctor . . .

Madalane's lips curled into a hard smile. The doctor was angry and frustrated that her medicine was powerless against Buck's illness. She still hoped to cure Buck Star with her tonics and eliminate Celeste's power over her husband. She would fail, but Madalane would not be satisfied with that meager victory. She had already decided that before Celeste and she left the Texas Star behind them, the woman doctor would not only lose her battle against them, she would lose all else as well.

Madalane turned toward Celeste as she left her husband's room. Celeste's beautiful face was flushed with anger as she hissed, "The old witch! Doc Maggie thinks she can turn Buck against me, but she can't. I'll show her. I'll show them all."

Madalane indulged Celeste's fury. She allowed it full rein. Yes, Celeste would show them all. Madalane would see to that.

Pru sat at the table in her small, spotlessly clean kitchen, with Jeremy beside her and Cal Star across from her. She was comfortable and in complete control in the familiar quarters as she prepared to list chores for her new "hired man."

Comfortable and in complete control . . .

As Pru remembered vividly, that had not been the case when she first arrived at the Rocky W. She had been horrified at the overall deterioration of the ranch, but the condition of the ranch house had devastated her. It had been empty for such an extended period that birds and field rodents had taken up residence; and with a leaky roof that had contributed to its decay, the house had been dark, dank, and uninhabitable.

At the point of tears but determined not to let Jeremy see her distress, she had attacked the problems with determination. Weeks later, the house was still small and run-down, but it was also bright and tidy, where spotless bed linens graced the lumpy beds; where a lace tablecloth covered the scarred surface of the much-abused dining room table; and where her cherished family china—the only household item of true value that she owned—was carefully displayed on a rough but freshly painted shelf.

With a slow sense of disquiet, Pru looked at Cal Star where he sat opposite her. So, if she was so comfortable and in control in her small kitchen, why did this man's relentless aura leave her breathless? Why did he dominate the silence with the unyielding sense of purpose she read in his eyes? And why did she have the feeling that his honey-colored gaze could see right through her vacillating confidence?

Annoyed at her uncertainties, Pru raised her chin with determination. She was the boss here, and she was the one who was going to set down the rules.

Pru began purposefully, challenging Cal's gaze with her own despite the irritating ripple that moved down her spine as she said, "Now for your chores: I'll expect you to clean up the ranch yard, to muck out the barn stalls, care for Lulu and the horses when needed, and—"

"The horses?" Cal interrupted with a frown. "I didn't see any horses in the corral or the barn."

"I'm talking about Blackie, the horse that pulls my wagon, and the saddle horses in the pasture behind the barn."

"I didn't see any horses in the pasture either."

"They're out there somewhere. I saw them there a while back."

Pru saw the look that flashed across Cal Star's face, and she was momentarily dismayed. Surely he didn't expect her to check on the horses every day?

That had been Jack's job. He was the one who took care of—

The thought stopped her cold.

Cal began, "Before we go any further, there are some things I need to know. First of all, do you intend to make the Rocky W a working ranch again, or are you just passing through?"

"Passing through?" Surprised at the question, Pru responded, "Whatever gave you that idea? Of course, I intend to make the Rocky W a working ranch. It's Jeremy's and my home now."

Cal asked abruptly, "How big a herd do you figure you're running here?"

A slow flush suffused Pru's skin. "I'm not sure. Jack was supposed to give me a rough count, but he never got around to it."

"So you have no idea of the size of your herd." Cal's lips tightened. "How about the condition of the herd? How many yearlings do you have ready for market; how many cows heavy with late calves; how many calves ready for branding?"

Pru did not respond.

"Have you even thought about branding?" Exasperation ticked at his mouth. "It's spring, you know. That's one of the chores a rancher generally does in the spring—rounding up the calves and branding them so they won't be prey for any footloose wrangler handy with a hot iron."

"Oh."

Cal's gaze grew harder. "I'm thinking none of the other chores have been done either, like checking out the range stock to make sure weak cattle are taken care of, like checking the herd for screw worms, or inspecting the water holes to make sure the stock can find water."

"Jack never said anything about that."

Cal stood up abruptly and walked to the door, then took a few frustrated steps back. "Of course, none of those chores will be necessary if you don't have any cattle left. You do know rustling's been whittling down all the herds in the area."

"Jack mentioned it."

"But that wasn't your major concern." Cal stared at her incredulously, then said, "Forget about cleaning up the yard and mucking out the barn for a few days. The first thing I'm going to do is check to see if there are any horses in the pasture. If they're there, you can prepare yourself to ride out tomorrow, because we're going to check on your herd together. I'm thinking Jack just might have forgotten to mention that you don't have one anymore."

Pru struggled to maintain her dignity as she stood up and said, "That won't be necessary."

"It won't, huh?"

"I mean, it won't be necessary for me to accompany you. You can report back what you find."

"Really? What if I tell you you don't have much of a herd, and you find out a few weeks from now that, like Jack, I'm just taking you for all I can get by selling off your stock?"

Pru swallowed, tears building. "That won't happen. Doc Maggie recommended you."

"Somebody recommended Jack, I'll bet."

"Yes, but I trust Doc Maggie."

"I'm thinking you trusted that other fella, too."

Beginning to tremble, Pru said, "I would appreciate it if you'd tell me what you're trying to say."

"He's not trying to say anything, Mama!" Jumping suddenly between them, Jeremy rasped, "You leave my mama alone! She doesn't need you to tell her what to do!"

Pru placed her hands on Jeremy's shoulders. She could feel his small body shaking as she said, "I think it would be best if Jeremy and I stayed home while you checked the herd tomorrow."

Cal stared at her for another moment, then said with a touch of incredulity, "Don't tell me you don't know how to ride."

"Of course I know how to ride! I rode quite often with Jeremy's father."

"—or that you can only ride sidesaddle."

Pru took a breath. All right. She wouldn't tell him.

Cal gritted, "Do you have any riding clothes—*Western* riding clothes?"

"I'm a widow, Mr. Star, and I dress accordingly. I had neither the funds nor the time to shop for riding clothes before coming out here."

Pru felt her face flush as Cal eyed her disapprovingly from head to toe, then asked, "How long has your husband been dead?"

"That's none of your business!"

"How long?"

Pru maintained her silence, then heard herself say, "Four years."

She wasn't sure, but she thought she heard him mutter a curse word before he turned abruptly and walked out into the yard.

"Mr. Star. . . ." Pru called after him, "where are you going?"

He turned back slowly toward her. "I'm going to see if I can find two horses in the pasture. Then I'm going back into town."

"But your chores . . . Lulu will need milking again later."

"You can take care of Lulu."

Pru started to protest, but decided against it. No, she wouldn't give him the satisfaction.

Mounting without waiting for her response, Cal rode out into the pasture and disappeared from sight.

Pru looked down at Jeremy as he said in a trembling voice, "I don't like him, Mama. You should tell him to go away."

Unable to respond, Pru was still standing in the kitchen doorway when Cal came back into view, leading two horses behind him. She waited until he took them into the barn, then an interminably long period before he came out again and prepared to mount.

Unable to resist, she called out, "So the horses were there, just as I said they would be."

Cal looked back, his expression dark. "Lucky for you."

Pru responded curtly, "It's unnecessary for you to go back to town now. You'll lose too much time. There's a lot of work to do."

"I'm going."

She added more forcefully, "I *am* your employer, you know."

With a look that was suddenly fierce, Cal strode back toward her. He stopped so close that she could feel the pure, male heat radiating from his body as he growled down at her, "Let's get something straight once and for all. Whether you know it or not, you're in a damned lot of trouble here on the Rocky W."

"My mama knows what she's doing! She—"

A glance from Cal halted Jeremy's tirade, allowing him to continue, "So I'm telling you now, this is the way things stand. If you don't start acting like a rancher and start getting things done around here, you won't have a ranch anymore. *Comprende?*"

"Mr. Star—"

"My name's Cal."

"I prefer Mr. Star."

"I don't."

Pru raised her chin. "All right, but I want you to remember my name is *Mrs. Reynolds.*"

Cal responded coldly, "That's fine with me."

Ignoring his comment, Pru repeated, "There's no reason for you to go back to town tonight."

Effectively dismissing her response, Cal said, "I don't know how long it'll be before I get back, but I'll make my bed in the loft." He added with a touch of sarcasm, "The reason I'm making that clear is because I don't want you aiming that shotgun in my direction if you hear me coming in after dark."

"You needn't worry about that, Mr.—Cal. And you can be sure Jeremy and I will manage quite well without you."

Stepping back without another word, Pru ushered Jeremy into the house and closed the door behind her. Jeremy was voicing his angry protests when the sound of Cal's departure faded into the distance.

Cal stood in the doorway of Doc Maggie's office. His broad figure was silhouetted against the bright, late-afternoon sunlight as he said, "What did you get me into, Doc?"

"What are you talking about?"

Doc Maggie's full face was a study in innocence, but Cal wasn't buying it. He had grown increasingly angry as he rode back to town. The memory of *Mrs. Reynolds's* stiff figure standing in the doorway was burned into his mind, and the echo of her autocratic tone scratched along his spine. The woman was impossible—bossy and determined to have her way although she was at a total loss when it came to ranching. Knowing Doc Maggie the way he did, he had the feeling she had been aware of the widow's irritating qualities before she mentioned his name.

"What am I talking about?" Cal strode into Doc's office, his expression tight. "I'm talking about the widow."

"Oh, that. Pru told me she had fired Jack Grate—

which I approved of, by the way. I don't know why she hired that fella in the first place. He certainly wasn't a good—"

"Stick to the point, Doc."

Doc shrugged. "Like I said, she told me she needed help and she needed it fast. You told me you'd be looking into finding a spot to hold you over while you were here, and it seemed to me like you two were a good fit."

Cal questioned, "Did you ever have a serious conversation with that woman?"

"Many times."

"About the Rocky W?"

"There wasn't much to talk about. She doesn't seem to know a lot about ranching."

"Oh, you caught that, did you?"

"She needs help. I figured you'd be the right fella to give it to her."

"There's more to it than that, and you know it." Cal scowled, "Jack Grate was probably robbing her blind, and she didn't have the sense to realize it."

"That could be true, but—"

"She's more concerned about cleaning up the barn and fixing up the ranch yard than she is about her herd."

"She's an Easterner, Cal."

"You're damned right." His lip curled with disgust. "Did you know she only rides sidesaddle?"

Doc restrained a shudder and attempted a smile. "Like I said, I know she doesn't know a lot about ranching."

"She doesn't know *anything* about ranching."

"You're going to help her, aren't you?"

"That isn't what I came back to Lowell for."

Doc sobered at that, then said, "I'm sorry, Cal. I thought I was doing you both a favor."

All anger draining away in the face of Doc's apology, Cal responded, "I guess I'm sorry, too. I'm sorry I took out my frustration on you, but that doesn't change how I feel about the widow."

"Pru."

"*Mrs. Reynolds*, as she chooses to be called."

Doc Maggie's smile was weak. "So, what are you going to do?"

"I'll help her out as best I can until you can find somebody to take over full-time."

"Until *I* can find somebody?"

"You found me, didn't you?"

"Yes, but—"

"Listen, Doc, this Rocky W business aside, I came back here in order to find out some things about my pa."

Cal noted the immediate change in Doc Maggie's demeanor—the sudden tightening of her jaw and the hard look in her eyes as she said, "I was meaning to talk to you about your pa, too. I was called out to the ranch today because your pa had a bad spell this morning."

Cal tensed. He wasn't accustomed to hearing his father spoken of in Doc's solemn tone of voice. It gave more credence to Sheriff Carter's obvious belief that his pa wouldn't last much longer.

Cal asked abruptly, "I need to know straight out—is my pa dying?"

"I don't know how many times I've asked myself that same question, Cal. I suppose if I could pin down the cause of his sickness, I might have an answer for you—but I don't."

"Doc—"

"If you're asking me if he'll die if he continues on like he is, the answer is yes—but I'm not sure how long it'll take. With this sickness coming out of nowhere, the only thing I can say for sure is that it's not contagious."

"No offense, Doc, but did you ever think of telling my pa to go somewhere to have another doctor take a look at him?"

"No offense taken, because I've told that stubborn old man to do that more times than I can count. He's dead set against it."

"Why?"

"Your guess is as good as mine."

"What about his wife? Can't she convince him to do it?"

"I figure you still haven't met Celeste."

"Meaning?"

"Celeste can convince your pa to do just about anything she wants him to."

"So?"

"So, she doesn't want to."

"What are you saying?"

"Just that. She seems content to watch sympathetically while he keeps getting worse." Doc paused. Seeming hesitant, she continued, "I've got something else to say, too, so here goes. I think Celeste is up to something—her and that servant of hers. I never did like the way that Madalane woman looked at me, like she was laughing at me or something. I just don't trust either of them."

Cal's frown darkened as he asked, "Is there any talk circulating about my pa's wife in town—about her maybe having a fella on the side somewhere?"

Doc gave a caustic laugh. "You have to be foolin'! There isn't a fella in Lowell that woman would consider good enough for her."

"Only my pa."

"Only him."

Cal nodded. He considered Doc's responses in silence, then ventured unexpectedly, "About Taylor . . ."

"I don't know where your brother is, Cal. I haven't heard from him in a long time. The last letter I wrote to him came back marked 'address unknown.' "

"I guess it's up to me, then."

"What are you going to do?"

"First off, I'm gong to introduce myself to my pa's wife."

"I thought Buck nearly threw you off the place."

"If what you just told me is true, he's not in any shape to try that right now."

Doc cautioned, "You need to remember something else I said, Cal. I don't know what's wrong with your pa. I can't tell how he'll react to too much stress, so—"

"I'll take it easy, don't worry."

"But I do worry, Cal. About you, and your pa."

"And Taylor."

"Him, too."

A smile briefly altered Cal's sober expression. "You're a fine old lady, you know that, Doc?"

Doc's response was spontaneous. "I take exception to that. I'm not *old*."

Out on the street minutes later, Cal considered Doc's reply. Doc and his pa were about the same age, but if he were to compare the way they looked, he'd say his pa was twenty years older.

That thought was still nagging him when Cal emerged from the general store a few minutes later. A package in hand, he turned toward his waiting horse.

"Well, it looks like you've got your mind set on where you're going."

Cal knew that voice.

He turned toward it and smiled broadly at the three cowpokes who stood a few yards away. Closing the distance between them, he shook their hands each in turn and said, "Damn if you boys aren't a sight for sore eyes!"

Josh, dark, with a perpetual beard, was smaller than he remembered. Larry, light-haired and freckled, was a little thinner. Winston was just Winston—big and brawny with a ready smile. He had grown up working beside them on the Texas Star. Strangely, seeing them now, he felt he had really come home.

"Seems like you growed up some since we seen you last."

Nodding in agreement with Larry's comment, Winston added jokingly, "I'm thinking I can still take you on, though."

"You're looking more like your ma than you ever did."

That last comment from Josh was sobering. It tightened Cal's throat before he said, "I was disappointed when I didn't see you fellas at the Texas Star yesterday."

"Yeah, well, Larry, Winston, and me figured it was time for us to move along."

"Why's that?" Cal pressed, "You fellas worked at the ranch for about as long as I can remember."

"Too long, maybe."

"Meaning?"

"Meaning too long to take what your pa's new wife and that servant of hers was handing out."

Cal waited for Josh to continue.

Speaking in his stead, Winston interjected, "That lady puts on a good front, but she's like a rattler, all coiled up and ready to strike when you ain't looking. She started out smiling, then ended up all but accusing Josh, Larry, and me of rustling Texas Star cattle."

"Pa didn't believe her, did he?"

Josh shrugged. "I don't know how to answer that, Cal. That wife of his has him wrapped around her little finger. Truth is, we probably wouldn't have paid her any mind if your pa had stood up for us.

But he didn't, so we figured it was time to move on."

Cal was stunned.

"We couldn't figure it out," Larry said. "Your pa didn't hire any wranglers to take our place, and he should've, since he's so short-handed. Mitch, Big John, and Randy stayed on out of pure orneriness, but I'm not sure how long they'll last. When I talked to them a while back, they was pretty fed up with your pa's wife ordering them around and interfering with their work."

Larry paused, then said, "You rode out to the ranch. You saw it. It's a helluva mess, ain't it? Mitch and the boys are disgusted. And to top it off, they ain't been paid in months."

Cal took it all in, then asked, "Where are you boys working now?"

"We've been working on the Reemes place." Josh shrugged. "Can't say we like it much. Ethan Reemes works us hard, then acts like he done us a favor taking us on. We might be moving on soon."

"I'm sorry to hear that," Cal said, his words heartfelt. "I guess it was a real stroke of luck, us running into each other today."

"Is that what you're thinking?" Winston laughed. "You didn't run into us. We came to town especially looking for you when we heard you was back." His smile dimmed. "We figured we owed it to your ma to welcome you home, because we figured your pa probably wouldn't."

Larry asked unexpectedly, "What did *you* think of your pa's new wife?"

"I haven't met her yet. Pa just about threw me off the place before I could." Cal continued with a frown, "I figure it's time I should, though. I was heading out there now."

"I guess we're not the only ones who've been filling your ears about her, then."

When Cal chose not to reply, Winston said, "Good luck to you. I figure you'll need it." He asked in afterthought, "Are you staying in town?"

"I hired on for a while at the Rocky W."

"Hell, no! Not the Rocky W!" Winston added with a shake of his head, "You're going to be needing more than luck there."

Saddened when their conversation drew to a close, Cal watched briefly as the cowpokes headed for the saloon at the end of the street. More determined than ever, he turned toward his horse.

The sun was setting when Celeste looked out the window at the sound of hoofbeats and saw Cal Star approaching the ranch house. Buck was resting fitfully, still weak after his collapse earlier that day. She had been about to take him the light supper Madalane said she had prepared especially for him. That comment had raised Celeste's brows, but Madalane had only smiled. She hadn't bothered to challenge Madalane's statement. She had depended on Madalane's expertise for far too long to question her.

Celeste assessed Buck's elder son with a critical eye as he drew closer. He was a bigger man than her husband: taller, more heavily muscled. He wore his hat pulled down low on his forehead, shadowing his face, but she could see the sun-streaked hair that hung down over his collar, and a flash of his determined expression. It had surprised her while covertly watching the heated exchange between father and son the previous day that the fellow bore so little resemblance to Buck. When she'd first met her husband, Buck had had dark hair, pale eyes, and handsome features; in contrast, his elder son's hair was shades lighter, his eyes a peculiar and oddly arresting shade of gold, and his features consummately masculine, rather than handsome. Her sexual response to Cal Star had been sharp and immediate. She had known in an instant that if he had been any other man than Buck's son, she would've found him irresistible.

Celeste dismissed her lingering regrets and studied Cal more closely. He was completely at ease in the saddle. From the way he held his impressive frame, and from the set of his chin, she guessed he would be at ease in any situation. That trait worried her.

At her elbow, Madalane commented sharply, "What is *he* doing here?"

"Doc Maggie probably told him his father had a bad spell. He most likely came to find out if Buck is nearing the end so he can claim his portion of the ranch." Celeste's expression grew obdurate. "That will never happen."

"No, it will not." Madalane smiled unexpectedly. "But if he is anything like his father, you'll have no problem handling him. I will leave that to you, of course. That is where your expertise is unmatched."

In silent agreement, Celeste checked her shadowed reflection in the glass, then stepped out boldly onto the porch as Cal drew near.

Cal drew back on his mount's reins, slackening his pace to allow himself a few moments to study the woman who appeared on the ranch porch as he neared. He had no doubt who she was. It was his father's new wife . . . and she was beautiful.

Cal studied her more closely. Her stature was petite, and with blond hair that glistened in the fading rays of the sun, an exquisitely sculpted face, and a lush figure, she was one of the most femininely appealing women he had ever seen. He momentarily pitied the poor, sick old man his father had become—a man who knew that with every passing day, the distance between his young wife and him grew irrevocably wider.

The woman addressed him directly as he drew up alongside the porch, saying, "My name is Celeste Star. You're obviously Buck's elder son. I'm sorry we didn't have the opportunity to meet when you came to see your father yesterday, but I thought at the time it would be best if I allowed you two to speak alone."

Cal dismounted with a nod, then said, "I don't think our conversation would have been any different if you had been there, but I can understand your feelings. Since you seem to know how things went yesterday, you know my father and I didn't have much of a chance to talk. I'd like to see my father to find out if we could do better this time."

"I suppose it would be best if we dispensed with pretense." Celeste's smile was appealing. "I'm sure Doc Maggie told you Buck was taken ill this morning. The boys brought him back to the house unconscious." A frown creased her brow. "I told Buck he wasn't well enough for a full day's work, but he didn't agree. Unfortunately, Doc Maggie had to confirm my conclusion before Buck would listen."

"Where is he now?"

"He's in bed. He's not feeling well. It's a bad time for you to try to talk to him."

"I'm here now. I want to see him."

"I'm sorry. I can't allow it."

"It isn't a matter of your giving permission," Cal responded. "I don't intend to wait until you—"

The screen door squeaked open behind Celeste, halting Cal's response. Buck's face was chalk white, his step unsteady as he walked out onto the porch and said, "What's the rush to talk to me? Are you afraid I'm going to die or something?" He gave a harsh laugh. "You didn't seem to give a thought to that during the years while you were gone."

"Pa—"

"Celeste is right. I'm too tired to talk."

Cal looked at his father. Celeste had moved close to him. She had slipped her arm through his and was pressing herself against his side as she looked up at him almost worshipfully. The adoring look on her face was so obvious, it made him sick.

Cal pressed, "We have some important things to talk about, Pa. The condition of the ranch, for one."

"All of a sudden you're concerned about the Texas Star, too, huh?" Buck gave a caustic snort. "Hell, that's a joke."

"You weren't having rustling troubles when I left."

"A lot of things have changed since then."

"Well, I'm here now, and I can help."

"I'll handle things fine without your help, just like I handled everything else."

"It doesn't look to me like you've been handling things too well for a while."

"Is that right?"

"The ranch is in bad shape, Pa. If you'd take an honest look around, you'd agree." Cal hesitated, then said, "Ma wouldn't have wanted to see it this way. She loved this ranch."

"I told you not to mention your ma to me!"

Cal took a breath and forced himself to say, "Bonnie loved this ranch, too."

"Get out."

"Pa—"

"Get out, damn it! I don't need you to come here and remind me of things I'd rather forget!" Buck took a shaky breath. "As a matter of fact, I don't need you at all!"

"Pa—"

"Get out of here, or I'll get my gun and drive you out!"

"Please leave," Celeste interrupted softly. "You're upsetting your father."

"Don't waste your breath on him, Celeste! He isn't worth it."

Cal's jaw tightened as Buck's knobby hand closed over Celeste's. His father's color was fluctuating dangerously, and his thin body was beginning to tremble.

Cal said abruptly, "All right. Have it your way, Pa. You always do."

Cal mounted and headed back down the trail without waiting for Buck's reply. He didn't look back as the screen door of the ranch house slammed loudly behind him.

"Hey, wait up, boy! I need to talk to you."

Cal reined back at recognition of the familiar voice. A slow smile replaced his frown as he extended his hand in greeting to the cowpoke who reined up beside him. Randy, the oldest of Buck's cowhands, had been at the Texas Star from its inception. Cal didn't know his age, but except for a few extra gray hairs and a deepening of the lines around his eyes, the smiling cowhand was still the same slight, fit fellow who had helped him break his first bronc.

Randy shook his hand with a smile. "Welcome home, Cal. Sorry to see you under these circumstances, but me and the boys are sure glad you're back."

"Thanks, but the way my pa is talking, it doesn't look like my being home will make much difference to anybody here."

"I was riding up on the other side of the barn

while you and your pa were conversing, and I didn't have to strain my ears to hear what you were saying. I'm telling you, Cal, don't listen to a word the boss says. If Big John and Mitch were here right now, they'd say the same thing. It's that wife of his who's making him talk that way. She's trying to drive us all off the ranch—everybody who cares about what's happening here."

"What are you saying, Randy?"

"I'm saying that woman has the devil in her. Your pa ain't been himself since the day he married her."

"She can't do anything that Buck won't let her do."

"You're wrong, Cal." Randy shook his head. "Believe me, you're wrong."

"I know, she has him wrapped around her little finger."

"All of that and more."

"I don't understand what you're saying."

"I'm saying your pa ain't himself, being sick and all, and that woman is playing on his weaknesses. Yet underneath it all, he knows how things have been heading, and he knows he's losing control. He needs your help, but he's too damned proud and stubborn to admit to you that he can't handle everything by himself."

"I can't help him if he won't let me."

"Yes, you can."

Cal did not respond.

"Listen here, Cal." Randy's mustache twitched as he continued more slowly, "The truth is, Mitch, Big

John, and me have just about had it with everything that's been going on here. We was about to give up on your pa until this morning when he rode out to work with us. Hell, he was as weak as a kitten, but he kept pushing himself, roping those calves and herding them into the corral. He didn't give in until his body couldn't take it no more and it just gave way. He cares about this ranch, Cal. And it ain't because he wants it for that wife of his. I'm thinking in the back of his mind, he knows as well as everybody else does that if she could, she'd sell the ranch out from under him and be back in New Orleans with all those highfalutin friends of hers as quick as her legs could carry her. No, he's hoping to save the Texas Star for other reasons that matter to him down deep—like this was the place him and your ma picked out together, where they hoped to raise their family, live the rest of their lives, and see their kids follow after them."

"It didn't work out that way, Randy. Ma and Bonnie are dead, Taylor's gone, and Pa's got himself a new young wife. There's nothing left of the way it used to be."

"Don't give up on your pa, Cal. If he hasn't given up after all the things that have been happening these past years, there must be a reason."

"I don't know, Randy."

"It ain't been easy for him. I get the feeling that it wasn't until your ma was gone that your pa realized how much he had without appreciating it."

"You couldn't prove it by me."

"Because of the way he was acting?"

Cal didn't bother to reply.

"Your pa never did do things the way most people thought he should. I'm thinking your ma was the only person who ever really understood him."

"It looks like his new wife understands him pretty well."

"She knows how to handle him, you mean . . . how to make him do what she wants whether he likes it or not."

"Buck never did a damned thing that he didn't want to do."

"Maybe the old Buck didn't."

"He couldn't have changed that much."

Randy's gaze silently challenged Cal's response before he asked abruptly, "Where are you staying?"

"I took a temporary job at the Rocky W."

Randy raised his bushy brows in wordless comment, then said, "Sleep on what I said, boy. And remember what the Texas Star meant to your ma. I get the feeling nobody would be happier than she'd be now to see you come home."

Cal could not reply.

Similarly affected, Randy offered simply, "She was a good woman. There wasn't a man on this ranch who didn't think she was the best thing that ever happened to your pa. I don't figure any one of us will ever forget her."

When Cal still did not respond, Randy concluded, "I have to go. Mitch and Big John will be getting back to the ranch about now. Your pa's wife and that servant of hers will start wondering where I am if I don't show up with them. I'd rather not have them know I was talking to you. I'm not about to give them any more reason to get me fired. Your pa needs every friend he's got."

At Cal's silence, Randy tipped his hat. "You know where to find me if you need me."

Disturbed, Cal was still staring after Randy when he disappeared around a bend in the trail.

Chapter Six

He hadn't slept well and his mood was foul.

Cal stood up slowly, his frown dark as he glanced around the barn loft where he had spent the night. He had come to realize during the night that Jack had been right again. The loft was as good a place as any to sleep if a man had a bottle of red-eye or a woman to share it—but he'd had neither, and he had spent the greater part of the night struggling to get comfortable while his mind ran in dizzying circles.

He had thought about the people who had welcomed him home, people he trusted, who all shared the same opinion of Buck's beautiful young wife. He had reviewed his short meeting with her over and over again in his mind in an attempt to dispense with any preconceived prejudices—but the result was always the same. He didn't believe anything about her.

About halfway through the night, as his father's

angry parting words echoed in his mind, he had begun asking himself why he was staying on. As daylight dawned, however, the answer was still the same: *two lonely graves.*

The widow had then begun inching back into his mind. It had annoyed him that she could enter his thoughts while so many other issues were pressing, but she had remained there, constant, with her wide gray eyes and sober expression. He had wondered unexpectedly what it would take to make her smile—and he had then wondered why he wondered.

Dependable. He couldn't seem to get away from that description of himself, which he had come to despise. In the case of the widow, however, he supposed it was true. She was irritating, autocratic, and just about the bossiest woman he had ever met, yet with the help of Doc Maggie and her use of the word *dependable*, he had become somehow responsible for her. Still, there was something about the widow that tugged at a part of him deep inside. For the briefest moment, he had thought he glimpsed the woman hiding underneath that stark black dress, a woman who—

Cal turned at the sound of a step on the loft ladder. He frowned as a sandy-haired head came into view.

Gaining the loft level with a surprisingly agile leap, the slingshot kid glared up at him and said boldly, "My mama told me to come up here to get you, but I didn't want to, because I don't like you."

Cal scowled. "No? Why's that?"

"Because you think you can fool me like you're fooling my mama, but you can't. I know what you did."

Cal's limited patience waned. "Look, little boy—"

"My name's Jeremy."

"Look, Jeremy, I'm not in the mood for one of your tantrums."

"I don't care what you're in the mood for, mister." The boy stared up at him with more courage than sense as he went on, "I'm not in the mood for you, either. I told Mama to make you go away, but she won't listen to me."

The widow was smarter than he'd thought.

Jeremy's eyes narrowed. "I heard you laughing at my mama. You made fun of her!"

"I did what?"

"I saw you come out of the saloon after Mama fired Jack. You were in there laughing at her with everybody else. Everybody there thought what she did was so funny, but it wasn't. Mama almost cried when she found out Jack bought things for himself all over town and told everybody Mama said to buy them, so she'd have to pay for them."

"So, that's what she was so mad about."

"You knew that already. I heard Jack bragging about it in the saloon when you were in there."

Cal thought back. Jack had held the attention of the bar for a while, but Cal had no idea what the braggart had said before the widow strode through the door. He remembered the laughter that followed her exit, though.

Jeremy was visibly trembling. The boy was so mad that he was ready to fight the world for his mother . . . when all he had to protect her was a slingshot and two tight little fists.

"I didn't laugh at your ma, Jeremy."

"You did, too. I heard you!"

"You heard the other men laughing, but you didn't hear me. I wasn't part of it. I didn't know your ma well enough to find the situation funny."

"You were in there—"

"And I left because I had better things to do."

"But—"

"Look, Jeremy, it looks like we got off on the wrong foot. You thought I laughed at your ma, when all I was doing was minding my own business; and I thought you were a spoiled kid, when you were just trying to stand up for her."

Jeremy appeared unconvinced, and Cal said, "Look, you know Doc Maggie, don't you?"

"Yes."

"Do you like her?"

Jeremy nodded.

"Do you think she'd tell your ma to hire somebody she couldn't trust?"

The boy hesitated.

"I'm thinking Doc Maggie is probably the best friend your ma's met since she came to Lowell. Am I right?"

Jeremy nodded reluctantly.

"So, why wouldn't I be your ma's friend, too?"

"Because Mama doesn't even like you!"

That was a good reason.

Cal forced a smile and responded, "I'm not trying to make your ma like me. I'm just trying to help her—because Doc Maggie asked me to."

Jeremy studied him intently. The boy's brown eyes bore into Cal for long moments before he muttered, "Mama says everybody deserves a second chance . . . even though Jack said they don't. Jack said—"

"I don't want to know what Jack said."

"But—"

"And I don't think your ma does, either."

Appearing to accept Cal's comment, Jeremy said, "All right. I'll give you a second chance like Mama says, but you'd better hurry up, because she's making breakfast and she said for you to come down." He added, "But you'd better wash your hands and face first, and scrape off that beard. Mama told Jack she wouldn't stand for slov . . . slovenliness."

Cal watched as Jeremy made his way down the ladder and walked out through the barn doorway. It had been years since somebody had told him to wash his face. He supposed it was the least he could do, especially in light of the surprise the widow had in store for her.

"Do you honestly expect me to wear these things? They're men's clothing."

Cal allowed the widow's question to hang unanswered in the air of the small kitchen as he readied his reply. He had waited until the widow had served him a surprisingly good breakfast, which he and Jeremy had eaten side by side in a newfound truce. He had then placed the package from the general store in front of her. She had opened it and looked at the folded pants and shirt, and the boots and hat lying on top.

She had reacted predictably, and now he responded, "They may not be fashionable, but they'll suit you a lot better while we're riding than that widow's outfit you're wearing."

"I'll do quite well with my present attire, thank you."

Cal's patience rapidly eroded as he replied, "I hate to tell you this, *Mrs. Reynolds,* but there isn't a sidesaddle to be found in Lowell. You're going to have to ride astride, like the rest of us poor old Texans." He added deliberately, "And black isn't the best color to be wearing when you're riding in the hot Texas sun all day—even if you are a widow."

"I said, I'll manage."

Stubborn, stiff-necked, bossy. Fine, let her have it her way.

Cal nodded. "Anything you say, *boss*. I'll be waiting outside."

They were riding in the relentless morning sun an hour later when Cal glanced again at the widow and silently groaned at the sight of her. Back straight and chin high, she was bumping along the uneven terrain with a determined expression belied by the trickles of sweat trailing from the damp, dark hair underneath the broad-brimmed black hat she wore, and the perspiration that stained her high-necked, long-sleeved black dress.

He recalled that Jeremy and he had been mounted and waiting when the widow emerged from the house as if dressed for an afternoon tea, with a ridiculous picnic basket in hand. She had struggled to mount her horse with growing frustration, until he had finally dismounted, swung her up onto the saddle, secured her basket, and while ignoring her frantic efforts to arrange her skirt modestly, had mounted his own horse and clucked their party into motion.

The situation had gone downhill ever since.

A glance at Jeremy revealed the boy was doing quite well on the mount he was riding. The horse was smaller than average, with a placid manner that had evoked the boy's confidence. The sound of the widow's backside slapping the saddle with painful consistency, however, had not ceased.

Somehow he had the feeling it was going to be a long day.

"How much longer until we find the herd, Mr. . . . Cal?"

Pru broke the silence of the miserable, seemingly endless ride. Despite her denials, she had agreed with Cal the previous day when he said she needed to take a more active hand in running the ranch. She had trusted Jack and sat back, expecting him to care as much as she did about the ranch's future. She now knew how great a mistake that had been.

Pru glanced at the big man riding so easily beside her. She studied his casual and masterful handling of the powerful animal he rode, as if it were simply an extension of himself. His horsemanship was in direct contrast with her own awkwardness at riding astride and the constant, rhythmic contact between saddle and derriere that was growing more painful by the minute.

Humiliating was the word that best described her inability to mount earlier that morning. She remembered the impatience Cal had barely managed to conceal when he finally dismounted to swing her up onto her horse and seat her astride. And she remembered thinking that was the last time she'd be beholden to him.

She had soon realized, however, how wrong she had been.

They had been traveling for an endless period on Rocky W land that she could not remember ever seeing before. Strangely, every tree, every rock, every rise of ground they passed looked the same as the one before. She knew that if her new "hired hand" should abandon Jeremy and her right now, she'd have no idea how to find her way home.

Pru silently sighed. She was a novice rancher—a tenderfoot, in Texan terms. She needed all the help she could get. She was determined, however, that she wouldn't fall into the same trap she had fallen into with Jack. *She* was the boss on the Rocky W, and she intended to make sure Mr. Cal Star remembered it.

Annoyed that Cal had not yet responded to her question, Pru said, “I asked you a question, *Cal.* How long will it be before we reach the herd?”

She was unprepared when Cal responded with tight-lipped anger, “Maybe Jack could answer that question better than I can, *Mrs. Reynolds*, since I haven’t seen anything so far that would make me think you still *have* a herd.”

“Of course I have a herd!” Pru replied with a confidence she did not feel. “Jack . . . or somebody would’ve told me if I didn’t.”

“Ma’am . . .” Cal’s honey-colored eyes held hers coldly. “That ‘somebody’ who should’ve told you just might turn out to be me.”

Pru was stunned into silence by Cal’s reply. She was still mulling over his response when she saw Cal grow suddenly alert, then turn his mount toward a stream a distance away. He kicked his mount into a gallop toward it, and Pru gasped aloud as her horse sprang into motion to match his pace.

Gripping the saddle horn with frightened desperation, uncertain exactly when her hat flew off her head and her high-buttoned shoes flew out of the stirrups, Pru barely restrained a scream. She glanced at Jeremy, who flew past her with a wide grin and a loud “Yahoo!” as he followed Cal toward the stream. She was still clutching the saddle horn when her mount came to so sudden a halt at the stream that she almost flew over his head.

Cal had already dismounted and was inspecting the herd of cattle watering there while she was still struggling to catch her breath.

Pru swallowed tightly as Jeremy jumped down from his horse and ran to join Cal. Determined to do the same, Pru swung her leg over the saddle and slipped to the ground to the accompaniment of a loud ripping sound. She refused to look back at the portion of skirt trailing limply behind her as she started toward them on wobbling legs.

She had almost reached their side when Cal looked up. She said in an effort to distract him from her obvious discomfort, "So, I *do* have a herd after all."

Damn!

Cal looked at the widow as she approached. She had lost her hat, her hair was hanging in windblown strands, her face was sunburned and sweaty, her ripped skirt was trailing raggedly behind her, and she was walking like each step would be her last.

And she had the nerve to speak to him in a tone that implied, *I told you so.*

He was unaffected by the note of uncertainty that entered her voice when she added, "This *is* my herd, isn't it?"

Cal allowed himself a few moments to gain control of his irritation as he pulled himself up to his full height, then said, "Ma'am, if this is all there is to your herd, you're in more trouble than you know."

Cal turned back toward the cattle watering

nearby. He mentally counted the calves in immediate view before adding, "But if this bunch is representative of what we'll find elsewhere on your spread, I'd say you have some heavy work ahead of you on the Rocky W."

"I'm afraid you'll have to be a little more explicit than that."

Explicit.

Right.

"In plain language, ma'am, this small bunch of cows and calves looks to be healthy enough, but you'll need to have a roundup to find out for certain where you stand. And by the looks of the number of calves I see here, you'll be needing to do some heavy branding soon."

"Oh. That's good." She appeared relieved. "Shall we start back after we eat?"

Cal stared at her.

"Well?"

Cal continued to stare.

Pru struggled to retain her composure. They were seated underneath a shade tree near the stream where they had found her cattle watering a short time earlier. The picnic basket was open and almost emptied, and Jeremy was noisily consuming the last of the chicken she had packed—but she had been too uncomfortable to eat.

She couldn't be sure how far they'd ridden that morning, but her fair skin was afire from unaccustomed exposure to the sun; the high neckline and long sleeves of her black dress had turned the garment into an oven that was cooking her tormented flesh more efficiently with every degree the temperature climbed; and the fine leather of her high-buttoned shoes had become soaked with perspiration and were now squeezing her tortured toes. To add to her torment, her backside was numb, her legs stiff, and her inner thighs felt as if they had been rubbed raw.

Miserable and short of patience, Pru replied sharply to the comment made a few moments earlier by the hired man who seemed to know more about her ranch than she did.

"What do you mean I'd have to hire wranglers for a roundup? I can't afford to do that. Couldn't you handle the roundup yourself?"

"No."

"Why?"

Cal looked at her assessingly, then said, "Maybe we're getting ahead of ourselves here with talk about hiring wranglers. After we look around a little more today—"

Pru felt a flush of panic. "You mean we haven't finished looking yet?"

"Ma'am—" A familiar impatience flickered in his irritating honey-eyed gaze as Cal responded, "There aren't any more than twenty-five or thirty head watering down there by the stream. You won't need to hire wranglers if that's all there is to your herd. But since we haven't covered even half of your property yet, there's a reasonable chance there are more."

Pru felt a sinking sensation in her stomach. "We haven't covered even half of my property yet?"

"You have no idea how much land you own, do you?"

The touch of incredulity in his tone annoyed her, and Pru countered angrily, "No. Do you?"

"Yes, I do. I grew up in these parts. I know exactly where your property begins and ends."

"Oh. I suppose that's why Doc Maggie recommended you."

"And because he's *dependable*, Mama. Remember she said he's *dependable*."

Pru did her best to ignore her son's comment as a thought struck her. "Your name is Star. You wouldn't be related to the fellow who owns the Texas Star, would you?"

Cal's expression hardened. "Buck Star is my father."

She pressed unthinkingly, "Then why—"

"My pa and I haven't seen eye to eye for a while."

Unwilling to admit to the sudden cramp in her calf that stole her breath, Pru gasped, "So you probably know where the rest of my herd will most likely be located."

"I suppose so."

"Then we can go directly there and finish up."

Cal's assessing gaze narrowed. "Look, if you'd rather go back to the ranch house now—"

"No."

He nodded. "All right. There's a watering spot not far away that's big enough for the greater part of your herd to gather. I'm hoping to get a good idea of how hard your herd's been hit by rustlers when we get there."

"Not too far away . . ." She prompted, "Like over the next rise?"

"A little farther. We'll probably have plenty of time to do what we came out to do and get back before sundown."

Before sundown . . .

Pru swallowed and turned hopefully toward her son. "If you're too tired, Jeremy, we can finish up another day."

"I'm fine, Mama." The boy wiped his hands on one of the napkins she had packed and continued earnestly, "I'm having a good time. Cal already showed me how to recognize the Rocky W brand. He told me the best way to use a branding iron so the brand will set well, too."

Pru's nose twitched. That must've been while she had been limping around, trying to get their picnic lunch ready.

"Mama?"

Pru restrained a sigh. "I'm glad you're having a good time, dear."

She inwardly groaned as Cal said, "We'd better get going if we want to get back before dark."

She drew herself shakily to her feet.

"Are you all right, Mama?"

"I'm fine, Jeremy."

"Carry the picnic basket for your ma, Jeremy."

"That isn't necessary," Pru snapped.

Pru was still standing beside her horse, trying to determine the best way to mount, when Cal came up behind her and swung her astride with no apparent effort. She watched enviously as he lifted Jeremy up into his saddle as well, then mounted in a fluid movement so graceful it took her breath away.

An inexplicable quiver moved up her spine when Cal glanced back toward her and their gazes inadvertently met. Ignoring her reaction, Pru followed behind as he and Jeremy moved forward.

Cal looked down at the sun-drenched stream below the rise where their small party sat mounted. Cattle stretched out before their eyes in a glorious fan of motion, and relief flooded his senses.

"Look at all those cows!" Jeremy exclaimed. "Are they all ours, Cal?"

"They're on Rocky W land, so they're yours unless their brands say different," Cal replied.

"I can't believe it!" The boy turned toward his mother, who sat her horse in silence. "Look, Mama, all those cows are ours!"

The widow nodded, and Cal's stomach gave another sickening lurch at the sight of her. She sat perched uncomfortably in the saddle like a hot, miserable black crow. From the looks of her, she ached from head to foot but was too stubborn to admit it. He had ridden back to find the hat that had blown off her head during the ride earlier, but it had provided her little protection from the relentless Texas sun. He had wanted to turn around and head back to the ranch house a dozen times, but the widow's stubbornness had kept them pressing on. He had told himself she was only getting what she asked for—another of Jack's comments that had rung with annoying familiarity in his mind—but he had gained little satisfaction from the thought.

"Should we go down and check the brands, Cal?" Jeremy prompted.

"Why don't you go ahead and do it, Jeremy?" Cal suggested encouragingly. "You know what to look for. I'll be down in a few minutes."

"I don't want him to go alone." The widow was adamant. "If the herd should start running—"

"There's not much chance of that. He'll be fine."

"Can I go, Mama?"

"No."

"The boy will never grow up if you don't—"

"Jeremy is *my* son—"

"All right."

His expression tight, Cal spurred his horse toward the herd. He had wanted a few minutes to talk to the widow alone, to discuss his concerns about her physical condition plainly, without the boy listening to their every word, but she'd made that impossible.

Cal slowed his angry pace at the sound of Jeremy's horse behind him and allowed the boy to ride up alongside. The boy surprised him by saying, "Don't be mad at Mama, Cal. She thinks I'm only a little boy and she has to take care of me. She doesn't know I'm almost grown up."

Relenting, Cal responded, "Your ma's right when

it comes to that, Jeremy. She does need to watch out for you a little while longer."

"Maybe . . ." The boy frowned, "But I wish I could hurry up and grow. When I'm as big as you, she won't have to worry anymore because I'll take care of *her.*"

Bittersweet remembrance tugged at Cal's mind. He recalled the many times he had stood beside his mother, knowing she restrained tears after a "discussion" with his father. He remembered promising himself that when he was big enough, he'd make sure she didn't have any more reasons to cry.

Pointing to a nearby steer, Jeremy shouted suddenly, "Look, that big cow has our brand on her! I guess this herd is ours, all right."

So it was.

Cal had firmly established that reality and assessed the condition of the herd when he finally rode back up the rise. One look at the widow and he realized she had been sitting her horse in the blazing sun since they had left her. He saw the shaky smile she offered her son, and snapped into motion the moment before she began swaying in the saddle.

Beside her instantly, Cal swept the widow off her horse and carried her into the shade of a nearby tree. He pulled the annoying black hat off her head and threw it onto the ground. Her face was stark white underneath spots of blotchy, sunburned skin as he sat her back against the tree trunk and began unfastening the buttons at her throat.

The widow attempted to push away his hands as she rasped, "I . . . I'm fine."

"No, you're not. You almost passed out because you're overheated. You need to let your body cool down."

"My body's fine, and I did not"—she took another gasping breath—"almost pass out."

"You didn't, huh?"

"Are you all right, Mama?"

"Get the canteen for your ma," Cal ordered. "She needs a drink of water."

"I'm not thirsty."

"Do what I said, Jeremy."

Jeremy ran back toward the horses as Cal began unfastening the buttons at the widow's neckline. Her eyes dropped weakly closed as he unbuttoned the first, then the second and the third. His fingers trembled as he unbuttoned the fourth, exposing a white vee of delicate skin and the rise of firm, white breasts.

Cal took a shaky breath and wiped the sweat from his palms, then attempted to push up the long sleeves of her dress. Prevented by their narrow cut, he slipped his fingers inside the cuff, unconsciously noting the weak throbbing of her pulse against his forefinger before he ripped the cuff open wide.

"What are you doing?"

"You need to cool down." He pushed up one sleeve, then the other. "It looks like you didn't have sense enough to find some shade for yourself while we finished with the herd. Did you bother to drink any water?"

"I wasn't thirsty."

The widow looked at her son as he approached. She accepted the canteen he handed her and said, "I'm fine, Jeremy, really."

"Take a drink." Cal's voice was gruff.

"I said I don't—"

"Take . . . a . . . drink."

"Maybe you should listen to Cal, Mama," Jeremy interjected. "You don't look so good."

"I told you, I'm fine."

"But you look bad."

The widow took a sip from the canteen, then said, "See, I'm fine."

Cal directed, "Take another drink."

The widow raised the canteen to her lips and drank more deeply. A few drops slipped from the corner of her mouth and trickled down her neck onto the white skin exposed at her neckline. He watched, almost mesmerized, as they disappeared in the swell of soft flesh.

"She'll be all right, won't she, Cal?" Jeremy's voice snapped him back to the present. The boy's small face was tight. "She's not going to die or anything . . ."

"Your ma's going to be fine. She's just overheated."

"I'm not . . . overheated."

Ignoring her denial, Cal untied the bandanna from around his neck, soaked it with water from the canteen, then ran it across the widow's forehead. He saw the relieved sigh she withheld as she took a deeper breath.

He soaked the bandanna again and ran it across her fluttering eyelids, unconsciously noting the way the moisture clung to the thick fringe of dark lashes lining her light eyes, and the way it beaded on her smooth, sun-tormented cheek. He took a breath as he ran the cloth across her parted lips and her tongue reached out spontaneously for moisture.

Jeremy crowded closer and Cal said reassuringly, "Your ma will be fine in a few minutes. She just needs to rest."

"I'm fine now." The widow opened her eyes and made an attempt to rise.

"Sit still." Cal's soft command jerked the widow's gaze toward him. "I'll tell you when you're ready to move."

"I said—"

"I don't care what you said. I can see what you look like, and you can't. I'll let you know when you're ready to ride."

Jeremy interjected, "You'd better listen to him, Mama. You look pretty bad."

The widow's weak gaze was caustic. "Thank you, dear."

"You're welcome, Mama."

Cal turned to Jeremy and said, "Your horse is looking a little tired. Why don't you tether him down by the stream where he'll be more comfortable. We're going to stay here for a little while."

Jeremy jumped to do his bidding. Cal waited only until the boy was out of earshot before he turned back to the widow and said, "I don't expect to argue with you in front of Jeremy again, so I'm going to set things straight right now. You nearly got yourself sunstroke because you're so damned determined to do things your own way, and I'm not about to let anything like that happen again."

"I don't like cursing."

"What you like doesn't matter right now. You're going to do what I tell you to do until we get back to the ranch house—and you're going to do it without protest, do you understand?"

"No, I don't. You don't give the orders. I do."

Stubborn . . . bossy . . . relentless.

He snapped, "That's fine with me, but Jeremy's scared. He already told you he thinks you look bad. He's one step away from panicking, and if he does—"

"All right." The widow's gaze flickered revealingly before it dropped away and she mumbled, "You win."

Cal did not reply. He had glimpsed it again, the flash of vulnerability in the widow's eyes. He resisted the sudden inexplicable desire to console her, to stroke back the strand of dark hair adhering to her cheek and whisper that he wasn't trying to win. All he really wanted was—

"I tied my horse up like you wanted."

Cal sat back as Jeremy returned, his youthful face tight with anxiety. Keeping his tone casual in an attempt to be reassuring, Cal said, "When I was your age I used to take off my boots and walk in the shallow part of the stream to catch the little critters swimming there. It's a good way to cool off."

Jeremy looked back at his mother. Noting his hesitation, Cal urged, "Jeremy might enjoy that, don't you think so, Mrs. Reynolds?"

"Go ahead, Jeremy." The widow forced a smile. "I'll be fine."

Cal wet the bandanna again as Jeremy turned obediently toward the stream. Cal ran the cloth across the widow's forehead and cheek.

"I'm all right. You don't have to do that."

"Close your eyes and rest, then. We won't be staying here long."

She protested determinedly, "We can leave right now if you want."

"Just do what I said."

Discouraging further conversation, Cal put the bandanna aside and sat down beside her. He leaned back against the tree trunk, stretched out his legs, tilted his hat down over his eyes, and folded his arms across his chest.

Cal closed his eyes, but the last thing on his mind was sleep. He had made a mistake. Somehow he had let the widow's hostility affect his judgment. He knew better than to let that happen.

. . . a widow who don't have a man and figures she don't need one . . .

Cal frowned. Damn that Jack!

* * *

Barely an hour had passed since the widow's bout of weakness, but her color was almost normal and her eyes were clear.

Cal stood up and called down to Jeremy where he was busying himself in the stream, "Bring up your horse. We're going to ride back now."

Cal assessed the widow as she struggled to her feet. He glanced at Jeremy as the boy led his horse back toward them, then untied the other two horses secured nearby. He fastened the reins of the widow's horse to his saddle.

"What are you doing?" She frowned as he approached. He refrained from responding and swung Jeremy up onto his saddle. She pressed, "Why did you tie my mount's reins to your saddle? You're not going to lead my horse and have me trailing behind you as if I were a child, if that's your intention."

"It isn't."

The widow gasped as Cal swept her off her feet and sat her astride his saddle. She gaped as he mounted behind her.

"What do you think you're doing?"

Cal slid his arm around her waist and adjusted her back against him to more comfortably share the saddle. He felt her instinctive resistance as her body met his, and he replied, "You're still weak and we have a long ride ahead of us. We'll be riding in the sun all the way, and I'm not going to take the chance you'll fall just so you can prove a point."

"What point would that be?"

"Do I need to answer that question?"

The widow drew herself up ramrod stiff as Cal urged his mount into motion. He said with a touch of sarcasm, "This isn't an English riding school, Mrs. Reynolds. If you'd loosen up a bit, your backside won't clap against the saddle the way it did all morning."

The widow gasped. "I did not *clap*!"

"The truth is, Mrs. Reynolds, you sounded like an audience of one."

The widow's response was inaudible, and Cal said, "Just relax and close your eyes. It's a long ride home."

He was right. It *was* a long ride home.

The sun was dropping into the horizon when the ranch house came into view at last, and Pru unconsciously sighed. Cal's arm tightened around her waist when his horse surged to a suddenly faster pace. Thrust back against the hard wall of his chest, she was acutely aware that he seemed unaffected by her weight, just as he had while supporting her sagging frame during their endless ride.

Not that she had been uncomfortable sharing his saddle. Quite the contrary. Despite herself, she had gradually relaxed—so much so that she had dozed. To her chagrin, she had awakened to find herself resting with her head back against Cal's shoulder and her lips brushing his neck with each rhythmic sway of his mount. Her lips tingling, she had pulled herself erect.

"Did you have a nice rest, Mrs. Reynolds?" Cal whispered.

A nice rest . . .

Relieved to be in the ranch yard at last, Pru waited as Cal dismounted, then turned to lift her to the ground. A fleeting wave of nausea buckled her knees when he put her down, and she gasped. Catching her, he swung her up into his arms.

"I'm fine." She protested with growing embarrassment, "Really, you can put me down."

"If you don't mind my saying so," Cal replied, "I've come to realize I can't trust your word on that."

"I said—"

"I heard you."

Cal started toward the house, then turned back to Jeremy to say, "Take your horse into the barn and give him some feed. I'll take care of your ma."

Pausing in the kitchen, Cal said abruptly, "Which bedroom is yours?"

"Put me down. I'm fine, I told you."

"I know what you told me." His arms were bands of steel that held her helpless as he continued, "Now I want you to listen to what *I'm* telling *you*. You need to rest for a while."

"I'm not sick."

"I didn't say you were, but being overheated the way you were—"

"I wasn't overheated!"

"What would you call it?"

"I was . . . overly warm."

Cal continued more firmly than before, "Being

overly warm takes a lot out of a person. If you rest a while, you'll be as good as new."

"I'm as good as new now."

His patience obviously expired, Cal said, "Which bedroom is yours? The first one?"

Striding toward the first doorway, Cal entered and glanced around him at the flowery quilt on the bed and the feminine articles on the dresser. He then carried her to the small mirror on the wall and said, "Take a look at yourself and tell me you're fine."

Frowning as darkly as he, Pru looked into the mirror and gasped aloud. She saw blotchy color, dark circles under her eyes, wispy strands of hair hanging from her formerly neat bun, and a tattered and torn dress that looked almost . . . indecent!

"Right." Cal's jaw was tight as he placed her on her bed and began removing her shoes.

"I can do that."

Silenced by his cold glance, Pru sat immobile until her feet were bared and he said, "Lie back and be quiet. I'll tell you when to get up."

"But . . . Jeremy's hungry."

"I said—"

"All right." Surrendering to another sudden wave of nausea, Pru lay back and gasped, "But I'll only rest for a few minutes."

Pru closed her eyes to the sound of Cal's footsteps leaving the room, and the irritating thought that he was right again. She did need to rest.

But only for a little while.

* * *

He had become a nursemaid.

That thought rankled as Cal glanced out the kitchen doorway into the fading twilight. He then looked back toward the two bedroom doorways where silence reigned.

Mother and child were tenderfeet. Exhausted after a long day in the saddle, they had both fallen into a sound sleep. The widow had actually been asleep before he'd cleared the doorway of her room. She had not heard her son enter the house; nor had she seen Jeremy peek into her room to reassure himself that she was all right before declaring that he was hungry. Feeling the rumblings of hunger himself, Cal had sent Jeremy to the hen house for some eggs while he milked a bellowing Lulu. He had then cooked the eggs and some bacon he had found neatly stored, sliced the loaf of bread he had also discovered, and served some of Lulu's fresh milk to wash it down.

Jeremy's head had been nodding before his plate was emptied. Cal had sent the boy to his room while he settled the horses for the night, and had returned to find him sleeping soundly.

The house was quiet . . . too quiet. He had kept himself busy cleaning up the kitchen, but that chore was done, and there was still time to think—thinking that Cal knew would cause him trouble.

But the thoughts came anyway. He remembered the sweet sensation of holding the widow in his arms as she had shared his saddle, as she had relaxed back against him in sleep, nodding with the horse's sway, her lips grazing his throat. He remembered the scent of her, all sunshine and purely female as her hair brushed his chin. He recalled the fluttering of her dark lashes the few moments before her luminous eyes gradually opened and she looked up at him in a rare moment devoid of caution and restraint. He remembered wishing that moment would last, wishing she weren't a widow who mistrusted him and every man, and wishing he weren't a man who had returned to Lowell to settle a lifetime of regrets.

Cal took a breath and glanced at the first bedroom doorway. He also remembered carrying the widow into her room, and the horrified gasp she had uttered when she saw her disheveled reflection in the mirror. What she didn't realize was that her dishevelment and the vulnerability it exposed raised emotions of another kind in him—and thoughts too dangerous to entertain.

His musings interrupted by the sound of movement from the widow's room, Cal walked to the doorway and glanced into the semidarkness. The widow was stirring restlessly in sleep, and he frowned. It had been obvious to him that the only reason she had agreed to rest was because her suddenly rebelling stomach hadn't allowed her to do otherwise. He wondered if her discomfort was worsening. If she was getting a fever . . . if the heat had affected her more seriously than he had realized.

Cal moved to the widow's bedside and felt her forehead. It was cool to the touch.

Relieved, but somehow not yet ready to leave her, Cal crouched beside the bed and studied her shadowed face. She looked so young and defenseless in sleep, so different from the person she struggled to portray. He touched the dark, silken strands stretched across her pillow, remembering the scent of her hair as her head had rested against his chin. He trailed his fingertips against her cheek, recalling the sweet weight of her head lolling back against his shoulder. Her lips parted unexpectedly with a mumbled word, and he leaned closer to hear her. Her warm breath brushed his mouth, and he breathed it in, savoring its scent. Suddenly unable to deny a longing for more, he brushed her mouth lightly with his—but his lips clung. He wanted . . . he needed . . .

Cal sprang back from her abruptly, as if burned. What was he doing? Was he crazy? This woman was weak and defenseless. She was also a cranky widow who mistrusted all men, including him—a woman intent on proving to him she was the boss—so intent that she had made herself sick while trying.

Unable to make himself move despite his self-recrimination, Cal watched as the widow stirred, then slowly opened her eyes. She struggled to focus in the semidarkness, and he offered hoarsely, "You were restless. I thought you might be sick."

The widow blinked, momentarily disoriented, then glanced at the window.

"Did I fall asleep? Is it night?"

"Yes."

"Jeremy . . . where is he?"

"He's asleep. He couldn't keep his eyes open at the table."

"You made him something to eat?"

"I was hungry, too."

"Oh."

"Do you feel all right?"

"I'm fine."

Of course.

Silence.

"Thank you for feeding my son."

Cal did not respond.

"I . . . I'm glad we found the herd today."

More silence.

"We can talk about the roundup tomorrow."

Cal did not move.

"I'll see you in the morning, then."

He couldn't go yet.

Cal heard himself say, "I think we need to settle something first."

The widow took a shaky breath. "What?"

"Say my name."

"C . . . Cal. Your name is Cal."

Unable to stop his gaze from dropping to her lips, he responded more gruffly than he intended, "That's right . . . and your name is Prudence."

Silence.

"Good night, Pru."

"Good night."

Cal forced himself to his feet and turned toward

Chapter Seven

Celeste struggled to maintain a smiling facade as she and Buck traveled the sun-swept, dusty trail back to the Texas Star. She glanced at Buck who was sitting beside her, wagon reins in hand, looking healthier than he had in months.

Would she never be rid of him?

". . . and Mitch and Big John could sure use the help. I'm thinking they'll be glad to have the boss b ack in the saddle again."

Celeste raised a hand to her upswept curls as Buck continued his nauseatingly cheerful monologue. She then adjusted her hat. Both actions were ploys to allow her a few more minutes to regain control of her raging emotions. Buck had insisted on riding into town that morning to save Doc Maggie the trouble of coming out to see him—because he felt so "well." He had been elated when Doc Maggie confirmed that his health seemed to be improving and he was well enough to rejoin his men in modest ranching tasks.

The aging doctor had appeared so pleased with herself that Celeste had almost retched. She had wanted to scream out the truth to the overweight, overbearing female physician who barely disguised her dislike of her. She had wanted to taunt the woman with the truth that her "doctoring" had nothing to do with the apparent improvement in Buck's health. She had wanted to shout that *she* was the reason her husband had regained enough strength to be fit for the saddle again.

That truth galled her. *She* was responsible for her husband's sudden upsurge of good health, when all she truly wanted was to see him lying in a cold grave.

Gradually regaining her self-control, Celeste slipped her hand through the crook of her husband's arm. She maintained her smile with pure strength of will as she clutched his bony limb close to her breast. Warmed by her touch, Buck looked down at her with a loving smile, and Celeste almost laughed aloud. Men were idiots! She manipulated them like puppets on a string—while despising them every step of the way.

Was there no man smart enough to match the wit and cunning of a woman?

Was there no man *her* equal?

Celeste leaned against her husband and clutched his arm intimately closer. When he reacted visibly to her touch, she concluded that if there ever was a man who might be her equal, it most certainly was not he.

An image of Cal Star, tall and powerful, appeared unexpectedly before her mind, as it had countless times since their meeting a week earlier, and Celeste gritted her teeth tight with frustration. She recalled the stretch of his shoulders, the depth of his muscled chest, his long-legged stride. Despite herself, she had pondered many times how it would feel to be wrapped in the embrace of those powerful arms; how it would feel to cup the manly bulge below his belt in her palm, to caress it warmly while she waited breathlessly for his response. She had wondered if he would melt at her touch like all the others before him. She then remembered the look in his eyes when they had conversed, and her musings had ceased.

Damn that Cal Star to hell! Buck had been so physically weak. He had been confused and so close to succumbing to her seemingly innocuous persuasions that she had been almost able to smell the success of her quest. Cal's return to Lowell, however, had changed everything.

Celeste remembered Madalane's irritation at being instructed that while Cal was still in the area and while Buck still refused to discuss his will, she must suspend the "tonics" she secretly administered to Buck. She had not wanted to provide Cal an excuse to remain in Lowell. For that same reason, she had told Derek to stop his rustling activities on the Texas Star. She had learned on their short trip to see Doc

Maggie, however, that her restraint had been wasted.

Cal was still in town, and had no intention of immediately leaving.

". . . and I got to admit I was surprised when I heard Cal was working on the Rocky W."

Snapping back to the present at the mention of Cal's name, Celeste offered, "Why should you be surprised, Buck? Cal is your son; and Lowell is his home. He was bound to return sooner or later."

"The *Texas Star* is his home—but he seemed to forget that for the last nine years."

"From what you've told me, it was more a matter of his running away than forgetting—but I suppose I might've run away, too, if I had killed my sister."

"Bonnie fell into the well. It was an accident."

Celeste shrugged. "An accident that maybe wasn't an accident at all."

Buck's frown was dark. "What are you saying?"

"Nothing . . . nothing, Buck." Celeste shook her head, avoiding his gaze with feigned regret. "Just forget what I said."

"I asked what you meant."

"I don't . . ." Celeste sighed. "I don't want to cause any more hard feelings than already exist between you and Cal, dear."

"I want to know what you meant."

Celeste replied with affected reluctance, "It just seemed strange to me how your son tried to shift the blame for your daughter's death onto you."

"It wasn't my fault Bonnie was killed."

"I know that." She paused again, then asked, "I just wondered—was there any jealousy between Cal and Bonnie?"

"Jealousy?"

"I mean, it's obvious to me how much you loved Bonnie. Did Cal resent your affection for her?"

"Are you trying to say—"

"I'm not trying to say anything, except the way he tried to switch the blame for her death onto you, and that talk about receiving a letter about Bonnie that brought him home—well, it all seemed to me like some kind of an excuse so he could come back to claim a share of the ranch that he had made sure would be larger than it was originally expected to be."

"If that's what he wanted—a bigger share of the ranch—why didn't he stay?"

"I don't know. Maybe because he didn't realize how badly you would react to Bonnie's death."

Buck did not reply.

"Buck, dear—" Celeste stretched herself up to press a kiss against his lined cheek. She concealed her revulsion as her lips brushed his papery skin and whispered, "I'm sorry. Just forget what I said. I don't know how we got on this subject. You were so happy before we started discussing Bonnie."

Buck looked down at her, then said abruptly, "I'm happy whenever I look at you, darlin'."

"Oh, Buck . . ." Easily summoning tears, Celeste whispered, "Forget what I said, please. Maybe Cal really did have good intentions in coming home.

Maybe he just wants to forget how his neglect of Bonnie caused her death. Maybe he's tired of remembering Bonnie would be alive today if it wasn't for him."

"I'll never forgive him for Bonnie's death."

"That's so sad, but I can imagine the horror of seeing Bonnie's twisted and broken body lying at the bottom of the well is an image you'll never forget. I can understand how it's burned into your memory, how it haunts you. I can even comprehend the uncertainties that must plague you when you start thinking maybe it *was* your fault she's dead; maybe if you hadn't gone into town to drink that day and left Bonnie in Cal's care, he wouldn't have had the chance to send her off alone so she could get killed. But that was Cal's fault, not yours. He's the one responsible for Bonnie's death. He knew it, too. That's why he ran off like a coward. Nothing he can ever say will change what he did."

Buck did not speak, providing Celeste the opportunity to continue in a voice trembling with suitable emotion, "But I want you to remember—even if you don't have your darling Bonnie anymore because of Cal, you do have *me*."

"Celeste, darlin' . . ."

Tears brimmed in Buck's bloodshot eyes, and Celeste inwardly smiled. Yes, he was a fool. If she wanted to, she could continue this horrendous masquerade forever. But she *didn't* want to, and with any luck, it would soon be over.

Celeste rested her head lightly against Buck's shoulder as the wagon continued on.

With any luck . . . and a little careful planning.

Pru busied herself around her small kitchen. She glanced out the window as Jeremy rode through the pasture at a pace that made her heart pound with anxiety. She was about to call out to him when she heard his joyful "Yahoo!" and she changed her mind. He had been riding most of the morning on the horse Cal had picked out for him on the day of their fateful journey to assess her herd. Horse and boy appeared at ease with each other, a perfect match that had brought new enjoyment to Jeremy's day, even if she still could not quite manage to watch him with complete peace of mind. She wondered why she hadn't thought to have Jack pick out a horse for Jeremy.

Jack . . . of course. She had depended on him, and he hadn't been worthy of her trust.

Cal's tall, sober image returned abruptly to mind, and Pru felt a new heat suffuse her sunburned skin. During the week since she and Jeremy had gone out with Cal to assess the herd, she had attempted to avoid thinking of the mortifying events of that day. The image of her disheveled reflection in the mirror upon returning to the ranch house, however, remained too vividly clear in her mind.

Pru took a deep breath. It was Cal's fault that she had been so stubborn, of course. If he hadn't looked at her as if astonished by her stupidity every time she spoke . . . if he hadn't always contradicted what she said . . . *if he hadn't been right at every turn*, she supposed she wouldn't have acted that way.

She also wouldn't have nearly collapsed in his arms from the heat, or been a burden to him for the entire duration of the ride back to the ranch house. Nor would she have found herself in such a state of exhaustion upon reaching home that she was unable to take care of her own son.

Pru closed her eyes with a silent groan. Those memories tormented her still. Yet somehow clearer and stronger was the memory of Cal crouching beside her bed in the darkness. The sound of his deep voice as he had talked to her. The unspoken intimacy of that moment had shaken her deeply—yet in the time since, all that seemed to remain of that intimacy was the sound of her name on Cal's lips.

Pru.

Her throat inexplicably tight, Pru glanced out the window toward the sun, which was rapidly rising to the midpoint in the morning sky. Breakfast that morning had been a strained, silent affair like all their breakfasts. Cal had left immediately afterwards, as had become the norm. She supposed he would return later with a report of the work he had either done, or had decided needed to be done. She had noted his apparent frustration as his list of things that needed doing had grown, and the strange estrangement between them had expanded as well.

Pru sighed. Cal had left that morning with no explanation as to where he was going. A pail of fresh milk indicated that he had milked Lulu before departing, but that was all she knew.

Questions buzzed in her mind, questions that had been met with more of Cal's silences. What about the roundup he had talked about, and the branding that he had said was so necessary? She had no idea of the timing involved, or if some unspoken deadline was indeed slipping away. She had become acutely aware of the countless chores that had gone untended before Cal arrived on the ranch—chores presently beyond her ability to accomplish and which would go untended until Cal returned.

The thought nagged: *if* Cal returned.

Pru closed her eyes. Cal had made it plain from the beginning that his stay at the Rocky W was temporary. She had never asked, but she knew that personal issues would determine the timing of his departure. Yet with every day that passed, with every new revelation of what lay ahead for her at the ranch, she—

Oh, drat!

Pru blinked back tears. The truth was, her total ignorance about ranch affairs left her totally dependent on Cal—just as she had been totally dependent on Jack. The situation was intolerable. She couldn't allow it to continue. *She* was the owner of the Rocky W, and if she was going to make a life for Jeremy and herself here, she had to learn everything that being a rancher entailed.

Pru raised her chin. So if Cal *didn't* come back

some day, she would be perfectly capable of getting along without him.

The sound of hoofbeats raised Pru's head toward a group of riders approaching the ranch house. There were four of them. Riding with their backs to the sun, they were not immediately identifiable, and she reached spontaneously for the shotgun she had brought in from the barn.

Yes, she was the one responsible for the new life she had undertaken, and she'd be damned before she'd let this last chance of a decent future for Jeremy and herself slip away.

With a deep breath, and new determination, Pru stepped boldly onto the porch and faced the riders as they approached.

She was the boss of the Rocky W.

Whoever they were, she'd make sure they knew it.

She had that shotgun in her hands again.

Cal frowned at Pru's stiff figure as his small party approached the ranch house porch where she stood. The sight of her sparked a spontaneous heat inside Cal, despite his annoyance, and he struggled against it. He glanced at the men riding beside him when she raised her gun in their direction. They slowed their pace. They had no idea what she had in mind. Nor did they know she couldn't hit the broad side of a barn if she tried, but she was putting on a good front, and he was perversely proud of her.

He glanced at the men again as they rode into the

ranch yard and Pru lowered her gun. He wondered what they saw when they looked at her. Did they see only a woman dressed in severe black, with her hair tightly bound and her sunburned face composed in a frown?

He wondered if they had noticed the brief flicker in Pru's light eyes when she recognized him as one of the riders, or the way she had released a small, relieved breath.

He had noticed it. He fought the emotions she evoked in him as he dismounted.

Aware that the other men had dismounted behind him, Cal addressed Pru flatly.

"I figured it was time to hire the wranglers you need, so here they are. Their names are Josh Tinker, Larry Meade, and Winston Small." He turned to the men beside him. "Boys, meet the lady who owns the Rocky W, Mrs. Prudence Reynolds."

"Ma'am."

"Nice to meet you."

"Pleasure, ma'am."

Pru nodded. Cal saw the resentment she struggled to conceal when she said, "I'm pleased to meet you, but I hope Cal explained the situation here when he hired you. I can't pay you a salary right now."

Cal took an impatient breath. "We'll talk about the particulars later."

"We don't have a decent bunkhouse either."

"The loft will do for the boys and me until we can get the bunkhouse fixed up."

"You'll be working strictly for room and board for a while."

Cal asked flatly, "Do you have anything else to say before we get started?"

Pru shook her head, then amended, "I will, of course, provide your meals at the times you stipulate. When would you like that to be?"

Cal responded, "Sunup and sundown will do, as usual. Is that all?"

When Pru nodded, Cal turned back to the men and instructed, "You can put your bedrolls in the barn for the time being."

Waiting until the three men had slipped from view, Pru demanded, "How could you do that? How could you hire wranglers without talking to me first?"

Cal saw the flush that transfused Pru's face. She was angry. He supposed she had a right to be, but he had no time for her anger. He responded sharply, "What did you want me to discuss with you?"

"You could at least have told me you were going to hire them this morning."

"Why? Did you have a choice?"

"*I'm* the boss on the Rocky W, not you!"

"And *I'm* the foreman—that was the stipulation when I agreed to Doc's crazy scheme, if you remember."

"That doesn't mean—"

"That means *I* make the decisions on what needs to be done to put this ranch back into decent shape."

"With *my* approval!"

Distracted as a shiny wisp of hair fell loose from Pru's tight bun, Cal noted the way it curled against the fragile column of her throat. He remembered—

Annoyed by his temporary distraction, Cal frowned and responded, "With your approval? Why? Would it have made any difference?"

"Maybe not, but—"

"*Maybe not?*"

"*I* own the Rocky W, Cal." Pru's jaw was tight. "I want you to remember that."

"Do you want me to remember, too, that you didn't even know if you had a herd when I got here?"

Pru did not respond, but her expression remained the same. More angry than he knew he had a right to be, he snapped, "I can fire these fellas as easy as I hired them, if that's what you want."

"That isn't what I want."

"What do you want, then?"

The question hung on the air between them.

Cal eyed Pru's slender figure. He silently wondered if she had any idea what she wanted, because he was beginning to get a pretty clear idea of what *he* wanted.

"All right, you win."

There it was again—*you win*. He didn't want to win. He just wanted—

Pru continued, "I don't know anything about ranching, but I want you to remember *I'm* the boss here. *I* make the final decisions, and we don't do anything without *my* approval."

Cal nodded. "That's all right with me. Do you want to hire these wranglers?"

"Yes."

"That's good. What else do you want to approve of?"

Pru's small nose twitched. "They do know what they're getting into, don't they?"

"They're experienced wranglers. Just one look around was all they needed to understand your situation, but they're good men. They aren't afraid of hard work. They'll settle for room and board for the time being, then a portion of the proceeds when you sell off your first herd—if that's all right with you."

"I suppose."

Cal stared at her coldly.

"Fine."

"Then we'll start rounding up the calves and getting them ready for branding."

Pru nodded.

Cal was intensely aware that she was still standing, stiff and angry, in the same spot he had left her when he and the men remounted and rode off.

Celeste pushed open the cabin's squeaking door and paused briefly to acclimate her eyes to the darkness within. She gasped when she was grasped from behind and dragged off her feet. Tossed roughly onto the cot, she grunted when a male body fell heavily atop hers. Wet lips crushed her mouth as a hard male bulge pressed almost painfully against the juncture of her thighs.

Celeste opened her mouth to the wet kiss. She welcomed the groping hands that tore at her skirt, pushing it upward and tearing at her undergarments. Her heart jumped a beat when the musty air of the cabin met the moist delta and a stiff male organ probed her ruthlessly. She stretched her legs wide to accommodate it, then grunted aloud when it was jammed home inside her.

Meeting the harsh, jolting sexual thrusts with a corresponding heat, Celeste grunted and gasped, her excitement mounting as the frenzied rhythm grew more fierce. Aware that she would soon reach climax, she opened her eyes to see the face of her lover. The savage lust on Derek's coarse, heavy features pushed her over the edge, and she called out as his moan echoed loudly in the silent cabin.

Breathless, suddenly disgusted with the primitive copulation she had just indulged in, Celeste attempted to push Derek off her. When she could not budge his heavy body, she looked up at him with a frown.

He said, "I ain't done yet. That was too fast. I figure you had something important in mind for me to do, or you wouldn't have hung that kerchief in your window telling me to come to our little hideaway. You want something from me, and you know I don't do nothing for nothing."

Celeste barely withheld a sneer as she said, "You're right." She forced a smile. He was crushing her with his weight, but she'd suffered worse. It occurred to her she might even get some pleasure out of what the bastard had in mind for her later.

That thought sending a rush of heat through her veins, Celeste continued, "There's been a slight hitch in my plans. I want you to take care of it for me."

"Tell me what the problem is, and I'll tell you what it'll cost you."

"The widow's ranch—the Rocky W. I want you to hit it and hit it hard."

"Hell, that's already been done! We took all we can from that ranch. The rest of the Rocky W herd is scattered all over that spread of hers. The boys and me would have to do a regular roundup before we could put enough beeves together to make it worthwhile—and that's too much like work, as far as I'm concerned."

"That was before the widow got herself a foreman."

"A foreman! That skinny witch can't afford to hire nobody with the condition that ranch is in."

"She's paying him off somehow." Jealousy at that thought tightened Celeste's jaw as she continued, "I found out this morning that the foreman got three other wranglers to work for her, too."

"She must be a busy woman."

Derek appeared to be giving his last comment some thought, and Celeste laughed confidently. "Forget it. She's not as good as I am. I can guarantee that."

Derek stared down at her. He was salivating visibly when he said, "What do you have in mind?"

"The Rocky W wranglers will be trying to whip the

ranch back into shape. I want you to cause them as many problems as you can, but let them finish their roundup. When they're done, you'll have a big enough herd to make the rustling worthwhile."

"Why the sudden interest in the Rocky W?"

"It's not the Rocky W I'm thinking about. It's the new foreman, Cal Star. He's my husband's son. He's in my way, and I want him out of town as soon as possible. He doesn't have the stomach for trouble, so if you make it hot enough for him on the Rocky W, he'll run. That's his specialty . . . running."

"He's that kind, huh?"

"A shame, too, considering what he looks like."

"Got your eye on him, have you?"

Celeste purred, "Derek, honey, I haven't got my eye on anybody but you. Do we have a deal?"

He scrutinized her expression for a silent moment, then nodded.

"That's good. I know I can depend on you. You never let me down."

Celeste's voice dropped lower. "Now . . . tell me what I can do to boost your enthusiasm. I've got plenty of time to make you happy." She reached for his male organ. It was already hard. A thrill shot up her spine as she rasped, "Just say the word, and it's yours."

She didn't have to wait long for an answer.

Cal paused to allow his mount a moment's rest as he scanned the pasture, then looked back at the holding corral the boys and he had repaired. It was a sorry sight with its hastily mended, uneven fencing, but it was strong enough to hold the calves until they could be branded and returned to the cows bawling to them from outside the enclosure.

They'd been working the smaller herd that had lingered by the closest stream. A late start had limited their progress, but Cal was fairly certain they'd be able to finish branding the calves before nightfall.

Cal scowled. He glanced at Winston, who was feeding the fire and checking the branding irons resting there. Cal wondered how long it had been since Old Man Simmons had used those irons. From the look of things, he had let everything lapse and had just let nature take its course during the final years of his life. Cal supposed he'd find out if he was right when he and the boys started rounding up the herd and checking for brands more closely, but judging from the ranch's degree of neglect, there'd be a need for more branding than he presently cared to speculate about.

Of course, the rustlers might have already made off with a lot of the unbranded cattle.

Cal paused at that thought. How had he gotten so deeply involved with Pru and the Rocky W, anyway? He had come home to talk to his pa and put the past to rest. When he arrived and saw the condition of the Texas Star, it became obvious that more than talk was needed. His pa needed help, and Cal knew he could provide it. He wanted to help his pa. He *needed* to help him—for both their sakes.

Cal's scowl deepened. What he didn't need was an entanglement with a stubborn widow that would cloud his mind when he should be thinking about a way to get around his pa's fascination with his young wife—when he should at least be finding a way to have a conversation with his father that didn't end in shouting and recriminations.

But it wasn't working out that way. In the time since his disastrous outing with Pru and Jeremy, he had been able to think about little but the widow. He remembered the foolish pride that had held Pru sitting stiffly on her mount in the full sun, just to prove herself. He recalled her determined effort not to surrender to her discomfort. Most vivid in his mind, however, was the brief, recurrent flash of vulnerability in her eyes that she'd been unable to disguise. It ate at him in silent moments. It raised a need to touch her, to console her, to hold her close and see those light eyes look up at him openly, without the shield she kept between them. He seemed unable to dismiss the memory of holding Pru in his arms as they had shared his saddle. The firm pressure of her tight, rounded buttocks pressed against him, and the sweet weight of her firm breasts against his forearms as she relaxed in sleep, had confirmed the fact that she was all woman underneath that baggy widow's garb she wore.

She had felt so right in his arms as he had carried her into her bedroom. Remembering those moments while he had crouched beside her bed, whispering to her in the semidarkness, he had begun wondering what would have happened if he had—

Cal cut short that thought as he had done countless times previously. He had no time for Pru or any woman. He had come home to put an end to years of aching guilt that still tormented him—and to discover who had sent him that cryptic note about Bonnie, and why.

"It looks to me like you ain't too happy a fella."

Cal turned toward Josh as the bearded wrangler drew his horse up alongside him. Shaken from his thoughts, Cal scrutinized his companions. He hadn't thought twice about where he'd find the ranch hands Pru needed to get the Rocky W back into shape. He remembered Ethan Reemes. Everything the boys had said about the man was true. Josh, Larry, and Winston weren't the kind to deserve the treatment Reemes handed out. He knew they hadn't spoken lightly when they said they'd be moving on soon. He also knew that leaving the area where they had worked for so many years wouldn't be easy.

The solution had been obvious. The Rocky W needed them, and they needed the Rocky W. He had also known that their acceptance of the terms of their employment was an unspoken statement of their trust in him. They knew they'd get paid for their work because he'd make sure they did.

Cal replied belatedly as Josh awaited his response, "I don't look like a happy fella, huh? I'm thinking you wouldn't be too happy, either, if you were me right now."

Josh responded with a half smile. "I figure there's

a lot of things you could be meaning by that, and I'm not about to guess exactly what you're referring to right now."

Cal's frown deepened. "The truth is, I'm still not sure how I got involved in this mess. I was talking to Doc Maggie one day, and the next day, here I am, trying to whip the Rocky W back into shape—when all I really came home for was to settle things with my pa."

Josh's smile faded. "I'm thinking as bad as things look here, it'll be a sight easier for you to shape this place up than it'll be to get past that wife of your pa's in order to talk to him. She's a determined woman."

"I found that out the first time I talked to her."

"She likes having your pa under her thumb."

"Pa's a sick old man."

"She don't seem to mind that at all."

"Meaning?"

Josh shrugged. "I don't know, but it seems to me, the sicker your pa gets, the more he tries to please that woman . . . and the more she seems to enjoy it."

"You mean—"

Josh shook his head. "It's nothing either me or the boys can put a finger on. I don't like her much, so my thinking might be prejudiced. All I know is that the Texas Star started going downhill the moment she married your pa, and she doesn't seem to give a damn."

"Pa's got resources. I don't understand why he doesn't use them to get the ranch back in shape. If money's the problem, he can just borrow against the next roundup."

"Rustling's hit him hard. He lost a lot of stock to diseases over the past few years, too. I'm thinking he's tapped out from trying to replace what he lost."

"He can borrow against the land."

"He already did that."

"The bank knows he's good for his debts. The Texas Star is the biggest ranch around."

"The bank doesn't know nothing of the sort—not anymore. From their point of view, your pa mortgaged his land, then got too sick to take care of business the way he should. Right now, even if he was his old self, he doesn't seem to have the money to hire the ranch hands he needs to do the job—and there isn't a wrangler in the territory who'll hire on at the Texas Star knowing he might never get paid."

"None of that would've stopped Pa before. He would've found a way."

"Like I said, your pa ain't the man he used to be."

Cal's frustration surged. "I need to talk to him. I need to try to make him see—"

"What good would that do right now, Cal? You're committed here, and it's going to be a while before you can get the Rocky W back on its feet."

"That's where you're wrong. I told the widow my job here was temporary. I told her I'd stay just until she could find somebody to replace me."

"Is that right?"

"Yeah, it is."

"You think she'll be able to do that—replace you, I mean?"

"I figure after you're here a little while, maybe you'd be interested in taking the job."

"Ohhhh, that's what you were thinking," Josh said.

"That's right, that's what I was thinking." Somehow defensive, Cal continued, "Look, Josh, I'm not trying to saddle you with this place. I'll do my best to work things out here first. And Pru isn't a bad sort. She's just . . . well . . ." Cal halted, then said bluntly, "All right, she's pigheaded and determined to prove she's the boss, even though she doesn't know one end of a steer from another. That makes it hard to talk to her sometimes, but . . . I'm working on that. Anyway, like I said, I only came back to settle things with my pa."

"That might take longer than you think, with the rustling and all."

"Maybe, but Sheriff Carter's looking for some outside help. I'm hoping he'll get the rustlers under control."

"Like you said—maybe."

Their conversation halted abruptly when Winston signaled the irons were ready. Cal glanced up at the position of the sun overhead. They had a few hours left—enough time to finish branding the calves already penned before they headed back to the ranch house for the night. It would be a start.

Dismounting at the corral with Josh beside him, Cal approached the bawling calves. He signaled to Larry to rope the first calf as he jumped the fence with Josh beside him while Winston readied the branding iron. At the calf's side, Cal grabbed the protesting animal, one hand on its flank and one near its foreleg. Leaning back, he heaved the calf over on its side, then reached up to grasp its foreleg and hold it down while Josh grasped the hind leg and stretched it out to provide a flat surface for Winston to set the brand.

The branding smoke billowed up, hot and acrid with a smell of singeing hair that burned his eyes as Cal awaited Winston's signal to release the calf. Stepping back at Winston's nod, Cal watched the calf spring to its feet. He ran his forearm across his tearing eyes, then went still at the unexpected sound of Jeremy's voice behind him.

"Did you see that, Mama? Did you see it? Cal lifted that calf right up in the air and flipped him over!"

Turning, Cal saw Pru and Jeremy sitting their horses a little distance away. He blinked as Pru slid down from the saddle. He eyed her from head to toe as she walked toward him wearing the riding clothes he had bought for her, then silently cursed.

That had been a mistake. A big one.

The male clothing—baggy pants, an oversized shirt—could not conceal the length of Pru's long, slender legs, the generous breasts that bobbed against her shirt at every step, or the narrow waistline where she had strung a cord through the pants beltloops in order to gather in excess inches of material. With a flat-brimmed hat covering dark hair, which she wore in a single braid down her back, and Texas boots on her feet, she no longer gave the appearance of a sorry black crow.

And there wasn't anything skinny about her.

With a quick glance toward the men, Cal saw they were as fascinated as he. Irrationally angered by that realization, he snapped, "What are you doing here?"

"What do you think I'm doing?" Pru's response was equally sharp. "I'm observing the branding procedure."

Observing the branding procedure.

Cal saw the smile that ticked at the corner of Josh's lips. He replied, "You mean you're checking up on us."

"That wasn't my intention."

"If you're not, I'd say you're wasting time when you could probably be doing something useful back at the ranch house."

"Excuse me, Cal." Pru's lips were tight. "But this is *my* ranch. I have the right to ride wherever I want on it."

"There's no need for you to be here. The boys and I can carry on fine without you."

"Maybe you can, but I'm staying anyway."

Jeremy interjected anxiously, "We needed to come, Cal. Mama needs to learn about things on the ranch. She doesn't know anything about branding, you know?"

Pru warned, "Jeremy . . ."

"She says she's going to ride out with you and the boys every day, so she can learn what ranching is all about . . . so she won't be so *dumb*."

"Jeremy!"

Cal glanced at Pru. Her face was flaming.

Totally without a response, Cal turned back to the men and signaled for Larry to rope the next calf. Cal had heaved the second calf onto its side and was holding it immobile with Josh's help when he heard Jeremy say, "Cal's strong, isn't he, Mama? I haven't ever seen anybody stronger than he is. Do you think I'll be as strong as he is someday, so I could do that?"

No response.

The smell of singeing hair was again burning his eyes when Cal heard Jeremy prompt, "Mama? Do you think I could?"

"Probably . . . if you wanted to."

"But you couldn't, Mama,'cause you're a *girl*."

Cal looked up at that. His gaze locked with Pru's for an extended second, and the heat that surged inside him had nothing to do with branding.

'Cause you're a girl.

Yes, damn it, she sure was.

Pru walked toward the dining room table, a steaming pot of stew in her hands. She deliberately avoided looking at the four men seated there as she returned to the kitchen for biscuits, fresh butter, and a jar of the precious strawberry preserves she had brought from home. She had a monumental pot of coffee freshly brewed on the stove, and a spice cake waiting for dessert.

Pru frowned as she took her seat and the men commenced eating. She was uncertain why their reaction to the first supper she'd served them was making her so nervous. Perhaps it was because Cal's reaction to every question she had asked during the branding had been so clipped. Perhaps it was because Jeremy had gradually gravitated to Cal's side, seeming to resent her questions as much as Cal did. Perhaps it was because by the end of the day, she had felt completely unnecessary. Or perhaps it was because she needed to provide a good meal for the men just so she could prove she was good at *something*.

"This is a fine stew, ma'am."

"It sure is—real good."

"Best stew I've had in a dog's age."

Pru forced a smile and nodded in response to the men's comments, aware of the color creeping up her neck. She hadn't realized she had been so obviously awaiting their approval.

"It sure is good, Mama," Jeremy added, directing his next comment to the men with whom he had so easily bonded during the afternoon hours. "Wait until you taste my mama's spice cake. She made it special. She doesn't know much about ranching, but she sure knows how to cook."

Mumbles of agreement sounded around the table, breaking the uncomfortable silence, but Pru did not look up.

Relieved when the meal was finally over and the men had left the house, Pru turned to the dishes. She had finished washing them when the sound of a step behind her alerted her to Cal's presence. She turned to find Cal standing so close behind her that she could see the brown specks in the glowing gold of his eyes as he said, "We have some things we need to straighten out about the way things are going to work around here, and I figure this is as good a time as any."

Pru responded spontaneously, "I'm not in the mood to argue with you, Cal."

"I don't expect an argument."

"You don't?"

"I'd like you and Jeremy to ride into town tomorrow to pick up some supplies the boys and me will be needing."

Pru searched his sober expression, then asked, "Do you really need supplies, or are you just trying to get me out of the way so I won't bother you when you work?"

"You didn't bother me."

"I did too."

"I said you didn't."

"Then why were you so short with your answers to my questions?"

"It could be because you asked too many."

"I thought you said I didn't bother you."

"You didn't, but your questions sure as hell did."

"Cal—"

"Look, Pru," She couldn't be sure, but it seemed Cal moved even closer as he said, "I can understand how you're thinking. You need to learn about ranching, and there's only one way to do it." He corrected himself. "No, maybe two. By watching, and by asking questions. All I'm saying is, I think you'd be better off using the first way to find out what you want to know, and forgetting the second, because your questions are getting in the way of us doing our work."

He was so close his body heat scorched her. The scent of the soap he had used to clean up before supper teased her nostrils. He smelled clean . . . and totally male.

"Pru . . . ?"

She swallowed, then nodded. "That's reasonable. I'll try to limit my questions."

"And I think you should find yourself some suitable clothes."

"Wh . . . what?"

"Those clothes you're wearing—"

Pru glanced down at her baggy pants and shirt. She retorted, "You bought them!"

"Yes, but they don't look like I figured they would. I'm thinking you need to be wearing proper clothes when the men are around."

"Are you saying the men were laughing at me because of what I'm wearing?"

"No. They aren't laughing."

"What are you saying, then?"

Pru waited for a response that did not come, then gasped, "Are you saying . . . saying these clothes look *indecent* on me?"

"What I'm saying is, a woman like you has to be careful how she dresses."

"A woman like me?"

"A young, good-looking woman."

"I am not good-looking!"

"You're not?"

"I . . . I'm a widow!"

Cal's gaze held hers. She could sense the words he withheld, and a slow trembling began inside her. She started when he reached into his pocket unexpectedly, then handed her the slip of paper he withdrew.

His voice was gruff. "This is a list of the supplies we'll be needing tomorrow. If you'll ride into town and get them, the boys and me won't have to waste time doing it."

Pru scanned the list. Wire, nails, horse liniment, fly repellant . . .

"Fly repellant?"

"For screw worms."

Screw worms.

"While you're at it, you'd better stock up on supplies for your kitchen. The boys are hearty eaters. They'll clean your kitchen out in a couple of days."

Cal's chest was heaving. His gaze was intent on her face, and he was frowning darkly. Suddenly as breathless as he, she nodded.

He added, "Don't forget the clothes."

"But I—"

"Just do it!"

Cal stepped back abruptly. "We'll be leaving at daybreak."

Pru nodded again. She was still unable to respond when he walked out the doorway.

* * *

Cal strode across the ranch yard toward the barn. Twilight had faded into night, and he had bolted away from Pru in the kitchen like a jackrabbit in tall grass.

He took a stabilizing breath.

That had been close.

It had been a long day branding calves, especially with Pru watching every step of the way. His resistance wasn't what it should be, and another minute looking down into those clear gray eyes and he'd have had her in his arms.

And that would have been a mistake—for both of them.

Chapter Eight

Madalane's handsome features drew into harsh lines as she faced her mistress across the shadowed bedroom Celeste shared with her husband. Buck had ridden off with the hands for the day's work while Celeste lay still asleep in their bed. It was hours later, and Madalane had entered the room to find Celeste barely able to open her eyes, so exhausted still from her previous day's encounter with the crude degenerate, Derek.

The memory of Celeste's flush when she returned from that tryst sent a cold chill down Madalane's spine. The man was foul. She had accepted the necessity of Celeste's collaboration with him, but she now recognized an unexpected danger.

She had seen the signs before, when Celeste was the most celebrated woman in Miss Ruby's House of Pleasures. Celeste was *enjoying* the depravities into which she sank with Derek—more with each encounter. She feared for Celeste and for the future they had both worked so diligently to attain.

As Madalane watched, Celeste rose from the bed, unmindful of her nudity. She walked to the washstand, poured water into the bowl, and splashed it against her flawless countenance. She patted her face dry with a fine linen cloth as she turned back toward Madalane.

Her fear expanding, Madalane said despite her awareness of Celeste's growing irritation, "You rely too heavily on the dependability of a coarse, ignorant thief whose only thought is for the stimulation of the moments when you lie together. Fool that you are, you lower yourself to his level in order to gain his cooperation!"

"A fool, am I?" Celeste's cheek twitched with annoyance as she spat, "I alone lifted us out of the New Orleans slums where we languished after my parents' deaths. I alone used my power over men to regain the position that was stolen from me as a child. Rather, it is the men I use who are the fools. They dance to my music, and Derek—as coarse and a vile as he is—dances so very well."

"He is coarse and vile—those are your words. He cannot be trusted to follow through on his promises."

"He has never disappointed me, and the reason is simple. *I* have never disappointed him." Celeste laughed. "I renew my power over him each time we lie together. I hold him in the palm of my hand." She laughed again. "In so many ways."

"Listen to me, Celeste." Madalane's expression

grew intense. "We have come too far to risk all when we are so close to achieving our ends. I have seen to it that your bank account in New Orleans has grown as the fortunes of the Texas Star declined. I have carried each deposit there myself, as you directed, and your future is already secure. Should that fool betray you—"

"He would not."

"If he should—"

"If he should, my dear Buck would never believe him."

"Buck's son would believe him!"

"It wouldn't matter if the whole world believed him; Buck would not, I tell you!"

"You depend on the devotion of your husband—a man whose infidelity to his previous wife was the root of the very deprivations you seek to avenge."

"Madalane"—Celeste's voice grew insidiously sweet—"you do not understand. It is my husband's infidelities that make him *mine*."

Madalane's body twitched with suppressed fury. Her gaze scorching, she said, "I see danger in your future. The fool Derek will betray you!"

"You see nothing!"

"You must listen to me! I speak for your own good!"

"You are growing old, Madalane"—Celeste swept her with a deprecating gaze—"while I grow more beautiful and secure in my power over men each day."

"I will remind you of this moment when the time is right."

"That time will never come. Derek will do what I ask of him. I've made him too weak to do anything else."

"I tell you—"

"I'm tired of your whining! It is time for you to listen to me." Her face flushing with the heat of her anger, Celeste grated, "My dear stepson's return was more timely than either of us realized. When he shows his true colors, when he deserts his father a second time, when he abandons the responsibilities he has assumed at the Rocky W at the first sign of trouble, Buck won't be able to deny his son's true character any longer—not even to himself. He'll make any changes I suggest in his will because he'll be too ashamed not to. Then we'll be totally free of him at last, and free to return to the life that we were both born for."

Her naked breasts heaving with the passion of her words, Celeste rasped, "Make ready your tonics, and when my husband's 'strange illness' strikes again, we'll see to it that he does not recover."

Madalane did not respond, and Celeste snapped, "You bore me with your predictions of doom. Go away! I don't choose to scowl today."

Madalane turned obediently toward the bedroom doorway. She heard Celeste's annoyed mumblings as she pulled the door closed behind her. She listened outside, waiting for the mumbling to cease. Celeste was angry, but she would soon consider more carefully all that they had discussed. If she did not, and the crude thief Derek did indeed become Celeste's enemy, Madalane would dispose of him herself.

Madalane drew herself up proudly. Despite her mistress's angry words, Celeste could not do without her. They shared a special bond that would bind them forever close. Celeste knew that as well as she. Celeste also knew her dear Madalane would do whatever was necessary to protect them.

Yes . . . anything.

It felt strange riding alone into town.

Dressed in her familiar widow's attire, Pru glanced at the sunlit terrain, then at the empty spot beside her where Jeremy usually sat. Her young son had been up at dawn, fully dressed and seated at the table when the ranch hands came in for breakfast. He had begged to be allowed to ride out with them, and she had been adamant that he should stay home.

Somehow she hadn't expected Cal to take Jeremy's part. She hadn't expected him to say, "The boy needs to learn about ranching if he's going to run the Rocky W someday." She wasn't sure if it was that thought, or the nodding agreement of the hands around the table that eventually changed her mind.

Presently, her feelings were mixed. Jeremy was only five years old. He needed to be in school more than he needed to be learning the workings of a ranch.

She had deliberately ignored her son's situation while struggling to find her own footing in their new life. It was a problem she knew she needed to face.

In any case, she missed Jeremy's company. The shotgun hidden underneath the wagon seat was a poor substitute for Jeremy's bright face and boundless curiosity.

Relieved when Lowell finally came into view, Pru navigated her wagon cautiously along the busy main street, then drew it to a halt in front of the mercantile store. She paused to check the list of necessary supplies Cal had given her: wire, nails, etc. Cal had added a few other items to the list, most of which she knew had been in the supply room when Jack first came to work for her. Since they weren't there any longer, and Jack hadn't made enough repairs at the ranch to have used them up, she was fairly certain he had found a more personally profitable use for them.

As if summoned from her thoughts, Jack appeared suddenly in her path as Pru stepped down onto the board sidewalk and turned toward the store. One glance at his unshaven face, slovenly attire, and leering expression, and she wondered how she had allowed herself to believe for a moment that he could be trusted.

Disgusted with him and with herself for having depended on him, Pru attempted to walk past Jack, only to feel him grip her arm to stay her. She shook his hand loose, feeling defiled as she snapped, "What do you want?"

"What do I want?" He laughed crudely. "You got a convenient memory, don't you? You owe me money for the work I done on your ranch."

"What work?"

"Don't be smart! You know what I'm talking about. If it wasn't for me, that ranch would've fallen apart around you, and you and that kid of yours wouldn't have lasted a week."

"No, I don't think so. It's more truthful to say that the Rocky W didn't fall apart *in spite of you*. And as far as my son is concerned, I've always provided for him without anyone's help, and I always will."

"Big talk . . . when you was as helpless on that ranch as a worm in a bed of ants."

The mental picture his words evoked curled Pru's lips with disgust. "I never was and never will be that helpless."

"Yeah? So you think everything's fine now that you hired Cal Star to work for you. You think he's a real man, huh, somebody who's going to get that ranch of yours back on its feet? Well, you got another think coming. A fella who kills his own sister ain't nothing to brag about."

"Kills his own sister—"

"That's right. Ask him. Go ahead. He'll tell you—and if he don't, anybody else in town will. That's why he can't step foot on his pa's ranch. That's why his pa can't stand the sight of him."

"I don't believe you."

"Why?" Jack stared at her more closely and said,

"Well, I'll be damned. He's been making up to you, ain't he?"

"Making up to me?"

Jack snarled, "Don't make out you don't know what I'm saying. I should've figured somebody'd try to get past that black dress and high-and-mighty manner of yours sooner or later, but I never figured it would be him."

"Get out of my way."

"Don't think you can act uppity with me just because you got somebody to stand up for you."

"I told you to get out of my way!"

"Yeah? What are you going to do about it if I don't?" Pru shuddered with fury as Jack grated, "You owe me money, and I expect to get it."

"I don't owe you anything! You've been adequately compensated for whatever little you did around the ranch by the things you charged to my accounts all over town."

"That was ranch business."

"That new silver-trimmed saddle your horse is sporting was ranch business?"

Jack did not reply.

"What about those hand-tooled boots and your new rifle? What about that horse you bought for the ranch that I never heard about, and still haven't seen although I got the bill? What happened to all those supplies you charged to me that somehow never made it to the ranch? And while you're at it, how about telling me what happened to the tools that were in the supply room at the Rocky W? Nobody can find them now."

"Nobody . . . you're saying your boyfriend can't find them tools."

"I don't have a *boyfriend*."

"Well, since you're from back East, you probably got a better word for how Cal Star takes care of you than I do."

Pru gasped.

Aware that their conversation was beginning to draw a crowd, Pru attempted to push Jack aside, only to feel him grasp her arm painfully tight as he said, "Just remember, *boyfriend* or not, I expect to collect the money you owe me—one way or another."

Her jaw firm, Pru jerked her arm free and walked into the store without a backward glance. She was shuddering when she reached the counter and Harvey Bower asked politely, "Something wrong, ma'am?"

Pru forced up her chin, handed him the list she clutched in her hand, and said, "I ran into a nasty varmint on the way here, but I'm fine now."

Oblivious to her meaning, the storekeeper responded, "A woman in these parts has to learn how to use a gun for her own protection, ma'am. I'm thinking you need to have somebody show you."

"I think I'll do that." Turning toward the storekeeper's wife when she walked up behind the counter, Pru said, "I'd appreciate it if you'd show me where you keep riding clothes suitable for Jeremy and myself. I have the feeling we'll both be spending more time in the saddle than I anticipated when I first came here."

"I'd be happy to, Mrs. Reynolds."

"Pru." Uncertain why she had never thought to say it before, she added, "My name is Pru."

The woman's smile broadened. "Just follow me, Pru, and I'll get you set up like a real Texan while Harvey is filling your order."

Pru turned back toward the storekeeper and said, "About my account . . ."

"Doc Maggie said you hired Cal Star to work on your place. He'll whip the Rocky W back into shape, so I'm not worrying about your account right now."

"Doc Maggie told you that?"

"She sure did. She told everybody else you owe money to in town, too. The doc never did agree with what some people said happened that day with Cal and his sister, even if he did leave town right afterwards. I figure her word is good enough for me."

. . . what some people said happened that day with Cal Star and his sister . . .

A chill ran down Pru's spine. She was about to reply when Agnes Bower addressed her husband with a frown, saying, "Just hurry and fill that order, Harvey. This lady doesn't have all day."

Pru followed behind as the woman turned toward the rear of the store.

. . . what some people said . . .

* * *

Jack stared at the store doorway through which Pru had disappeared moments earlier. He ignored the frowns of the townsfolk filing past him on the street as his inner rage expanded.

The uppity witch! Who did she think she was? He never did like the way she looked at him, like she thought he wasn't clean enough to come into that house she was so particular about.

So, she wasn't going to pay him. Well, he'd see about that. He had worked at the Rocky W long enough to learn some things, and there was more than one way to skin a cat. But first, he was going to teach her a lesson she wouldn't forget.

Jack started toward his horse with a hard smile on his lips. He was going to enjoy this.

"I hear Cal's back in town, Buck."

Buck turned sharply toward Big John as the burly wrangler drew his mount up beside him. The sun had almost reached the midpoint in the sky, and it was hotter than Buck remembered scouting a herd could ever be. His body was quickly heating to the boiling point, a fact that was emphasized by his realization that neither Big John, Randy, nor Mitch seemed to be suffering the same degree of discomfort.

Buck took a shaky breath. He had to face the truth. Whatever it was that was dragging his health down, he hadn't beaten it yet.

Buck swallowed. His mouth was dry and his head was woozy. He could remember a time when riding his own land had cured all his ills, when the sight of his cattle milling at the stream had lifted his spirits, when watching his two sons working the herd had seemed a promise of the future that would never dim, and when just the thought of the two smiling female faces that would greet his return home had made his heart proud.

Looking back, he wondered how he could ever have wanted more.

It had all ended so fast. First Emma, then Bonnie—and his world collapsed around him.

"Are you all right, Buck?"

"Sure I'm all right!" Buck mentally shook himself back to the present. An unyielding anger added sharpness to his tone as he responded, "I heard what you said, too. My answer is, yes, Cal's back in town. You know it, and I know it. But that doesn't mean he's got a chance of getting back on this ranch."

Big John's gaze was direct. "Why not?"

"I don't have to make any explanations to you."

"No, you don't, but you know as well as me and the boys do that we sure could use some help on this place."

"Not *his* help."

"Buck . . ." Big John's deep voice grew softer. "I was on the ranch that day it happened, you know. I saw Cal when he came back from town—when you all came back with Bonnie's body."

"I don't want to talk about it."

"It seems to me it's time you do."

"I said—"

"Cal was only a kid. I saw him go into the barn, and I went in after him to talk. He was sobbing so hard, he never saw me come in."

"We all did a lot of crying that day."

"He loved Bonnie."

"He got her killed."

"It was an accident."

"An accident that never should've happened! If it wasn't for Cal, Bonnie would still be alive."

"I'm thinking nobody blamed Cal more than he blamed himself."

Buck met Big John's gaze coldly. "We'll never know that, will we, since he ran off like a thief in the night before his sister was even in her grave."

"You might find out what he has to say about it if you'd give him a chance to talk to you."

"He doesn't deserve a chance."

"Don't be so mule-headed, Buck! Cal's your son, and he's come home to make things up. You need him now, and we—"

A new flush of rage coloring his face, Buck rasped, "I don't need him!"

"You only have two sons."

"I don't have *any* sons, and that's the last of it!"

Suddenly unable to bear the heat or the conversation a moment longer, Buck snapped, "You boys can get along without me up here. I'm going back to the house." He paused, then added in deadly earnest, "And if Cal sets foot on this ranch, I want you to drive him off with a gun if you need to."

"Buck—"

"Do you hear me?"

Big John sighed revealingly. "I hear you."

Buck turned his horse back toward the house. He rode recklessly fast, to escape the heat, to expel painful memories, and to return to the only person left who really understood him—his beautiful Celeste.

Jack approached the Rocky W ranch house as the sun reached its summit in a clear, intensely blue sky. His wet lips drew into a slow smile. The place was deserted, just as he had expected. He had passed Cal Star, the smart-mouthed kid, and a few wranglers down by the stream, and had taken care not to let them see him.

He'd been surprised to see the widow in town, but her timing couldn't have been better. Talk about the reasons the widow had fired him had gotten around, and there wasn't a rancher in the territory who would hire him. He was broke, thirsty, and mad as hell, and she'd been just the person he was looking for.

Jack thought back to the way she had looked at him when she stepped down from her wagon, as if he was lower than dirt, and a familiar fury rose. The snobbish witch had worked him like a dog to fix up that house of hers. She had only gotten what she deserved when he had helped himself to whatever he could around the ranch. She didn't seem to miss what he took, or she didn't much care. She had put more effort into fixing up the house than checking up on the ranch stock. He had taken his cue from her, telling himself that if she didn't care about the herd, neither did he. And now she didn't want to pay him.

He'd fix her.

And when he was done, if she still didn't want to pay him, he'd just do what he'd done before. He'd *take* what he had coming.

Jack pulled up at the ranch house rail and dismounted. He stepped up onto the porch and opened the door. He paused there a moment, smiling broadly, then walked inside.

Pru was still shaken from her encounter with Jack when the Rocky W ranch house came into view at last. She was glad to be home. Agnes Bower was a helpful woman. She had personally escorted her around the store to get the items she needed, had stood by as she had gone through the limited ready-made clothing stock available, and had offered comments on the color, size, and pricing of everything. She had even carried the items to the counter for her—all the while keeping up a running conversation about Pru's new "hired man."

The knot inside Pru tightened to the point of pain. She needed time to digest the startling facts that Agnes had recounted. Bonnie Star had been seven years old and in Cal's care when she was killed. Cal hadn't even stayed in town long enough afterwards to see his sister buried.

Pru was incredulous at that. She wondered why

he had left home without explanation . . . and what had prompted him, after all the years in between, to return. Somehow she could not equate the irresponsible boy he had then been with the confident, determined, dependable man he was now.

She remembered Cal's concern when her stubbornness the day they scouted the herd had made her ill. He had put her to bed and taken care of Jeremy. She recalled his gentleness when he'd crouched beside her bed, concerned that she was sick again. She remembered the sensitivity in his tone . . . the way he had stroked her hair as he looked down at her. The glowing gold of his eyes had been strangely clear in the semidarkness. The pure male scent of him had been somehow reassuring, as had the unexpected tenderness in his tone, which had touched a spot deep inside her. She remembered that for the briefest moment, she had almost wished—

Pru's mental meanderings halted as she pulled into the yard and saw the screen door of the house hanging limply on broken hinges. Her throat was tight when she drew her wagon to a halt and jumped down, then withdrew the shotgun from underneath the seat. Her heart pounded when she stepped up onto the porch and shoved the door aside.

Pru looked inside and gasped. She strove for control as she viewed the devastation within. The table and chairs had been broken and upended, the curtains torn from the windows and the glass broken, the dry sink overturned, food stores thrown against the walls and then trampled into the floor, pans and utensils dented and scattered . . .

One glimpse into the living room, and Pru emitted a sob. The worn furniture was slashed, the stuffing strewn about. The rug was shredded, and the lamps smashed.

She closed her eyes, unwilling to see more.

Cal unconsciously glanced at the sky overhead. He frowned at the realization that it was well past noon. The branding was not going as well as he had hoped. Rebellious calves and ornery cows had made the morning's work a trial. They'd already been behind schedule when they had paused for the noon meal and a headstrong cow had taken the opportunity to butt the weak, temporarily repaired corral fencing. She had broken through it before they'd realized what she was doing, releasing the calves, which had scattered as fast as their spindly legs could carry them.

Cal had been determined that wouldn't happen again, and had started back for the ranch house, certain Pru would have returned with the tools and supplies needed to make more suitable repairs.

Cal drew himself rigidly erect as the ranch house came into view. A warning tremor went up his spine.

Something was wrong. Pru's wagon was drawn up at the hitching rail outside the house, and the door was partially torn from its hinges.

Dismounting on the run, Cal drew his gun and entered the house. He paused, startled by the wreckage within, then called out, "Pru, are you in here?"

No response.

He walked cautiously forward, then halted at the sight of Pru sitting on the floor on the far side of the dining room. The broken pieces of her shattered china lay around her.

"Pru . . . ?"

She did not move.

Cal crouched beside her and turned her toward him. Her face was white and her eyes were dry, but the desolation in her voice tore at his heart when she said, "The china was all I had left of home. It was my mother's."

"Are you all right?" Cal's throat tightened when a single tear slipped down Pru's cheek. He slid his arms around her and drew her close as he whispered, "Tell me you're all right."

"Why would someone do this, Cal?"

"I don't know."

"Everything in every room is destroyed, even the bedrooms. It's all smashed, cut up, trampled. Jeremy's clothes, my clothes." She drew back with a half smile that wobbled. "All my widow's dresses are cut into ribbons."

He almost smiled back.

"Who did this, Cal?" Her trembling was beginning to worsen. "*Why* would somebody do this?"

Pru's tears were coming full force now. She was sobbing, shuddering, clutching him, mumbling incoherently, and he drew her closer. He knew how it was to feel desperate. He knew how despair shook a person to the core, how panic fostered a need to escape. But it was different for Pru than it had been for him. It was different, because she was in his arms, and she had him to protect her, to take care of her. He wouldn't let anything like this happen to her again.

He was whispering those words against her hair. He was holding her breathlessly tight as he brushed a kiss against the curling tendrils at her temple. He was smoothing the tears from her cheeks with his lips. He was stilling her quivering lips with his mouth. He was kissing her deeply, holding her, never wanting to let her go.

His mouth followed the delicate line of her throat. He pressed loving kisses against her shoulders, the hollow at the base of her throat. Working aside the buttons she had loosened due to the heat of the day, he tasted her breasts, reveling in their sweetness.

Pru lost herself in the heat of Cal's loving ministrations. It felt so good to be in his arms—safe, wanted, protected—to be a part of something real and vibrant. She wanted him to hold her. She wanted him to love her, to make this beautiful moment drive harsh reality from her mind.

She surrendered to the loving heat rapidly consuming her. She accepted his kisses. She felt his hunger as he stroked her flesh. She shared it with growing fervor, returning kiss for kiss, caress for caress.

The blazing gold of Cal's eyes was mesmerizing as he lowered his weight upon her. She felt his hardness probe the moist delta between her thighs, and she gasped as he entered her in a quick, facile movement. Exhilaration shuddered through her as she raised herself to meet his intimate thrusts, instinctively joining the rhythm of his lovemaking.

The wonder soared higher.

Cal's breath brushed her cheek as he paused at the brink. She heard his incoherent whisper the moment before he came to sudden, ecstatic fulfillment in a rush that sent her spiraling.

Pru returned to reality slowly, to the wreckage surrounding them. Suddenly stunned by her behavior, she reached for her dress with tears welling.

"No, not yet." Cal turned her toward him. He scrutinized her silently, then forced her to meet his gaze as he said, "You're not 'the widow' anymore, remember? You're Pru Reynolds, and you have the right to let someone make love to you." He whispered, "I want that someone to be me."

"I'm sorry." Aware that she was trembling, Pru rasped, "I don't know what . . . how this happened."

"I do."

"It shouldn't have happened." Pru reached again for her dress. "It was a mistake."

"No, it wasn't."

"I need to dress."

"And I need to keep you here with me a little longer."

"Cal, I—"

"Shhh . . ." Cal brushed her mouth with his. "It happened because it needed to happen, Pru, because it was meant to happen ever since the first moment I met you."

"No, that isn't true."

"It is."

"No."

Turning her toward him, Cal slipped himself inside her. Her eyes fluttered shut as her body closed around him and he whispered against her lips, "See how right this is?"

A familiar heat surged to life anew, and Pru did not reply to his question. He was moving inside her. He was whispering in her ear. Time and space slipped away, leaving only the power of the moment and Cal's need for her—a need as powerful as her own. She responded with spontaneous ardor as the heat of their joining rose to a loving inferno, then burst into a sudden cataclysmic culmination that left her again breathless in his arms.

Pru's eyes were closed, her breathing ragged when she felt Cal take her hand. She opened her eyes as he pressed her fingertips to his lips. She noted the moment when his gaze focused on her forearm, when his expression hardened and he questioned, "How did you get these bruises on your arm?"

Frowning, she stared at the deep purple marks she hadn't noticed before. She searched her mind for the answer, then went still.

"I asked you how you got these bruises."

"I fell."

Cal's gaze turned to ice. "I'm not blind, Pru. These

finger marks are plain enough to read. Somebody hurt you."

"It was an accident. It's not your problem."

"Answer me."

"Cal—"

"Tell me who did it."

"Jack wanted to talk when I met him in town. I didn't. He got angry when I tried to walk away from him."

A flush of color flooded Cal's face. He said unexpectedly, "Get dressed. We have a lot to do here before everybody gets back. You don't want Jeremy to find his home looking like this."

Cal drew her to her feet. He clutched her against the powerful, naked length of him, brushed a kiss across her lips, and whispered, "Remember, you're not 'the widow' anymore."

"But—"

Deliberately cutting her response short, Cal handed her her dress.

Pru dressed quickly, eyes averted. Cal was fully dressed as well when she looked up and he said, "Let's get this place cleaned up."

Grateful for the return of a normalcy she could comprehend, Pru worked silently at Cal's side. They had done all they could when his strong arm slipped around her waist from behind. She felt his lips against her hair, and she was unable to protest when he turned her to face him and covered her mouth with his.

Enveloping her totally in his embrace, consuming

her reservations with his lips, Cal drew back at last to whisper, "Remember, you're not 'the widow' anymore."

. . . and you're mine.

Cal finished that last, recurring thought in his mind as he rode toward Lowell leading a packhorse. He had wanted to say those words a few hours earlier while he held Pru close and their loving was still fresh, but he had known it would be a mistake. It had happened so fast between them. One moment Pru was crying, and the next she was lying in his arms. Strangely, as well as he had known she needed him, he hadn't realized how much he really needed her.

That thought was sobering. He knew that a part of Pru regretted the intimacy they had shared. He had seen misgivings in her face when the men returned. He had heard it in her voice as she responded as best she could to the hands' startled reaction to the destruction in the house. He had felt it in the way she avoided him while trying to answer Jeremy's questions—but he dismissed it all. Her reaction was temporary. She had come alive under his touch. She would again.

He had known the moment he touched Pru that she was meant for his arms. She fit so naturally there. Despite the prudent upbringing that was so much a part of her character, she had reacted to him like tinder to a match. He had felt her shock at the intimate blaze that had resulted. He also knew that the heat of that blaze had frightened her in some ways, but he was determined to overcome her fears.

Cal's expression hardened as the lights of Lowell became clearly visible in the twilight. Pru had looked at him with uncertainty when he announced he was going into Lowell to replace the food and other supplies that had been lost. He had left the men with a few explicit instructions but had not bothered with further explanations.

Carefully scrutinizing the busy main street as he approached the general store, Cal noted that the daytime bustle of supply wagons from nearby ranches, of shopping women and energetic children, had all but disappeared. In their place, the evening traffic of bearded cowpokes out for a night on the town, and gaudily dressed saloon women all too willing to help them, had already begun. The number of horses tied at the hitching rail of the Last Chance Saloon indicated that business was vigorous despite the fact that the weekend was several days away. His gaze halted on a familiar mount, and his jaw tightened.

His expression sober, Cal dismounted outside the general store. Inside, he handed Harvey Bower the list of supplies needed, nodded politely at Agnes Bower, and within moments was on his way toward the bright lights and loud music emanating from the Last Chance Saloon.

Halting just inside the swinging doors, Cal scanned the room through a blue cloud of smoke. He saw crowded gaming tables, customers grouped in all manner of conversation, and saloon girls laughing and singing loudly to the bawdy tune being banged out on an ancient piano. His gaze settled on a familiar figure in the inevitable line of cowpokes at the bar, and a hard smile flicked across his lips. Jack was easy to spot. He stood at center stage, waving his arms broadly as he continued what was obviously a tale meant to entertain.

The loud round of laughter at its conclusion faded abruptly as Cal approached and halted a few feet from Jack's back.

Cal waited. It took no more than a few seconds for Jack to turn and face him. Sweaty, bearded, unclean, Jack addressed him with a smile, exposing yellowed, uneven teeth as he said, "Well, if it ain't Cal Star. We ain't never met, but from the look of you, I'd say you know who I am, too." He gave a short laugh. "Do you have something in mind? Maybe you're looking for some advice, seeing as you took over my job at the Rocky W."

"I don't need any advice from you." Cal's voice was cold. "But you're right. I did come in here looking for you. We need to talk, and it might be best if we stepped outside to do it."

"We ain't got nothing to talk about, because I ain't got no interest in the Rocky W anymore."

"That isn't the way I heard it." Cal's tone was clipped. "I heard you stopped Mrs. Reynolds this afternoon, looking for some money you said she owes you."

"She told you that, did she?" Jack nodded. "Yeah,

I did that. I didn't get my money, though."

"But you put your hands on Mrs. Reynolds, and you left the marks to prove it." Cal took a step closer. "I'm here to tell you, if you put your hands on her again, you'll answer to me."

"So, that's the problem. What's the matter? Saving her for yourself?"

Cal grated, "I came here to give you a warning, but if you'd like a lesson instead . . ."

A sneer curled Jack's wet lips. "How is the skinny witch? As cold in bed as she looks?"

Cal's roar of rage was simultaneous with the flash of fist that knocked Jack backwards against the bar. Squaring his stance, Cal was ready when Jack steadied himself, then leaped forward with a feral growl.

Jack never saw the second punch coming.

Cal turned toward the bar when Jack hit the floor. He rapped out, "Pour me a beer, Bart."

In tenuous control of his fury, Cal watched as the beer was poured. He then slapped his coin down on the bar, leaned over Jack's inert form, and splashed the full contents of the glass onto Jack's face.

Jack sputtered and choked. His eyes blinked open. Waiting until Jack's mind appeared clear, Cal growled down at him, "Touch her . . . mention her name again, and you'll answer to me. And if I find out you had anything to do with what happened at the Rocky W today, I'll be back. That's a promise."

Jack gulped.

"Did you hear what I said?"

Jack strained to catch his breath.

"I said . . . did you hear me?"

Jack nodded.

"I want to hear you say it."

"I . . . I hear you."

After allowing his gaze to linger a chilling moment longer, Cal walked out through the swinging doors.

Chapter Nine

"I didn't really want to tell you, Buck, but I couldn't sleep for thinking about it." Dawn was lightening the night sky as Celeste turned more fully toward Buck in the confines of their marriage bed. Aware that a shaft of pale morning light slanting through the window shade highlighted her exquisite features and outlined her rounded breasts through her sheer sleeping garment, she continued, "I knew you'd hear about it sooner or later, and I didn't want you to be angry because you were caught unawares."

Celeste waited for Buck's reply. She had gone into town the previous day. She had stopped in the apothecary shop to pick up the latest remedy Doc Maggie had prescribed for Buck. She had been glad to participate in the charade that the medicine was helping him, while knowing full well it would have little effect when the time was right for Madalane to resume dosing Buck with her "tonics." She had been stunned, however, to hear the story circulating around town from the busybody Jessica Crasswell.

Cal Star and the Widow Reynolds?

Celeste struggled with her reaction to that thought.

Tall and broad-shouldered, long-legged and tightly muscled, Cal Star was all male from the top of his sun-tinted hair to the tips of his well-worn boots. The idea that he had aligned himself with a skinny, repressed widow had been almost unbelievable.

Jealousy had followed close behind Celeste's incredulity. She had chafed at the notion that the widow had a man the likes of Cal Star servicing her, while she must be satisfied by the pathetic efforts of a scrawny old man whose limp male organ was a nauseating joke, or by the perversities of a lecherous degenerate whose sexual tendencies were brutish at best.

Determined to use the gossip to her advantage, Celeste scrutinized Buck's lined face for his reaction to her disclosure. She saw the dark circles underneath his eyes, the hollows in his cheeks, and the revealing twitch of his features. She continued with pretended anxiety, "You're not angry with me, are you?"

Buck responded tightly, "What my son does—how he conducts his life—isn't my affair."

"I know . . . I know." Celeste sighed. "I tried to tell Mrs. Crasswell that, but she said the whole town was talking about the way he's carrying on with the Widow Reynolds. She said he's flaunting their connection. She said he actually went into the saloon a week ago and assaulted the poor fellow who used to work at the Rocky W. Cal told the man *he* was taking his place, that the widow didn't want anything to do with him anymore."

"I told you, I don't care what Cal does."

"But Bonnie—"

Buck tensed. "What about Bonnie? She's dead and buried. She doesn't have anything to do with the widow and Cal."

"I know, but Cal's actions have started up all the old talk in town about the way he ran off after Bonnie died."

"That's over . . . old news."

"It isn't anymore."

Celeste could feel the trembling that beset Buck's thin frame as he snapped, "Cal never should've come back. I don't know why he did, anyway."

Celeste turned her head, avoiding Buck's gaze with calculated deliberation.

Buck scrutinized her for a few seconds before he asked, "What's wrong, Celeste?"

Properly distressed when Buck turned her back to face him, Celeste responded, "It's just that it upsets me to think that all this might be my fault."

"Your fault?" Buck shook his head. "Whatever gave you that idea?"

"N . . . nothing."

"Celeste . . ."

"I don't want you to be angry with me."

"Nothing you could ever say would make me mad at you, darlin'."

"It's just that . . ." Celeste paused, then continued in a rush, "I told you once before that I thought maybe Cal had been jealous of Bonnie."

Buck's expression tightened.

"I'm afraid this is all happening now because he's jealous of *me*."

"Of you?"

"He expected to come back and find you so lonely and glad to see him that you'd take him back with open arms. Instead, he discovered you have me . . . and a new life."

Buck remained silent.

"He's afraid he won't get back into your good graces now, because you don't need him."

"He'd be right if he thought that. I'm done with him."

"I think he figures that by causing gossip, all the old talk will start up again, and you'll *want* to talk to him."

"I don't know if I believe that."

"Why did he take up with the widow, then? Everybody says she's cold, plain, and sharp-tongued. The only other thing that could possibly have attracted him to her is the fact that her property borders the Texas Star and he'll be close enough to keep an eye on things here."

"Well, if that's what he's thinking, it won't do him any good."

"I know. I just . . ." Celeste looked up at Buck. A

tear trailed down her cheek. "I just feel so responsible."

"None of this is your fault, darlin'. You're beautiful and sweet, and you're innocent of any blame in this mess." Buck took a breath. His jaw firmed. "I'm going to talk to Cal."

"No, I don't want you to do that!" Suddenly afraid her strategy to keep Buck at odds with his son might backfire, Celeste clutched Buck's bony arm and rasped, "Promise me you won't."

"Cal's my son. I need to set him straight."

"Buck, please . . ." Using the full force of her tears, Celeste cried, "That's what he wants. I'd never forgive myself if he turned on you and something happened."

"Nothing's going to happen."

"Buck, please . . . promise me."

"Celeste—"

She sobbed, "Please . . ."

"Don't cry, darlin'. You know I can't stand to see you cry."

"If anything ever happened to you . . ."

"Nothing's going to happen to me."

"Promise me you won't go anywhere near Cal."

"Celeste . . ."

"Please . . ."

"All right, but don't cry. I won't talk to Cal. I promise."

"Just ignore the talk around town about Bonnie."

Buck tensed again.

"Don't give Cal the satisfaction of knowing he's affecting us."

Buck did not respond.

"Just make believe he doesn't exist, and he'll go away. You'll see. He'll just go away."

"All right, darlin'. Calm down. I'll do anything you want me to."

Celeste snuggled close to Buck. Silently repulsed when his bony arms drew her closer and he began caressing her, she felt bile rose in her throat. But he'd said it. He'd do anything she wanted him to do, and she'd make sure he kept his promise.

Cal Star didn't stand a chance.

Mitch halted in the process of saddling his horse. He stared at Buck for a silent moment as they prepared to ride out for the day's work. He had noticed Buck's preoccupied frown at the breakfast table, a frown he had carried into the barn when he came for his horse. He had asked Buck what was wrong, and Buck had told him.

Mitch said with open incredulity, "Where'd you get that idea? I heard that story, too, but Cal didn't do nothing wrong when he went after that Jack Grate who used to work at the Rocky W. The widow fired that fella because he was stealing. When he tried to get more money out of her, he put his hands on her—so Cal stepped in."

"That isn't the way I heard it."

"Then you heard it wrong."

"The folks in town are all talking about the way Cal's carrying on with that widow."

"Are they?" Mitch shrugged. "The town likes to talk. All I know is the widow needed help at the ranch, Cal needed work, and Doc Maggie put them together."

"Doc Maggie?"

"That's right. She knew the widow was as green as they come, that she needed somebody she could trust to handle the ranch for her. Cal was at the Rocky W only a short time when he hired Winston, Larry, and Josh to work there."

Buck grunted. "I thought those boys were working at the Reemes place."

"Not after Cal tapped them on the shoulder."

"They made a mistake if they're depending on him."

"I don't think so. He is already started getting the Rocky W back on track."

"You seem to know a lot about what's going on at the Rocky W."

"It's just next door, boss. And if I was you, instead of fretting about what people were saying, I'd be pretty proud of what Cal's done so far."

Buck's gaze turned cold. "Well, you aren't me, are you?"

There was no mistaking Buck's tone.

Their conversation abruptly concluded, Mitch tightened the cinch on his mount's saddle, slapped down the stirrups, and led his horse outside without bothering to reply.

* * *

"You will lose control of your husband if you don't do something soon."

Celeste's clear skin grew heated. She had stood on the ranch house porch with pretended concern as her husband rode off for the day's work with his men. After their dawn conversation about Cal, she had been confident that all would progress according to her plan—until the men disappeared from sight and Madalane began her tirade about the conversation she had overheard between Buck and Mitch in the barn.

Celeste's lips were tight as she snapped in return, "My husband sees no further than I want him to see."

"Blood is thicker than water, Celeste." Refusing to relent, Madalane continued, "Your husband still refuses to speak with you about his will. He does that for one reason only—because in the back of his mind, he hopes his sons will redeem themselves in some way."

"That's nonsense!"

"What other reason could there be?"

"My husband trusts me."

"He hopes to trust his sons again—the way he once did."

"Stop this nonsense! I won't listen to it any more. Just this morning I endured my husband's fumbling, pathetic efforts to prove his manhood. He failed, of course. He was apologetic, and I was *so understanding*. He is humiliated by his inability to perform his marital duties, which makes him even more malleable. He will do anything I ask to make up for his inadequacy."

"Cal Star is his son."

"His son whom he despises for killing his daughter!"

"It was an accident."

"Buck looks at it differently."

"There is danger in a father's love for his son."

"Buck has disowned his sons."

"He only fools himself."

"I tire of your warnings, Madalane!"

"We have come too far to lose—"

"Go away."

"You must make sure—"

"I said, go away!"

Her head high and her lips tight, Madalane turned abruptly toward her room. Trembling with ire, Celeste walked to the kitchen window and cursed aloud. Madalane was growing feeble—too old to remember clearly the power a woman could wield with her body.

Celeste smiled. Buck wanted her. He *lusted* for her. He dreamed of the day he would be man enough again to take her as he once did. Fool that he was, Buck did not realize that she would make sure that day never came.

Cal Star, however, was not that same kind of fool.

The truth of that statement knitted Celeste's brow with delicate lines of concern. Madalane was right, damn her! She needed to alter her plans—this afternoon, if possible. She'd hang a kerchief in her window, and Derek would be waiting at their rendezvous point.

Celeste frowned more deeply as a familiar tingling began inside her. Derek was lecherous, crude, almost barbaric, but he provided her with exactly what she needed—in so many ways.

Pru was in the yard. The morning sun glittered on her dark hair as she scattered feed for the chickens scratching the ground at her feet. Cal remained silent, uncertain. She didn't know he was there, watching her.

Pru was wearing a blue gingham dress she had bought for herself after the house was devastated and all her clothes were shredded. She had dispensed with the tight, severe hairstyle she had previously worn, and had taken to wearing her heavy tresses in a single braid hanging down her back that was easier to maintain. She did not seem to realize the impact of those simple changes—that the modest hairstyle framed her face with errant, curling wisps, accenting her delicate features; that the garment emphasized her slender proportions in a way her widow's attire never did; or that the simplicity of the garment's style allowed her youthful beauty to shine through, making her appear more a girl than a mature woman who carried heavy responsibilities on her narrow shoulders.

Cal watched her a few minutes longer. He ached to hold her. He yearned to smooth the frown from between her brows. He hungered to tease her lips with his kiss until they parted to allow him deeper access there.

He recalled the moments while Pru had lain in his arms. He remembered her swift intake of breath when their flesh first met. The sound was etched into his heart.

Pru had felt so right in his arms that he had realized in an instant that their union was inevitable. He wondered how that could have been so clear to him, when their intimacy had obviously left her feeling only discomfort.

Pru was avoiding him. She made certain they were never alone, and put distance between them when others were near. Her gaze skirted his whenever he attempted to hold it. The breach between them seemed to widen with each passing day. Unable to bear the situation for another hour and aware that he needed to talk to Pru alone, he had used a flimsy excuse to return to the ranch house a short time earlier, and had left Jeremy and the men at work on the range.

But still he hesitated. The situation between Pru and himself had seemed to worsen after she went to town to buy Jeremy and herself a change of clothes. He wondered what she had heard to affect the way she looked at him; if, perhaps, rumors about his past had resurfaced, causing her to doubt him.

Appearing to sense his presence, Pru looked up unexpectedly, then went still. She seemed unable to move as he approached and halted beside her.

She stepped back when he attempted to touch her, and said, "No, Cal . . . please."

His throat tight, Cal replied, "What's bothering you, Pru?"

She did not immediately reply, and he coaxed, "Tell me, please."

Pru's clear skin colored. "The whole town is talking about us. I could feel people looking at me when I went to town. I could feel them staring at me in the mercantile store. I finally visited Doc Maggie and asked her what it was all about. She told me."

"She told you what?"

"You shouldn't have gone after Jack, Cal! Talk about what you did to him in the saloon spread like wildfire in town, and what Jack said about us traveled even faster. You shouldn't have done it. You just made matters worse."

"The bastard got what he deserved. He won't come near you again."

Suddenly livid, Pru rasped, "I don't need you to fight my battles for me!"

As angry as she, Cal responded, "I suppose that's why that saddle bum felt free to put his hands on you."

"I handled it, didn't I?"

"By walking away and pretending there wouldn't be a next time."

"I would've handled it if there was a next time. I've always managed before."

"That was before."

Pru raised her chin. "Before what?"

"Before I made love to you."

Pru's fair skin flushed. "That was a mistake. It won't happen again."

"A mistake?"

"It never should've happened. It never would've happened if I hadn't been so badly shaken."

"You're saying I took advantage of you."

"I didn't say that."

"What did you say, then?"

"I said . . . I meant . . ." Pru was trembling. She closed her eyes. When she opened them again, she said, "I'm saying, however it happened, it can't happen again." She paused to regain control, then continued, "I came here to make a new life for Jeremy and me. I can't afford to associate myself with scandal."

Cal searched her gaze. "You're referring to the talk about Bonnie and me, aren't you?"

"No."

"Bonnie was my sister. I was eighteen years old, my brother Taylor was fifteen, and Bonnie was seven when my mother died unexpectedly."

"I don't need to hear this."

Cal continued resolutely, "My father was too stunned to think straight when my mother died, and Taylor, Bonnie, and I weren't much better. My father handled things by going into town and burying his grief in the closest whore."

"Cal!"

"He left me in charge of Taylor and Bonnie. That was his first mistake."

"I don't want to hear any more."

Pru turned to walk away, but Cal held her fast as he continued, "I wasn't up to the responsibility, and Bonnie died. It's as simple as that."

"Let me go."

"You wanted to know what everybody's talking about. That's it. I couldn't handle how it all happened, and I left town before Bonnie was put into the ground. My father never forgave me. He won't talk to me or let me on the ranch, although he sure as hell could use my help."

"Stop . . . please." Cal halted at Pru's plea, and she continued, "Your past isn't the problem. I'm only concerned about the future I'm hoping to make for Jeremy. I can't have people saying what they're saying about you and me, Cal. Jeremy will eventually hear it, and I don't want that to happen."

"Whatever they're saying in town, they're wrong."

"You know as well as I do that we—"

"Are they saying I made love to you?"

Pru took a shuddering breath.

"Are they saying it was beautiful between us?"

Pru could not respond.

"Did they say I've done nothing but think about holding you in my arms ever since—that I've been marking time until we could be together again?"

"Cal, please . . ."

"Please what, Pru? Please make love to you?"

"No."

"Please take you into my arms so we can both see if it could possibly be as good again as it was then?"

"Cal . . ."

Slipping his arms around her, Cal rasped, "I want you close to me, Pru. I need to know you want it as much as I do. Tell me you do, Pru."

"I can't do that, Cal."

"Yes, you can. Just say the words."

"Cal—"

"It's easy. Just say, 'I want you, Cal.' "

"Please, I—"

He was kissing her forehead, her cheek. He was brushing her mouth with his as he urged, "Say it, Pru. I need to hear you say it."

He felt her sigh. He tasted her tears. He sensed the crumbling of her defenses the moment before she whispered, "I do want you, Cal."

Those precious words.

Cal scooped Pru up into his arms. Moments later, he nudged the ranch house door open, then walked directly to the bedroom and placed her on the bed. He lay down beside her and slid his arms around her. He held his breath until she slid her arms around him in return, then welcomed his kiss.

Longing took them rapidly forward. Kisses grew heated. Caresses scorched. Pru's naked flesh moved against his—silk against steel—and wonder surged hot inside him.

Her moist heat closed around him, and all conscious thought fled.

Cal plunged deep and sure inside her with instinctive words of love, and his heart took wing.

He was flying high in passion's throes when he

heard Pru gasp, then heard his own rasping response as they soared in the wild glory of the moment, then dropped back to reality in the intimate haven of each other's arms.

Lying in the silent aftermath of their loving, Cal raised his head to look down into Pru's flushed face. He whispered against her lips, "Do you really care what people say, Pru?"

He saw the single tear that trailed from the corner of her eye the moment before she slid her arms around his neck, and the loving began again.

The bastard!

Crouched concealed a distance away, Jack felt a rush of pure rage. He had been watching Cal and the men working. He had followed Cal to the ranch house, and had seen his encounter with the widow with his own eyes—right until he carried her into the house! Everything he had said about Cal Star and the widow was true! That show Star had put on in the saloon had been strictly for the benefit of the town—so he and the widow could play their little games in secret—and he, Jack, had paid the price.

Jack touched his bruised jaw. The discoloration there was a vivid reminder to everyone who saw him that Cal Star had made him crawl.

No, Star wouldn't get away with it.

He'd get even . . . with both of them.

"We can't wait any longer. You have to do something quickly."

Derek returned Celeste's stare in the dim light of the filthy cabin. He responded, "I told you, I ain't taking my men over to the Rocky W unless there's something in it for us—and there ain't nothing there for us yet."

Celeste persisted, "Have you checked lately? The talk is that my *stepson* has been making rapid strides there."

"I don't need to check. That ain't my job."

"What is your job, then?"

Derek's smile was snide. "Making you happy's my job—and I know how to do it, too."

He took a step toward her, and Celeste sneered, "Oh, no, you don't."

Derek's smile faded. "What do you mean, *no*?" His expression hardened. "I don't need your approval. I can take what I want, anytime I want."

"You can take what you want . . ." Celeste challenged, "but it wouldn't be the same as if I was *giving* it to you."

"It wouldn't, huh?"

"You know what I can do for you, Derek." Celeste slid a lascivious gaze slowly down his body. When she looked back up into his face, he was salivating. She smiled. "That's right, I can make it real good for you if you do what I say."

"What have you got in mind?"

"I want you to raid the Rocky W tonight. I want you to unfix whatever my stepson has fixed—to take whatever herd he's managed to put together. I want you to leave nothing untouched, so he'll give up, turn his back, and ride off, just like he did when he was younger."

"That might turn out to be more work than it seems."

"You should be able to rustle a big enough herd to make it worth your while."

"For my men, maybe, but not for me."

"What do you mean?"

"You might have to coax me."

"Coax you."

"Yeah."

Forcing herself to ignore her surging response, Celeste replied, "I'll coax you, all right . . . but only if you raid the Rocky W *tonight*."

"I might not be able to get the boys together that soon."

"Tonight, Derek." She moved closer to him and began unbuttoning his trousers. "Tell me you'll do it tonight, or I'll stop right here."

He suppressed a groan as she caressed him. He swallowed hard as she manipulated him with expert hands. He finally gasped, "You drive a hard bargain."

"Tell me it'll be tonight, and I'll make it better for you than you ever dreamed."

He was twitching, sweating profusely, holding off for more, and Celeste silently swore.

She rasped, "You're going to lose your chance if you hold out any longer, Derek. Tell me it'll be tonight, and all your dreams will come true."

"All right. Tonight."

"That's what I wanted to hear."

Moving closer, Celeste whispered up into Derek's coarse features, "Get ready, because here it comes."

"What took you so long, Cal?" Jeremy spurred his horse toward him as he rode into view on his return from the ranch house. The boy reined up beside him, then looked up at the position of the sun and said, "You've been gone a long time. Me and the fellas were worrying."

Cal withheld a smile. The boy was riding like a native-born Texan. Jeremy had slipped into the habit of judging the time of day by the position of the sun, and was already identifying himself as one of the men. Cal was somehow proud. But Jeremy was asking questions that none of the other men would venture, and he needed to answer him.

"I couldn't find the tools I went back for." Cal motioned to the post-digger and other implements strapped to his saddle. "I wanted to check up on things at the ranch house, too. I wanted to make sure your ma was watching out in case anybody she didn't like showed up."

Jeremy's freckled face wrinkled in a frown. "You mean like Jack? He's the one who tore up the house, isn't he?"

"I don't know."

"Mama didn't say it was him, but I know she thinks it was. If I ever see him again, I'll fix him."

"No, you won't, Jeremy." Cal's expression was sober. "I already took care of it."

"I hope you fixed him real good!"

"Well enough that I think he'll stay clear of the ranch house from now on."

"Then why are you thinking Mama has to watch out?"

"I just want to make sure."

"Was she worrying because she thought maybe Jack would come back?"

"Maybe . . . but she's not worrying anymore."

"You made her feel better?"

Cal nodded. "I'm thinking I did."

"Then she's probably going to make something good for dessert tonight."

"Well . . ."

"Maybe an apple pie."

Cal remembered the apples he had glimpsed on the kitchen table as he and Pru had walked back from the bedroom. With the taste of Pru still fresh in his mouth, however, with her scent still clinging, and his desire for her endless, he hadn't been paying much attention to anything else.

He replied cautiously, "That might be her intention."

Turning back toward the men, Jeremy shouted, "We're going to have apple pie for dessert tonight, fellas, because Cal went back to the house and made Mama feel good!"

The men glanced up at Cal, and he silently groaned.

Jeremy's bright expression faded. "Who's supposed to stay behind to watch the herd while we eat supper tonight? Winston?"

Cal grew sober as he again scrutinized the herd of cows, calves, and yearlings they had managed to gather. He hadn't forgotten the rustlers rumored to be in the area, or the fact that the Rocky W and the Texas Star had been two of their favorite targets. As difficult as it was with so few men, he had worked out a schedule to guard the herd, and they had started running the animals closer to the house. He reviewed the schedule quickly in his mind and replied, "It's Winston's turn, all right."

Jeremy's light brows drew into a frown. "We have to tell Mama to save a pretty big piece of pie, then, because Winston's a pretty big fella."

"Right."

"Are you going to take over for Winston during the night?"

"No, Larry is."

"That's good. Mama will feel better if you're there."

"What makes you say that?"

"Mama trusts you, just like I do."

Cal's throat tightened.

"But you'd better hurry up and get back to the boys. They've been waiting for you, because they're needing your help." Jeremy paused and lowered his voice. "I'm not much help yet, you know, but I will be, someday."

Cal looked at Jeremy soberly. Yes, he would be, someday.

* * *

Derek rode slowly through the twilight shadows. He glanced at the men riding beside him, still uncomfortable with what had happened between Celeste and him earlier that day.

He frowned at the familiar stirring in his groin. Damn, that woman was good! She was full of surprises when they lay together, surprises that kept him guessing and wanting more. He'd never known a woman who satisfied him the way she did—but he figured that was the problem. She was *too* good.

Derek glanced up at the clear, star-filled sky, then back at his men. He hadn't wanted to hit the Rocky W tonight. Despite what he had said to Celeste, he knew he'd have no problem getting his gang together. The boys were at their hideout, like they usually were between nights on the town. They hadn't liked the idea of a last-minute raid on the Rocky W, either, but they had gone along with his plans like they usually did.

Discomfort nudged again.

It was no secret that Celeste's personal plans came first with her. That fact had never bothered him before, because Celeste's personal plans had put money in his pocket and her in his bed. As a matter of fact, he had considered the situation ideal when he'd first joined up with her, since the only provision she had made was that he keep her identity secret from his men. Then Cal Star came back into the picture and things rapidly changed.

Celeste was getting more tense with every day that

passed. She was beginning to push too hard. He didn't have to follow through on his promise to raid the Rocky W tonight—he knew that—but he wasn't yet ready to give up what Celeste had to offer.

But the realization that Celeste was controlling him grated on his pride.

A mumbling among the men turned Derek toward them with a frown. "Keep it down!" he hissed. "We ain't supposed to announce our arrival, you know."

He had known he was in for trouble when Sarge snapped back, "We've been riding for an hour and we ain't seen nothing but a few scattered beeves. Are you sure that new foreman at the Rocky W has put a herd together that's big enough to be worthwhile? That don't seem likely to me."

"We wouldn't be here now if there wasn't," Derek said. "I ain't never steered you fellas wrong yet, have I?"

When Sarge did not respond, Derek halted his mount abruptly. He wasn't accustomed to being challenged by his gang. They'd been together a long time and were comfortable with the way things worked—with Derek giving the orders and the boys taking them.

He eyed the men more closely in the limited light. Sarge was frowning. Harry's and Lefty's expressions were tight. Luke looked noncommittal.

Derek snapped, "What's going on here?"

Sarge's jowled face darkened. "The boys and me were just wondering who's really running things now."

"What're you talking about?"

"Look, you ain't fooling none of us, boss." Sarge nudged his mount up closer. Tall, unkempt, and intense, he was wanted by the army for desertion. He was also the most outspoken of the group. "It ain't no secret to us who's been letting you know where them herds were since we got to Lowell, and when was the best time to take them. It's been working out pretty good, and we didn't have no complaints until now, but she—"

"She?" Derek waited for a response.

"That Star woman you've been bedding."

"How'd you know about her?"

"You ain't exactly hid how you've been watching her window every day with that spyglass, or how you took off every time you got her signal, or how you came back most of the time smelling like you had a woman and telling us where we'd be hitting next."

"Smart fellas, ain't you?"

Sarge shrugged. "Like I said, we ain't had no complaints, and we figure we couldn't blame you for hightailing it to meet her since she takes such good care of you."

"So?"

"But we don't like jumping when she says jump."

"What're you talking about?"

"You met up with her this afternoon—we all knew that—but all of a sudden we got to drop everything and do what she tells us to do. We didn't have no time to scout out the herd like we usually do."

"The herd's where she said it is. We just ain't come on it yet."

"That don't mean nothing." Harry's bearded jaw twitched as he interjected, "We ain't had a chance to check it out, and we don't like riding blind."

"You ain't riding blind, because I know exactly where we're going—to get that Rocky W herd."

"Hell, that don't mean much, neither! The Rocky W's a big spread. That herd could be anywhere."

"It's by the old branding corral."

"The old corral close to the ranch house?"

"The ranch house is a couple of miles away from there."

"That's close enough."

"We'll move them out real slow. Nobody at the ranch will know we were there until the next morning when they see the herd is gone."

Sarge shook his head. "I ain't going."

Anger flushed Derek's thick features. "Scared?"

Sarge's eyes grew frigid. "Smart."

"You'd be smarter if you just shut your mouth and did what I told you."

Derek saw Sarge's hand move spontaneously toward his gun. His own hand moved a second faster and he warned, "It's fine with me, if that's the way you want it, but I'm telling you now, you'd be making a mistake."

Watching as Sarge's hand relaxed, Derek said, "Now you're making sense." He scrutinized the men with a glance, then said, "I ain't never steered you wrong, and I ain't going to this time. Yeah, you're right. That Star woman has been giving me most of the information I needed to hit the ranches around here. She's been giving me something private on the side, too—and she's real good."

The men snickered, but he remained sober as he continued, "She's got plans of her own that don't include that old man she married. I figure that's all right, because my plans with her ain't long-range, neither."

"What's she in such a rush for tonight?"

"That's her business. All she's asking us to do is a little extra work on the side when we get them cattle."

"Extra work . . ."

"Like smashing up that corral and whatever else those fellas fixed up."

"What's she got against the Rocky W?"

"Like I said, that's her business. But I'm telling you right now, if there ain't a decent herd waiting for us near the Rocky W branding corral, I don't expect to waste any time getting out of there." He paused and scanned the faces around him. "Does that sound all right to you?"

Lefty was the first to nod his assent. Luke and Harry followed. Sarge was last.

Derek almost smiled. He was the boss, and they knew it.

He nudged his mount into motion.

Pru turned toward the kitchen shelf with a freshly washed pot in hand. She slipped on water that had spilled on the floor and caught herself a moment before falling, then stood still for a silent moment and closed her eyes in an effort to regain control of her ragged emotions.

The men had been on time for supper, but she wasn't. Somehow she had been all thumbs around the house after Cal left her. Preoccupied with thoughts she couldn't seem to dismiss, she had tripped, dropped things, forgotten what she was intending to do . . .

Pru shook her head. And her distraction was getting worse by the minute.

The men had come home expecting to find dinner ready, but she'd been so far behind that they'd had to wait almost an hour to eat. Jeremy had complained he was hungry over and again, until Cal finally took him out of the kitchen to keep him busy in the barn.

Pru had been tense at dinner, but the meal was actually very good when she finally served it—or so the men said. Apple pie, Jeremy's favorite, had stopped his complaints, but her clumsiness continued. The reason was obvious. She was too intensely conscious of Cal's presence whenever he was near. In an attempt to dismiss the vivid memories of their intimate moments together that afternoon, she had deliberately avoided him in much the same way as she had before—a futile effort, when she couldn't seem to think of anyone or anything else when he was near.

Pru swallowed against the hard lump in her

throat. Even now, alone in the kitchen as the men conversed in the yard before retiring to the newly cleaned bunkhouse, the clumsiness continued. What was wrong with her?

Pru reviewed the situation in her mind as she had countless times before. She had been upset, alone, and frightened the first time Cal and she made love. With the destruction of her household lying around her, it had felt so good to feel his arms around her—but she knew that didn't really explain her actions. She'd been upset, alone, and frightened before, and had had men offer to console her, but she'd never been tempted to accept their consolation. She'd faced defeat after defeat without any thought of surrendering to an easier path.

It was Cal's fault. If he hadn't looked at her as if he couldn't bear her pain, as if he wanted to erase all the sadness from her mind, as if he wanted to protect her from everybody and everything that could possibly hurt her . . .

If he hadn't been so tender . . .

If he hadn't taken her into his arms with that soft rasp in his voice that had torn at her heart . . .

But there had been a morning, after that first time, when she had faced her regrets. She had told herself she was a widow, a mother, a woman with responsibilities—that Cal was a man whose past haunted him, who had warned her from the start that his stay was temporary, and whose life was even more uncertain than her own.

She had told herself she had Jeremy to think of.

She needed a secure future for his sake.

She had been so determined—until Cal took her into his arms again.

Pru gasped as her foot slipped out from under her, slamming her against the kitchen table with a crash. She looked up, rubbing her side, to see Jeremy in the doorway with Cal looming behind him.

"What's the matter with you tonight, Mama?" Jeremy was frowning, and so was Cal. "You're making so much noise in here."

"I slipped." She smiled. "On a wet spot on the floor. I'm fine."

But she wasn't. Cal was looking at her. His gaze searched her face, and she felt her throat choke tight. She needed to tell him that the same mistake couldn't keep happening, that they—

The bark of gunshots in the distance shattered the moment.

Pandemonium broke out as the rapid reports sounded again and again.

The men were mounting their horses as Cal snapped, "Stay here with Jeremy and keep your gun in hand. Fire in the air if you need us. The boys and I'll be back as soon as we can."

Pru was breathless, still hardly comprehending the rapid progress of events as their horses faded from sight.

Derek cursed aloud as bullets picked at the ground around him. He glanced at Luke, who lay motionless on the ground a few yards away, a gunshot wound in his chest.

It had all happened so fast. Derek had spotted the Rocky W herd just where Celeste had said it would be. His men had started toward it with soft whoops intended to start the cattle moving. Then gunshots had come out of nowhere.

The herd was guarded!

He had returned fire when Luke fell from his horse. Then, dismounting in the shadows, he had watched the gunfire bursts coming from a hidden position behind some boulders.

It was only one man, and Derek would be damned if he'd let some cowhand get away with taking down one of his riders.

Harry and Lefty dismounted behind him. With a nod, Derek directed Sarge to circle around the man guarding the herd from the left as he himself circled around from the right. He waited until the others were firing rapidly before signaling Sarge into motion.

Derek moved cautiously through the shadows. It was that bastard Cal Star's fault, he was sure. The widow didn't have enough sense to set a guard on her herd, and any hands she might have hired wouldn't have cared enough to tell her to do it. But Cal Star, trying to impress his father into taking him back, cared enough.

And he was going to pay.

Using the sound of the guard's gunfire to guide him, Derek moved gradually closer. With Sarge on one side and himself on the other, the guard didn't stand a chance.

He was close enough at last to see the guard's shadow as the fellow continued firing. He was a big man, all right, but big or small, they were all the same size when a bullet took them down.

Derek raised his gun. The fellow was shielded by a boulder. If he moved a few inches, he'd be—

Derek's head snapped toward the sound of hoofbeats approaching, toward the sight of horsemen riding hard and fast in their direction.

The Rocky W riders would be upon them in a few minutes.

Making a quick decision, Derek turned back in the direction from which he had come. The sound of his movement drew the guard's gunfire, and bullets began striking the ground close by. He had reached his horse and had mounted when the guard's gunfire switched to Sarge's direction. He heard an outcry as a bullet found its mark.

His fury knowing no bounds, Derek turned his mount toward the shadows and kicked him into a gallop. He glanced back when he heard hoofbeats behind him and saw Harry and Lefty riding hard in his wake.

Gunfire followed them, but Derek didn't stop. He pressed forward at breakneck speed until the Rocky W was far behind him.

Expressionless, Cal stood over the bodies of the two rustlers. He glanced up at Josh and Larry, then at

Winston, who stood a few steps to their rear.

"Do you know either of them?"

The men shook their heads, and Cal frowned. "You've never seen either one of them before?"

"No."

"No, sir."

"Me neither."

Cal looked back at Winston. "Did you see them when they first rode up? How many of them were there?"

"There was five of them, I think. They came riding up and started moving the herd on the quiet. They didn't expect somebody'd be on guard. I fired a couple of warning shots, and when they started firing back, I took aim. The first fella fell right away. I got the second one when I realized they was circling around, trying to get me from behind."

Cal swore low in his throat. He was about to reply when the clatter of hoofbeats turned him toward two riders approaching. He tensed when they became identifiable.

Waiting only until Pru and Jeremy drew up beside them, Cal looked at Pru and demanded, "What are you doing here? I told you to stay back at the house."

Pru sat stiffly without responding as Jeremy said, "We had to come, Cal. The gunfire stopped, and Mama was afraid somebody got killed."

"Somebody did." Aware that the men had formed a line shielding the two bodies from the boy's view, Cal looked back at Pru and snapped, "Get Jeremy out of here. This is no place for him."

Pru turned to Josh and said, "Take Jeremy home for me, Josh." She took a short breath, "You'll be needing to come back here with the wagon anyway, to take away the . . . debris."

"I want you out of here, too, Pru." Cal was adamant. "Now."

"No."

"I said—"

"This is *my* ranch, Cal." Pru's pale face twitched. "And I'm not a child."

His hesitation brief, Cal turned toward Josh and ordered, "Do what she said. Take Jeremy home with you and come back with the wagon. We'll wait here."

"I don't want to go back now, Mama!"

Pru replied flatly, "You're going anyway."

Pru dismounted when Jeremy and Josh had ridden out of sight. Cal saw her face turn even paler when she said, "I want to see them."

"That's not a good idea, Pru."

"I need to see them."

Cal motioned for Winston and Larry to step aside. He felt Pru's shock when she saw the bodies. His arm went out to support her when she said, "They're strangers to me. I don't know either one of them."

He turned her away, his arm tight around her. She was shuddering, and he moved her off to the side, uncaring of the men's knowing glances when Pru looked up at him and whispered, "I was afraid, Cal. I was afraid one of those fellows lying there might've been you."

Chapter Ten

"The whole town's talking about Cal, Buck."

Buck looked at Doc Maggie as she said the words he had heard too often before. When she rode up the trail toward the ranch house a few minutes earlier, he had felt her assessing him with a professional eye as he walked across the yard toward her buckboard. He had the feeling she saw right through his effort to conceal his burgeoning fatigue.

He had started the day at sunrise, working with his men on the range, but his attempt to put in a full day's work had again proved too much for his weakened constitution. He had returned to the ranch house by early afternoon.

Exhausted, and not in the mood for gossip, Buck responded sharply, "What Cal does or doesn't do isn't my business anymore. I thought I made that pretty clear to you the last time we talked."

"I guess you didn't make it clear enough, or I wouldn't have driven this buckboard an extra hour out of my way on a busy day, just so I could tell you what happened on the Rocky W."

"I told you, I'm not interested."

"Really?" Doc Maggie persisted, "Even if I believed what you're saying, that wouldn't stop me. You've been thinking only the worst of Cal for more years than I care to count. It's time you started seeing him for the man he is, not the man you think he is."

"Does that mean you came out here to tell me something good about him?" Buck gave a caustic snort. "That's a real change of direction from the way the gossip's been going since he came back."

"What gossip are you talking about?"

"You know as well as I do what I'm talking about—Cal and the widow."

"All I know about Cal and Pru Reynolds is that she and her son needed help out on the Rocky W, and Cal needed a job. Did you know he's already shaped up a good enough herd on the Rocky W that rustlers tried to move it out from under him?"

Buck frowned.

"Aren't you going to ask me what happened?"

"I figure you'll tell me."

"Cal took care of it."

"What're you saying?"

"Your son brought two dead rustlers into town this morning. Seems those fellas didn't consider Cal would be smart enough to put a guard on the herd. The guard took a warning shot when they showed up, and then the fireworks started. Cal rode up with his men and chased three of the rustlers off. The other two weren't so lucky. As it turned out, the only thing those fellas ended up getting from the Rocky W was a fatal dose of lead poisoning."

"You sound mighty happy about that for a woman who's supposed to be concerned with saving lives."

"Tell me something, Buck." Obviously irritated by his remark, Doc Maggie snapped, "Is that your way of weaseling out of accepting the fact that your son has whittled down a gang that's been plaguing the area for months, when nobody else hereabouts even managed to set eyes on them?"

"I ain't weaseling out of nothing." As irritated as she, Buck countered, "It just seems pretty funny to me that everybody in town is calling Cal a hero today, when yesterday they were all whispering about the scandal he's causing with that widow."

"What scandal?"

"Don't make out you don't know, Doc."

Doc's expression tightened. "Gossip is gossip, but I can personally attest to what I'm telling you now. If it wasn't for Cal and his men, those rustlers would've gotten off with Prudence Reynolds's herd, and that would've been the end of the Rocky W."

Buck did not respond.

"You should be proud of Cal. Even Sheriff Carter was running around in circles trying to catch those rustlers."

Still no response.

"You're a stubborn man, Buck Star."

When he still did not reply, Doc Maggie scrutinized him more closely and said, "All right, so you don't have to listen to me when I talk about Cal if you don't want, but you'd better start listening to me when I warn you about your health. I'm the doctor, remember—and I'm telling you now, you look damned bad. You're pushing yourself too hard—trying to do too much, too fast."

"I'm fine."

"I don't believe a word of it." Doc Maggie paused a moment, then snapped, "Are you taking your medicine?"

"You mean that worthless stuff you prescribed for me that Celeste makes me take every morning and night?"

"Stubborn old coot! Just remember, listening to me when I talk about Cal's one thing, but you'd better pay attention when I tell you—"

"I know, you're the doctor."

"I sure as hell am!" Doc Maggie stopped for a breath, then said, "Stop in for a checkup the next time you're in town."

"I—"

"Remember. I'm the doctor! Goodbye."

Doc did not wait for Buck to reply as she turned her buckboard without another word and started back down the trail.

Buck stared after her, frowning.

And she had the gall to call him a crazy old coot.

He remained pensive as Doc's wagon turned out of sight. He didn't care what she said. She was asking too much of him to waste even a minute being proud of a son who was responsible for his sister's death.

. . . Wasn't she?

"Things are getting rough, Pru. I don't want you staying out here alone on the Rocky W when we're not around."

It was evening, the day after the rustlers had attempted to take the Rocky W herd. Cal had followed Pru into the ranch yard when she went out to toss the remains of the evening meal. Aware that Jeremy was with Winston and Larry in the barn dosing an ailing horse, he had taken a rare opportunity to speak to Pru alone.

Cal looked at Pru with growing uncertainty. She had turned to him instinctively after the shock of seeing the dead rustlers. She had looked up at him with the same look in her eyes that he had seen after they had made love, and he'd had all he could do not to take her into his arms then and there. Instead he had comforted her and calmed her fears, and had waited for a better moment. Then had come the morning after, when Pru had reverted back to the woman whose eyes barely met his.

Cal scrutinized her distant expression a moment longer, feeling at a complete loss. He needed to understand why he read deep feelings for him in her eyes one moment, only to see her avoid his gaze the next. His own feelings suffered no similar fluctuation. He had wanted her from the first moment he touched her. He wanted her now, even if he knew he dared not press her when her emotions were so uncertain.

With fear for her safety taking precedence over all else, however, Cal knew there was one discussion he could not put off any longer. He said, "I want you and Jeremy to stay in town for a while."

"What?"

"It's not safe for the two of you alone here on the ranch."

"Not safe because of what happened with the rustlers?"

Cal nodded.

"They won't try that again for a while."

"I wouldn't be too sure about that."

"They know the herd is guarded now."

"I made a decision when I took the rustlers' bodies into town this morning, Pru. I've already sent a telegram ahead to the railhead telling them to expect our beeves."

"What are you talking about?"

"We've managed to put together a pretty good herd for market. I would've preferred to wait a little longer before driving it to the railhead, but I don't want to take any more chances with the rustlers. You need the cash the sale will bring to settle some debts, and the market is good, so we're going to start the drive at the end of the week."

"Oh."

"That means we'll be gone a few days—maybe a week. I can't be certain how long. I'm thinking this won't be the safest place for you and Jeremy if it becomes general knowledge that you're here unprotected."

"I have my gun."

"Pru—"

Pru raised her chin in silent defiance. "Safe or not, the Rocky W is our home now, and this is where we're going to stay."

"You're not thinking this through, Pru."

"I said—"

"We still don't know who tore up the house, or why."

Pru did not reply.

"He could come back."

"Then I'll deal with him."

"Listen to me, Pru." Grasping her arms, Cal locked her gaze with his as he said, "I want you safe while I'm gone. I don't want to have to worry that you'll be waving that gun around when I know you don't stand a chance in the world of hitting what you're aiming at."

"I can take care of myself."

"If you say so." Cal's expression grew stiff. "But can you guarantee that you can protect Jeremy?"

"I . . ." Pru took a deep breath, unable to continue.

Cal pressed, "Don't be stubborn, Pru. It's not worth the risk. You can stay with Doc Maggie until we come back. She'll be glad for the company."

"All right." Cal's relief was cut short when Pru added, "I'll leave Jeremy with Doc Maggie, but I'm going with you."

"What?"

"You said yourself I have a lot to learn about ranching, and you admitted the only way to do that is to watch and ask questions. I can't do either of those things if I stay in town while you're taking care of the business end of ranching. Neither will I learn anything if I'm hiding while you're taking all the risks. This is my ranch. It's time I learned to run it."

"You can learn to run it, but not now."

"Now is the best time."

"No, it isn't.

Pru responded resolutely, "I'm going with you to the railhead."

"No! It's too dangerous. Besides, you'd be a liability. You can't ride worth a damn."

"I can sit a horse and keep him moving. Not much more will be asked of me, so that'll suffice."

"Pru, listen to me." Bonnie's lifeless face flashed unexpectedly before him—a sharp, cutting vision that almost stole his breath as he rasped, "I can't be sure what to expect on the drive. The rustlers are still out there."

"This is my ranch—"

"I won't take you along!"

"You don't have a choice."

"Don't do this to me, Pru."

"I'll drive into town and talk to Doc Maggie tomorrow."

Cal stared down into Pru's determined expression. It was happening again. He'd taken on responsibility for someone he cared about, for safety that would be almost impossible to guarantee. He whispered, "I'm asking you—"

"I'm going."

The finality of Pru's response tightened Cal's jaw as he turned abruptly and walked away.

"He ain't going to get away with it!"

Derek railed heatedly as he faced Celeste in the confines of their rendezvous cabin. Equally angry, Celeste held his furious gaze. She remembered her shock when Doc Maggie had ridden up to the ranch and told Buck that Cal had brought two dead rustlers into town that morning. Standing out of sight behind the screen door, she had eavesdropped on the whole conversation while Doc attempted to convince Buck that Cal was a *hero*. She had barely restrained herself from stepping out onto the porch and calling Doc Maggie the nosy old busybody she was, and demanding that she leave. She had then been forced to wait until Buck came inside and repeated the conversation to her. His casual comment that Cal had finally managed to do something right had struck a hard note of discord inside her.

She had silently cursed Doc then, infuriated at the realization that Buck was beginning to look at his son in a more positive light—which was exactly what the determined physician had intended.

Even more unsettling was the realization that if Doc's story was true, Derek might have been one of the two rustlers who had been killed.

Did she care?

The answer to that was simple. She needed him.

She had been forced to wait until the next morning, until she could raise her signal and then go to the rendezvous point to find out if Derek was alive to meet her. Yet finding him waiting for her there had only increased her wrath.

And his mood was as foul as hers.

Her patience nil, Celeste responded, "Is that all you've got to say, that Cal Star's not going to get away with killing two of your men? The whole episode was a disaster. Admit it. Cal Star outsmarted you! You not only failed, you made a hero of him in the bargain." She sneered. "I really must thank you for that."

Derek took a threatening step toward her. "Don't thank me. Thank yourself. It's your fault my men were killed. You said that herd was just waiting for us to rustle it. You never mentioned it was guarded."

"If you were smart, you would've checked out that possibility."

"There wasn't no time to check things out, and you know it. And because of that, two of my men are dead."

"There's only one person responsible for killing your men, and that person is Cal Star. He's the one you should be blaming, not me."

"The boys and me wouldn't have gone to the Rocky W if it wasn't for you."

"You didn't do me any favors, Derek, and don't pretend you did. You raided the Rocky W because you were panting for what I had to offer, and I made it worth your while. The thought of the profit you'd turn after selling off the herd was added inducement. It's not my fault if Cal Star outsmarted you."

"He blind-sided us with that guard!"

"That's too bad. So, what are you going to do about it?"

"You're a cold bitch, ain't you?"

"Some say I am . . ." Celeste's eyes narrowed as she returned, "And some say I'm damned hot when I want to be."

"Yeah . . . when it suits you."

Celeste replied haltingly, "It may surprise you, Derek"—she moved a step closer—"but you do something for me that most men don't when we come together. You make me forget the business end of the deal while we're skin to skin. You make me forget everything except how hot I can make it for both of us."

"Witch—"

"As a matter of fact, I'm thinking about it right now—how I could turn your anger into groans, and how you could make me forget the touch of my husband's shaky hands when you're on top of me."

"I didn't come here today with that in mind."

"No, but it's on your mind now, isn't it?"

Derek declined to reply, but Celeste saw the answer in his gaze, and she laughed. "All of a sudden it doesn't seem so important that two of your men were killed, does it?"

"It sure as hell does!"

"No, it doesn't." Celeste slid her hand under Derek's belt buckle into his intimate warmth. She held off only inches from his rapidly hardening male organ and whispered, "As a matter of fact, it's seeming less and less important."

Derek did not reply.

"You don't want me to stop, do you?"

"I said—"

She took a step closer and breathed up into his face, "I don't want to stop either, right now. I figure we could have a good time together with you being dead set for vengeance and me feeling the same—with both of us needing a satisfaction that'll unite our anger."

"I told you I didn't come here for that."

"But you didn't mean it, or you'd be pushing me away right now." Celeste ran her fingertips over Derek's male organ as it swelled up to nudge her hand. She rasped, "That's right, Derek. Hot, hard, and ready. I'm ready for you, too."

Derek grabbed for her, but Celeste slipped away. She said harshly, "But first we need to settle things between us—and the only thing between us right now is Cal Star."

"That bastard—"

"You want him dead, Derek. I can see it in your eyes. I want him dead, too. Once he's gone, everything will slip back to normal."

"I don't care about 'normal.' I care about the way he made me look bad in the eyes of my men. There's only one way to fix what he did, and that's to make him as dead as the men he killed."

"That's what I want to hear." Celeste's smile was hard. "Now all that's left to settle is how and when—and to make sure Cal's death doesn't raise any suspicion that I had a part in it."

"I don't give a damn about raising suspicion!"

"I do! When everything is taken care of and Cal is dead, I won't have any trouble getting my husband to change his will. Once that's done and I'm sure Taylor won't inherit, my husband will die unexpectedly. Everyone will call it a heart attack, and I'll be properly bereaved, so it's important that nobody even thinks to blame me."

"As if I care about that."

Celeste whispered erotically, "I could make you care." Derek went still. His passion bulged visibly, reassuring her as she pressed, "You know I can do it."

"Yeah, I know." Sweat appeared on his forehead as he hesitated a few moments, then snapped, "What have you got in mind?"

"I want you to raid the Rocky W herd again."

"And step into another trap? Hell, no!"

"I heard one of my husband's men telling him Cal wired the railhead yesterday when he brought the two bodies into town. He's going to be driving the herd there to get some working cash for the Rocky W. That'll be the perfect time to put a bullet in Cal Star and make it look like it all happened while you were rustling the herd. It'll be a good way to redeem yourself in the eyes of your men, too."

"I don't need to 'redeem' myself for my men."

"If you say so, Derek—just as long as Cal Star ends up dead."

Celeste waited endless moments as Derek withheld agreement. He said abruptly, "When's he supposed to drive the herd to the railhead?" Celeste closed the final distance between them. She moved her body against his in a way that stopped Derek's breath. He rasped, "You'd better be sure before you answer me, too. I ain't looking for no more mistakes."

"I'll get you the information, Derek. You can depend on me to do that." Her own body heat rising, Celeste rasped, "The question is, can I depend on you?"

Derek's stubbled cheek ticked.

"Derek . . . ?"

"Cal Star's as good as dead."

"You won't be sorry—not in any way."

"Yeah? So, show me."

As breathlessly anxious as he, Celeste did.

Doc Maggie scrutinized Pru's sober expression as the widow stood opposite her in her silent office. The change in Pru's appearance was startling. Wearing the gingham frock she had bought in the general store to replace her shredded widow's weeds, and the flat-crowned, wide-brimmed Western felt hat she had adopted to shield her fair skin from the hot Texas sun, Pru looked barely old enough to be the mother of five-year-old Jeremy. Somehow the uncertain, floundering widow who had arrived in Lowell months earlier had been replaced by a younger, stronger woman.

Uncertain of the wisdom of Pru's newfound conviction, however, Doc Maggie shook her head and continued, "You know I'll gladly keep Jeremy with me while you're gone, but I can't believe Cal thinks it's a good idea to let you ride along on the drive to the railhead."

"I didn't say Cal thinks it's a good idea."

"Then why—"

"It's my ranch, Doc. I make the decisions."

"It's always been *your* ranch, but that doesn't change the fact that you were barely hanging on until Cal took over. That should tell you his opinion is worth something."

"I didn't say it wasn't."

Confused, Doc shook her head. "So?"

"I need to go along."

"Why?"

"That should be obvious to a woman like you."

"To a woman like me . . . it should be, huh?"

"You've achieved success in a field where women aren't usually accepted. You know a woman can do whatever she puts her mind to. I'm going to learn how to run the Rocky W so I won't need to depend on anybody but myself for Jeremy's and my future."

"But Cal—"

"Cal made his position clear when he took the job at the Rocky W."

"And his position is?"

"He has some things to settle with his father.

That's the reason he came back. As soon as he clears them up, he'll put the Rocky W behind him."

"He told you that."

"He said he'd take the job as long as I understood it was temporary. That's clear enough for anybody to understand."

"Oh. I thought things . . . circumstances might've changed his mind."

Pru's face colored revealingly as she replied, "The only circumstances that've changed are that I've finally come to realize *I* need to change." Pru took a breath and continued, "I can't go on being 'the widow' for the rest of my life, Doc. I need to get past it. I made the decision to make the Rocky W my home, and I need to adapt to the change. I need to learn everything a woman born to ranching knows if I expect to survive here, and I need to start learning now."

"That's a tall order."

"I can handle it."

"Pru—"

"I *will* handle it."

Doc studied Pru's expression a moment longer. She read a resolve in her eyes similar to the determination she had experienced years earlier after her own dear Willie's death. Her eyes moistened unexpectedly. Somehow she had fallen into the same age-old misconception that she had resented years earlier when people had looked at her as "a woman who was left alone." She had thought Pru wouldn't be able to make a life for herself without a man's guidance. She had forgotten that intelligence and determination were formidable weapons in conquering adversities of any kind, and that a woman's inherent inner strength made those qualities almost invincible when she chose to use them. It was suddenly obvious that Pru had taken those qualities to heart in a new way.

Doc supposed that realization was a bit belated, but Pru was right. She did understand.

Doc replied with new certainty, "I know you'll handle it. And don't worry about leaving Jeremy with me. He'll be fine."

"I need to know something else, too, Doc." Pru took an unsteady breath. "I'm not unaware that there are risks in the course I'm taking. Aside from the problem with rustlers, there's the attack on the ranch house to consider."

Uncertain where she was heading, Doc did not reply.

Holding Doc's gaze steadily with her own, Pru said, "I need to know that if anything happens to me . . ." She paused, then hastened to add, "Not that I expect it to, but if it does—I need to know somebody will be there for Jeremy. There's nobody I'd trust more than you to take care of him."

Doc's throat choked tight.

"You don't have to answer me now. But I'd like you to think about it."

"Pru—"

"I just need to know—in case."

"Pru, I—"

"Take your time." Pru swallowed. "I know the answer isn't easy."

"It is for me." Doc Maggie covered the distance between them in a few steps and hugged her in a motherly embrace. She released her moments later and rasped, "I don't have to think about it. You'll never have to worry about Jeremy as long as I'm around, even if I don't expect you'll ever have need of my efforts."

"I know that, but thank you, Doc."

"No need to thank me."

"Thanks anyway."

Watching as Pru turned away from her with a stiff smile, Doc followed her slight figure as she stepped out onto the board sidewalk and pulled the office door closed behind her. It occurred to her that Pru might look like a girl now, but she had never been a more formidable woman.

She admired her; she sure as hell did.

Pru closed Doc Maggie's office door behind herself and stepped out onto the street. She ignored the speculative glances her new appearance drew from sharp-tongued matrons and interested cowpokes as she continued on down the street. She hesitated momentarily at the sight of Cal exiting the mercantile store where he had gone to get supplies for the cattle drive. Jeremy was walking beside him, and her throat tightened. They looked so comfortable together, Jeremy looking up at Cal with a newfound respect, and Cal looking down at him with sober interest. Her own reaction to the sight of the two males she suddenly realized were the most important people in her life, was not so casual.

Jeremy, freckle-faced and curly-haired, so young and so protective of her in his own childish way—she could not possibly love him more.

And then there was Cal.

Pru's eyes narrowed as she assessed the long-legged, self-possessed stride that set him apart from the crowd as clearly as his towering height and muscular physique. She remembered that the first time she saw him, she had been intimidated by the sheer power of his physical presence. Then she had become the focus of his intense, honey-colored gaze, and she'd reacted to her intimidation by boldly attempting to let Cal know that *she* was the boss, and *she* was in charge.

Her first mistake.

Her second mistake had been to put herself in a position where she could end up in his arms.

A familiar quiver ran up Pru's spine.

She had been so confused. She'd been unable to understand how she could be so determined one moment to maintain her position of authority over him, and then end up lying in his arms the next. She had told herself the first time it happened that it wouldn't happen again. She had told herself the same thing the second time. Then had come a twilight on the ranch when gunshots sounded in the distance and Cal rode out with the men toward unknown danger, leaving strict instructions for Jeremy and her to remain behind.

She had waited only until the shooting stopped to follow.

Her confusion had ended the moment she rode up to the branding corral, saw two bodies lying on the ground, then met Cal's burning gaze with her own.

Her relief had been so great when she saw him alive and well that she had realized in an instant she loved him. She had almost told him so when he slipped his arm around her and drew her away from the lifeless bodies of the rustlers.

But she hadn't. More rational thoughts had prevailed—like the realization that although Cal had showed her in so many ways how much he cared, his first priority still was to settle the darkness in his past. She knew it wasn't his fault. He wanted her, but the Rocky W and she were an interim circumstance while he struggled to settle a guilt he had suffered most of his adult life.

She knew all that, but it didn't stop her from loving him even as she realized he might eventually leave her.

And she needed to prepare in the only way she could.

Cal's expression was sober as she approached and asked, "Are the supplies for the drive loaded in the wagon?"

He nodded.

"Doc said she'll take care of Jeremy while I'm gone."

Jeremy burst out angrily, "I told you, I don't want to stay with Doc. I want to go with Cal and you."

"I'm sorry, Jeremy, you can't."

"I'm going with you!"

Cal interjected firmly, "No, you're not. You're five years old, Jeremy. Your ma doesn't feel comfortable taking you along yet. She'll let you come when you're older—when you're six or thereabouts." He looked at her coldly. "Won't you, Pru?"

Cal's stony glance hardened a painful knot inside her as Pru responded, "That sounds reasonable."

"But, Mama—"

"You heard your mother, Jeremy."

Jeremy's chin dropped toward his chest. "Yes, sir."

It was all Pru could do to maintain an unaffected facade. How had Jeremy's feelings for Cal reversed themselves so quickly, to the point where instead of challenging him on every point, he now accepted Cal's judgment without question?

She supposed she knew.

That thought lingered as Pru said, "Come on. Doc's waiting for you."

She glanced at Cal as Jeremy took her hand, but he had already turned toward the rail where his mount was secured.

The coldness remained.

* * *

"Hey, Jack, that's your replacement riding past on the street, ain't it?"

Jack Grate looked up at the Rocky W wagon as it rolled past the shadowed overhang where he lounged with cronies from his previous night's drunken spree. His lip curled in a spontaneous snarl at the sight of the widow and her son, with Cal Star riding guard at her rear.

His stubble-faced companion continued mockingly, "He's the fellow who paid you that visit in the Last Chance a while back, ain't he? How come he ain't saying hello?"

"Maybe I should call him for you," the second fellow interjected, joining the mockery. "The widow would probably like to say a few words, too."

Jack ignored their taunting and turned toward the swinging doors at the end of the street. His persistent hecklers followed as he pushed his way through the doors a few minutes later and headed for the bar. He signaled for a drink as the first fellow goaded Jack, "Oh, that's right, I forgot. Cal Star said you'd hear from *him* if you went near the widow again—so I guess since you've been keeping your distance like you were told, you're not too anxious for their friendship."

"You two ain't as smart as you think you are!" Jack spat, his temper flaring. "And that bastard ain't as safe as he thinks he is, neither."

"Oh . . . ho, are you making a threat against Cal Star?" The second fellow was grinning widely, enjoying his taunting as he continued, "You'd better watch out what you say, or that big fella might come and knock you flat on your back again."

Jack turned hotly toward them. "You're walking on thin ice, both of you. I ain't opposed to being the first to draw my gun, so unless you're ready to back up what you're saying, you'd both better hotfoot it out of here fast."

"Aw, come on, Jack." The first fellow's tone changed dramatically. "You know we was only kidding."

"Yeah, we was only joking."

"Maybe you was joking, but I'm not. Get moving!"

Jack's menacing stare followed his two tormentors as they turned toward the door and walked out of the bar without looking back.

"They ain't so smart."

That unexpected comment came from a dark-haired man standing a few feet down the bar, and Jack turned sharply in his direction. The man's coarse features were tightly set as he continued, "After what they said to you, if I was them, I'd be watching over my shoulder just to make sure that gun of yours stayed in its holster until I got out the door."

"They weren't afraid because they knew they were safe enough with witnesses around—but I guarantee they'll be looking over their shoulders while they're riding alone, or maybe walking down a dark street." Jack wasn't smiling. "That's my specialty . . . and they know it."

"You ain't past using situations to your advantage,

is that it?" The dark man smirked. "Some might say that's a coward's way of doing things."

Jack tensed. His hand moved toward his gun.

"But me, I say that's smart."

Jack eyed the stranger, then relaxed.

The other man pressed, "What's all this talk about Cal Star and you?"

"The bastard has it coming, and he's going to get it, too. I'm just waiting for the right time."

"What happened?"

"That whore widow told him some kind of story about me—so he jumped me when I wasn't looking, right here at the bar. Truth is, I wouldn't touch that witch with a ten-foot pole."

"Is that right?"

"She's got it coming, too. She owes me money, and I'm going to get it one way or another."

The dark-haired man nodded. "I don't like Cal Star much myself. I figure he's got something coming from both of us."

Jack eyed the stranger more closely. He studied the fellow's unshaven face and saw a coldness in the eyes looking back at him that reflected deadly sentiments not unlike his own.

Jack extended his hand and said, "I don't know your name, but I like the way you think. My name's Jack, and I'm pleased to meet you."

The dark-haired man accepted his hand and shook it firmly. His deadly gaze did not falter as he replied, "Pleased to meet you, Jack. My name's Derek—and the next drink's on me."

Chapter Eleven

Cal squinted and adjusted the brim of his hat lower on his forehead as he scanned the sunlit terrain with a watchful eye. Mitch, Randy, and Big John had agreed to oversee things at the Rocky W for the duration of their trail drive, relieving him of that concern. The herd was moving easily, and Larry, Josh, and Winston had settled into their positions.

Those concerns eased, he glanced to his right and anxiously studied Pru, who was riding a few yards away. They had started the drive out at daybreak, with Cal riding flank where he could most easily keep an eye on Pru and the herd. He was acutely aware of the difficulty involved in moving a herd of considerable size with limited drovers; and the sight of Pru, sitting her horse in unaccustomed Western riding clothes, wearing boots still stiff enough to chafe her heels, gloves too large for her delicate hands, and carrying gear on her saddle which she could not even name, tied his stomach into knots.

As they'd started off, Pru had lurched sharply forward on the saddle, almost losing her seat, and causing him to clench his jaw tight.

He had ridden to her side, silently furious with himself for having consented to take her along. He had barked orders for her to remain a safe distance from the herd and never to venture in among the cattle, whatever the situation. He had made it clear that if she strayed out of his sight, he would send her back to the ranch. He had deliberately reminded her that that eventuality would leave him even more shorthanded than he presently was.

Strangely, she had not even replied.

Cal looked at Pru a moment longer. They had been on the trail for several hours. It appeared she was traveling now with relative comfort, seeming to roll easily with the horse's sway. Her color looked good, and her expression was not tense. He wondered what she was thinking, then chastised himself. It didn't matter what she thought. It only mattered what she *did*—specifically that she followed his orders.

Cal forced his attention back to the herd. He didn't like having his concentration compromised by his concern for her, a concern which had not lessened despite the uneventfulness of the last few hours. He was keenly aware of the dangers this drive presented. In a way, Old Man Simmons's inattention to ranching affairs during the final years of his life had been to Pru's advantage. It had fostered herds of "wild stock" and yearlings which the rustlers had ignored because they were too unpredictable and couldn't be moved quickly and quietly. It was this stock that comprised the majority of the herd they were presently moving. Although the herd was traveling at a leisurely rate, he knew these cattle could be spooked by something as trivial as the sudden bucking of a horse or a startling sound. He knew too well the damage that churning hooves could cause, and how easily an inexperienced rider could go down in their midst.

A chill rolled down Cal's spine, and he glanced back at Pru again. She was so damned stubborn, so intent on learning everything there was to be learned about ranching—immediately, without delay—when he knew the accumulation of that knowledge could take a lifetime.

And then there was the possibility of rustlers.

Cal's frown deepened. Nobody had to tell him that traveling with a limited number of wranglers made the herd an excellent target. If all went well, they would reach the railhead in three days, but during that time, anything could happen.

Anything.

That truth added new anxiety to his concern as Cal spurred his horse to a cautiously increased pace.

Agitated, Celeste dug her heels into her mount's sides as she urged him along the narrow trail. She didn't like riding astride, and she didn't like it when things didn't go according to plan. It was midafternoon, and she had hung the signal in her bedroom window only minutes before leaving the house, uncertain whether Derek would see it in time to meet her when she arrived at the deserted cabin.

She had taken a risk in leaving the ranch house at such a late hour. With Buck's limited stamina, he would not be able to work the full day, and was possibly on his way back to the ranch house at that very moment. She was keenly aware that to raise suspicions with her absence could delay her plans for months.

Madalane's dark, angry expression returned to mind, and Celeste silently cursed. She had sent Madalane to town twice to get information on the Rocky W trail drive. The townsfolk were accustomed to seeing Madalane in the stores. Everyone spoke freely in her presence. The Rocky W wranglers would have had to come to town for the supplies they'd need on the drive, and with Agnes Bower's propensity for gossip, it should have been easy for Madalane to find out what she wanted.

Celeste's anger flashed hotter. Madalane was losing her edge. A few years earlier, Madalane would have had no problem in accomplishing the task she had been set. Instead, she had come back the first day reporting that Agnes and the usual fonts of information in town had been suspiciously quiet about the intended date of the Rocky W drive.

Celeste had decided to send Madalane back to town again earlier that morning, where Madalane had seen the widow's son walking with Doc Maggie, and learned he was staying with Doc because the

Rocky W trail drive had already begun.

She had been furious with Madalane for her inefficiency. She had not spared the woman's feelings, and Madalane had not hidden her anger at being so chastised—but Celeste didn't care. Madalane's ineptitude had afforded Derek an excuse to fail again. She needed to—

A horseman leapt unexpectedly out of the foliage onto the trail ahead, blocking her path, and Celeste gasped. She reached for the gun slung across her saddle, then frowned in recognition as she drew her mount to a halt and said, "What are you doing here, Derek? You know where we're supposed to meet. Someone might see us."

"You worry too much. Nobody's going to see us."

"I prefer to meet in the cabin."

"Not this time. I ain't giving you a chance to distract me."

"What is that supposed to mean? You sound like you don't trust me."

Derek shook his head. "I'm just smart. I've got important things to do, and I need to keep my mind on business."

"You're right. You have very important things to do." Celeste continued sharply, "I found out this morning that the Rocky W's herd is already on the trail. They have a head start on you, Derek. You're going to have to do some catching up."

"That ain't no news."

Surprised by Derek's reply, Celeste snapped, "If you know the Rocky W herd is already on the trail, what are you doing here? Why aren't you following them?"

"Why should I? Them wranglers can't travel fast with that herd of wild stock or them steers'll spook. The boys and me can catch up with them easy, and that's what we're going to do when the time is right."

"When the time is right? I don't want any slipups this time, Derek. I don't give a damn what you do with that herd, but I want Cal Star dead."

"You're a fine one to talk about slipups when you come here with information I've known about for days."

"You've known about it for days . . ." Celeste's jaw twitched. Madalane would hear about this.

"That's right. I got myself a new man who's real good at finding out things."

"A new man!" Celeste was incredulous. "You hired a new man now, somebody untried, when you need to do something as important as getting rid of Cal Star?"

"In case you didn't notice, I'm shorthanded with two of my men shot dead. So I got myself somebody who's as determined as I am that Cal Star don't come off that trail drive alive."

"I thought *you* were going to make sure of that, Derek. Or have you already delegated that task to somebody else you can blame if you fail again?"

"I ain't going to fail! And Cal Star ain't going to make it to that railhead, because we'll be waiting for him."

"He's already ahead of you on the trail, damn it!"

"I know my job. Don't you go telling me how to do it! Right now Cal Star's fresh and cautious. He's watching everything real close, expecting something might happen at any minute. I'm going to give him a chance to relax a little, so he'll think everything's going along without a hitch. I'll hit him late the second day, when his men will be looking forward to settling the herd down for the night and getting a good meal in their stomachs. The cattle will be used to running in a herd by then, too, which'll make them easier to move out once we get control."

"The widow's traveling with him, you know." The surprised flick of Derek's heavy brows was revealing, and Celeste sneered, "So, you aren't as well informed as you thought."

"It don't make no difference if that widow's with them. She's a tenderfoot. She ain't no problem—but I'm figuring Jack will be happy to take care of her, too. She's been stuck in his craw for a long time."

"Jack . . . ? Are you talking about Jack Grate, the fellow the widow fired from her ranch? He's the new man?"

"That's my business."

"I asked you a question."

"And I ain't answering."

"Derek, if you think—"

His expression suddenly rabid, Derek inched his mount closer and spat, "You ain't telling me nothing, you hear? This ain't like the last time, when you came to the cabin with all that talk about how easy it was going to be to rustle the Rocky W herd—

about how that herd was just waiting for us to take it. You talked me into it then because you was rubbing up against me and making me so hot that the last thing I was thinking with was my brain." He gave a harsh snort. "Not this time. I got a score to settle with Cal Star and his boys, and I'm not going to let nobody get in the way."

When Celeste did not reply, Derek sneered, "But if you get to feeling the need for a real man after everything is taken care of, I'll be happy to oblige."

Derek's comment was too close to the truth for comfort, and Celeste snapped, "I'll think it over."

"Yeah?" Derek reached out unexpectedly and jerked Celeste toward him. He crushed his wet lips against hers, almost gagging her as he thrust his tongue deep into her throat. He pulled back from her just as unexpectedly and spat, "Keep that in mind while you're 'thinking it over.' And just so you're clear about it, there's two of us now—Jack *and* me—who're going to make sure Cal Star don't make it to the railhead alive. So you can go back to that old man of yours without a worry; and while he's sweating on top of you, you can start dreaming up ways to show me how much you appreciate what I done for you."

Forcing a smile, Celeste replied, "You can depend on it."

Celeste's smile faded as she turned her horse. Silently cursing Derek for the brutish bastard that he was, she headed back in the direction from which she had come.

* * *

The sun had set, the cattle were almost settled down for the night, and the campfire was sputtering low when Pru scanned the faces of the men. They had already eaten their campfire meal and Winston was pouring himself another cup of coffee, but his large frame was sagging with fatigue. He had ridden behind the herd to keep the lagging cattle in line, and she now knew that a day spent in the endless cloud of dust the herd raised was more difficult than she had ever imagined it could be. Winston had dusted off his clothes and washed his face with a handful of their limited supply of water. She had heard him swear he would jump headlong into the stream when they reached it the next day—and she believed he would.

She had been impressed by the silent communication among the wranglers as the day had worn on; they seemed to understand what had to be done to keep the herd moving smoothly with a glance, a signal, or just keen observance of each other's actions. She realized, however, that appearances were deceiving, and that Cal had carefully planned both the pace and the route that the herd would take.

Josh was readying his bedroll, looking almost as tired as Winston. She glanced up at the herd and located Larry's shadowed figure as he slowly circled the steers. He was on the first watch. She had heard Cal give the order for Josh to take the second. Exhausted by the day's ride, she marveled at the men's stamina. Her respect for them grew greater by the hour.

Feeling the weight of someone's stare, Pru turned abruptly and met Cal's unsmiling gaze. It had not missed her notice that neither his attention to the herd, nor his silent scrutiny of her had lapsed during the endless day. She knew that fatigue would have no effect on his attention to his job, and she suddenly needed to explain that she regretted the burden she added to his responsibilities with her presence. But she also needed to make him understand that she wasn't doing it out of sheer mulishness, or to prove that she was the boss, but for the sake of the future—Jeremy's future.

Before realizing her own intent, Pru heard herself say, "I'd like to talk to you for a few minutes, Cal."

Cal held her gaze in silence, and Pru realized abruptly that he was considering refusing her. She swallowed, uncertain what she'd do then. She hadn't realized she was holding her breath until he nodded his agreement.

They were a short distance from the campfire when Cal turned toward her abruptly and said, "What do you want to talk about?"

"I'm sorry you're angry with me, Cal." Earnest, Pru continued, "I can see I'm a burden to you here. I don't think I fully realized that before." She almost smiled. "Another of the things I needed to learn the hard way."

When Cal did not reply, when he continued staring down at her with the same hard intensity she had seen in his eyes all day, Pru continued, "That's the problem, you see? I have so much to learn if I'm going to make it on the Rocky W. Unfortunately, this trail drive is lesson number one—and you're the teacher."

"I didn't sign on at the Rocky W to teach anybody anything."

"I know. You made your intentions clear the day you accepted the job. But I made things clear to you that day, too. I told you then that when all is said and done, I'm the one who's going to sink or swim on the Rocky W. I don't intend to sink here, Cal. And I need your help."

"My help . . ."

"I'm watching and learning, but it's the hard way again. You could make it easier for me."

"I thought I was."

"Cal . . . please try to understand."

"What do you want from me, Pru? A running commentary on what it means to be a wrangler?" Cal's expression did not change. "I don't have time for that, and I don't have all the answers even if I did."

"Don't be stubborn, Cal."

"*I'm* stubborn?" Cal's lips compressed into a tight line. He said abruptly, "What do you want to know?"

Surprised by his sudden compliance, Pru stammered, "Things like how you set up the responsibilities on the drive."

"I don't need to explain responsibilities to these men. They know how to hold their positions on the drive."

"Their positions?"

"Larry was on point today, Josh on swing, I'm riding flank, and Winston held up drag. Those positions will change tomorrow."

"Because?"

"That should be obvious."

Pru flushed, then pressed, "What do those positions mean?"

His patience obviously short, Cal responded, "*Point* heads the herd in the right direction. In order to handle that job, a man needs to know how to move cattle so they don't get off track. He also needs to know what's ahead in the country. But these are good men. Any of them can handle it. *Swing* keeps the herd strung out so it moves more easily, and stops it from cutting across trails when the herd changes direction. *Flank* keeps the herd moving and the flank narrowed down. The narrower the drag end of the herd can be kept, the better the stock will travel. *Drag* makes sure the lagging cattle—the weak and tender-footed stock—keep up."

"Oh."

"Anything else?"

"Cal—"

"I said, anything else?"

"How much longer do you think the drive will take?"

"Another day and night. If we don't run into any difficulty, we'll probably reach the railhead in three days."

Pru nodded, then said, "I don't want you to be angry with me, Cal."

Cal's jaw locked tight.

"Cal—"

"We're up at dawn tomorrow. You'd better get some rest if you intend to keep up."

"I'll keep up."

"You'd better."

His attitude was beginning to grate on her, and Pru replied, "I hope that's not a threat, because if it is—"

"Take it any way you want, as long as you're ready to go with the others."

"I'll be ready. Don't worry."

Cal's gaze locked with hers. "I won't waste my time worrying. I'll just send you back."

"That'll never happen!"

His gaze hardening, Cal turned back toward the campfire without bothering to reply.

Didn't she realize what she was doing to him?

The camp was asleep as that question echoed in Cal's mind. Pru lay wrapped in her bedroll across the campfire—as far away from him as she could possibly get. He watched as she breathed evenly in sleep. She was exhausted, but she hadn't fallen asleep easily, and he knew why. She was angry because he hadn't responded to her overture the way she'd expected.

Agitation twisted hot and sharp inside him even as he swept the campsite with a scrutiny that was more reflex than conscious effort. Satisfied that all appeared well, that Josh and Winston were snoring softly while Larry maintained watch on the herd, he looked back at Pru. Her dark braid glinted in the firelight as he ran his gaze along the delicate outline of her body underneath the blanket. He remembered following those slender curves with his palms, reveling in the velvet softness of her skin as she lay in his arms. He recalled caressing her with increasing warmth, searching out her moist female heat and stroking it gently. He remembered looking down into her face as she responded to his touch, watching as her eyelids fluttered and slowly lifted to reveal the heat of passion again rising in her eyes. He recalled covering her mouth with his—tasting her as his kiss pressed deeper and his stroking delved more intimately. The look in her eyes, the sudden flush of her skin, the exact moment when her passion surged out of control and she shuddered to fulfillment, returned so clearly to mind that his heart began pounding.

He remembered kissing her breasts as she strove to catch her breath, running his lips over her skin to taste the salty moisture on its surface, knowing a hunger for more. He had slipped inside her then, and had remained unmoving for long moments while he savored his possession of her—until she locked her gaze with his and rasped his name through parted lips. That simple whisper of sound had eradicated all conscious thought, had thrust him out of control and brought them both to a fierce, ecstatic culmination.

He wanted her. There was no other warmth he sought, no other taste he savored, no other hunger he hoped to sate—no other woman in the world for him but Pru. She was so near, yet there were miles between them that he dared not breach.

Bonnie's childish, smiling face flashed again before his eyes, and Cal felt his stomach clench tight. Pru believed in him, trusted him, was relying on him, just like Bonnie. He was responsible for her safety, just as he had been responsible for Bonnie's—and the truth was, he wasn't sure he could live with the torment of failure if it happened again.

Pru had said she now understood how she added to his difficulties by coming on the drive, but she didn't, really. He could tell by the uncertain way she looked at him that she didn't realize he had been conscious of her every moment of the long, grueling day; and that as night fell and they sat eating round the campfire, his only true hunger had been for her.

But memories haunted him. Shadows stood in the way. Images hovered between them—images etched so deep inside him that he was uncertain he could ever strike them fully from his mind. He wondered—

Roused from his thoughts by Larry's approach, Cal threw back his blanket. He stood up slowly, and shook his head as Larry started to approach Josh. Abandoning the attempt to sleep, he walked toward his horse to take the next watch.

* * *

"What are *you* doing in town so early in the morning?"

Surprised at Doc Maggie's brusque question, Buck paused in the doorway of her office, uncertain how to respond. The street behind him was bright with morning sunshine as he sought an answer to her sharp inquiry. He wasn't about to tell her that he had ridden off to work with the men as was his custom in the morning, but that he had turned toward town as soon as he was out of Celeste's sight—that he hadn't wanted to worry Celeste, but he figured he needed to see the doc. He'd been back on his feet long enough that he should have regained some of his stamina, but it wasn't happening. He wanted to know why.

Doc Maggie was waiting for his response when he replied with a question of his own.

"Did I hear you wrong, or did you tell me to pay you a visit the next time I was in town?"

"I did. But that didn't mean I expected you to show up at my door before the birds were up in the morning."

"It ain't that early, Maggie."

"It isn't?" Doc Maggie glanced out onto the street, where morning traffic had barely begun. "Could have fooled me. I haven't even had time to cook breakfast yet."

"Cook breakfast? I thought you gave that up after Trudy Bartlett opened her restaurant down the street."

"That may be so, but I've got me some company staying over, which changes things a bit."

Buck took a spontaneous backward step. Obviously embarrassed, he stammered, "Excuse me. I didn't realize I'd be stepping into . . . I mean that I'd be intruding into your *private* time. I'll come back later."

"Well, you're here now. Besides, my fella can wait. He's getting dressed now."

"Never mind, I can come back. I—"

Buck halted as Doc's curtained partition moved and a freckle-faced boy stepped out into sight. The boy's shoes were clumsily tied, his shirt was bunched up in his trousers, and his eyes still held a trace of sleep.

Buck glanced at Doc Maggie with a twitch of his lips. "A little young for you, ain't he?"

Doc Maggie withheld her usual smile.

The boy questioned abruptly, "Who're you?"

Buck responded, "Who's asking?"

"I asked you first."

"I guess you did."

"How come you aren't answering me?"

"How come a little boy like you asks so many questions?"

"I'm not a little boy."

"Oh, yeah, I forgot. You're Doc Maggie's *boyfriend*."

The boy turned back to Doc Maggie with a frown and whispered in a voice that carried clearly in the small office, "Is this fella all right in the head?"

Buck saw the smile that tugged at Doc Maggie's lips when she replied, "He's fine—just grouchy. He's a patient. His name is Buck Star."

Turning to Buck, she said, "Buck, this is Jeremy Reynolds. He's staying with me for a few days."

"Your name's Buck Star? Are you Cal's father?" Jeremy scrutinized him more closely, then deciding he was, continued without waiting for a reply, "I heard Mrs. Bower talking about you. Why don't you like Cal?"

"That's none of your business, *little boy*."

"It is too my business." The boy took an angry step. "Cal's my friend, and I need to know."

Buck frowned at Doc. "Who is this kid?"

"She already told you. My name's Jeremy Reynolds."

"Reynolds." Buck nodded in sudden realization. "The widow's son."

"Nobody's supposed to call Mama 'the widow' anymore. She doesn't like it. Her name's Prudence."

"That doesn't make any difference to me."

The boy stared at him, then said abruptly, "You're Cal's father and you're supposed to like him. How come you don't?"

"I've already told you, that's not your business."

Doc Maggie interjected, "Why don't you answer the boy, Buck?"

"Because I'll be damned before I'll stand here and be questioned by a little squirt just out of short pants!"

Undeterred by Buck's outburst, Jeremy continued, "Mrs. Bower said it was because Cal's sister got killed and you blamed him."

Heat flushed Buck's face. "I don't care what she said."

"She said it wasn't Cal's fault, but I didn't need to have anybody tell me that—and I'm only a kid. You're older then me and you're supposed to be smarter, so how come you blame Cal?"

Buck looked up at Doc. "I'm leaving. I'll be back when your 'company' leaves."

"Are you mad at me?" Beside him in a few steps, the boy took Buck's arm and said, "Cal won't like it if I got you mad."

"Is that what he said?"

"No."

"What did he say about me?"

"Nothing."

"So what makes you so sure you know what you're talking about?"

"I listened real close to what Mrs. Bower said."

Damned busybody . . .

"She said Cal felt bad about his sister getting killed—real bad."

"Like you said, you're only a kid."

"Maybe, but I know my mama didn't know anything about being a rancher before Cal showed up. Jack was supposed to be helping her, but he was stealing and running up bills that she had to pay. Then Cal came, and now she's learning to be a real rancher."

"Yeah . . . I heard."

"And I'm going to be a wrangler, too . . . when I get older."

Buck did not respond.

"You should be proud of Cal, Mr. Star. If I was his father, I'd be proud."

Ignoring him, Buck looked up at Doc and said, "I'll come back when you're not so busy."

"Buck—"

Doc Maggie took a step toward him, but Buck walked back out onto the street and didn't look back.

"We're in for trouble if we can't water these beeves tonight, Cal."

With Winston's comment ringing in his ears, Cal stared at the dry stream bed they had reached a short time earlier. He didn't like this. They had started the herd up at dawn and had deliberately driven the cattle on an indirect route to the railhead with the plan of thoroughly watering the animals before the last day's travel. But the stream was dry.

"Looks like Rob Tinker dammed up the stream again." Josh shook his head. "There was hell to pay the last time he did it, but he's a stubborn fella and set in his ways."

"That don't help us now," Winston added.

Cal glanced up at the sun rapidly rising in the cloudless sky. It would be hot soon. He questioned, "What about that water hole near Aaron Stills's place? Is it still in good shape?"

"It was the last time I passed by, but that's no guarantee."

"You'd be taking a chance driving this herd all the way up there if it ain't." Winston glanced at the herd rooting in the dry stream bed. "Them cattle are getting mighty restless."

Hesitating only a moment, Cal said, "I'll ride ahead and check on it to make sure. There's a stream up a little farther that might do if the water hole doesn't work out. It'll be a while before we have to make any decision about redirecting the herd, so you boys can keep it moving until I get back."

"Sounds like a good plan."

"That's all right with me."

"We'll be waiting for you, boss."

"I'm going with you."

Cal turned sharply toward Pru, who had sat her horse in silence since arriving at the dry stream bed. The last thing he needed was to have her with him after he had spent the night trying to get her out of his mind. He had almost hoped she'd wake up in the morning stiff, exhausted, and disheartened, so she'd ask him to let one of the men take her back to the ranch. Instead, she had awakened with the men, saddled up her own horse, and kept up without a word of complaint.

She was determined.

But so was he.

He returned, "No, you're not. You're staying here with the herd."

"I said, I'm going with you." The men turned their horses back toward the herd, leaving Pru alone with Cal as she continued firmly, "I told you how I feel about this, Cal. I need to learn everything I can on this drive."

"Like checking on a water hole?"

"And maybe learning a little bit more about what this country is like along the way."

"No. You're staying with the herd."

"I *own* the Rocky W, remember?"

"That may be so, but you're not the boss on this drive. What I say goes, and I say you're staying with the men."

"Why are you so angry with me, Cal?" Pru's fair skin flushed unexpectedly and her voice grew hoarse. "I've done all I can to make you understand how important this drive is to me. I don't want to be in a position where somebody like Jack can take advantage of me again. Can't you comprehend that?"

"I need to move fast. You'll hold me back."

"I've kept up so far."

"That's not much of an accomplishment with the herd traveling as slowly as it is."

"All right. Maybe you're right. Maybe I will hold you up. If I do, you can leave me behind and pick me up on the way back to the herd. Does that satisfy you?"

"You're expecting me to leave you behind in open country?"

"I have a gun. I can protect myself."

"I've seen you shoot, remember?"

"I'm going with you. I can't learn anything by staying behind with the herd."

"You won't learn anything if I have to leave you behind halfway to the water hole, either."

"I'll take my chances."

Pru's lips were set in a firm line. He was wasting time arguing with her.

"Well?"

Cal snapped, "Make sure your gun is loaded. If you can make enough noise with it, you might not have to worry about hitting anything when I leave you behind."

He saw the anger that flashed in her eyes when she replied, "I'll keep up with you, damn it! And my gun *is* loaded."

Not bothering to respond, Cal turned with a last signal to the men and headed his mount northward.

Derek rode at a moderate pace. He glanced uneasily at the men riding beside him. Somehow, the last thing he had expected was that friction would develop between them, but he supposed he should have realized it might. Lefty had made no secret of his resentment at the way things had worked out when Sarge and Luke were killed. His grumbling increased when he learned they were going to go after the Rocky W herd again, and Harry had joined in. When he came back from town with Jack in tow, it was the final straw.

Both Harry and Lefty had taken an instant dislike

to Jack. They said Jack was a braggart and they didn't trust him, that he would let them down at the first sign of trouble. Derek had told them it didn't matter what they thought. They needed another man to help move the cattle, and Jack was that man.

They had finally accepted his explanation, but their silence since mounting up that morning spoke more clearly than words.

Determined that their attitude wouldn't affect the outcome of their venture, Derek began, "We should be spotting the herd in an hour or so. That'll give us time to set things up."

"You'd better hope this works out better than it did the last time." Lefty's stare was critical. "We can't afford no more mistakes."

"Don't worry about mistakes. I got everything planned out fine."

"What's to plan out?" Suspicion tinged Harry's voice. "We go after the herd and use our guns if anybody gets in the way."

Derek slanted Jack a revealing glance, and Lefty snapped, "You ain't only got rustling the herd in mind, do you? Your 'girlfriend' gave you another chore to do."

"Shut up."

Lefty continued with growing heat, "I don't care how good she is in bed. I don't like working for a woman, especially that Celeste Star!"

"Shut up, you fool!" Derek glanced at Jack's surprised expression. The sleazy bastard had picked up on Celeste's name, and Derek had no doubt he'd make good use of it if the opportunity presented itself. Celeste would blame him. Not that he cared, but he wasn't ready to give up what Celeste had to offer; not yet.

Derek continued, "You two don't have to worry about anything except getting that herd. I'll take care of everything else."

"Sure . . . like the last time."

His expression deadly, Derek said, "It ain't going to be nothing like last time. That herd's as good as ours right now—but if you don't like the way I'm running things, you can turn your horse around and go back the way you came." Derek's thick features tightened further. "But I want to make something clear right now. If you try doing things your own way once we get started, I won't wait for one of them wranglers to put a bullet in you. I'll do it myself! Is that understood?"

Derek scanned Harry's and Lefty's faces, then looked at Jack and saw his sneer. The bastard was enjoying this!

Derek waited a few seconds longer, then saw Lefty nod. Harry's nod followed. The bastard Jack was still sneering.

Forcibly subduing his anger, Derek said, "All right. We all know what we got to do. Like I said, that herd's as good as ours."

The day was growing hotter and his horse was slowing. Pru and he had been riding nonstop for the past half hour. Aware that his mount was tiring, Cal slowed him to a more modest pace. He glanced at Pru, who was riding a few feet to his rear. To her credit, she had kept up with him, but he could see it hadn't been easy for her. Her face was flushed and damp, and she was frowning.

Cal drew his mount to a halt and waited for Pru to rein up beside him. He said gruffly, "Take a drink. You've been riding hard and you're overheated. You need to cool off."

Pru replied stiffly, "I'm not overheated."

"It seems to me I've heard that before."

"That was then and this is now. I'm a different person than I was—and I'm not overheated."

"Take a drink anyway."

"You're my foreman, Cal. You're not my nursemaid."

"Take a drink."

Pru's jaw tightened. "How much farther is it to the water hole?"

"We'll be there in five minutes or so."

"So why are we stopping?"

"We're waiting for you to take a drink."

Rolling her eyes with frustration, Pru unscrewed the top of her canteen and drank long and deep. Water trickled down her throat from the corner of her mouth. It disappeared in the neckline of her shirtwaist, stirring memories best left forgotten, and Cal took a stabilizing breath.

Finished, Pru said, "I took a drink. Are you satisfied now?"

In response, Cal spurred his mount into motion.

He looked back at Pru when they approached a familiar rise. She was right behind him. He had known she was too stubborn to give up, and that had been his first reservation about taking her along. The second was his concern about her reaction if they arrived at the water hole and found it dry.

"What's the matter, Cal?" Pru urged her mount up to Cal's side as he slowed his pace. "Don't tell me you want me to take another drink."

"No." Cal did not smile. Instead, he eyed her flushed face, noting the little curling tendrils that had formed at her hairline. He remembered brushing them with his lips.

"Cal?"

"The water hole should be at the bottom of this next rise."

Pru caught her breath. "You're sure?"

"Of course I'm sure."

"So what are we waiting for?"

Holding her gaze with his, Cal said, "I wanted to make sure you knew—to give you my promise that we'll get the herd to the railhead whether there's water down there or not."

"You said you'd get the herd there. I haven't doubted it for a minute."

"It's just that simple, huh?"

"For me it is."

"Did you ever stop to think it might not be wise to trust in me so much?"

"No."

Cal's voice deepened. "Why, Pru?"

Pru evaded responding as she nudged her mount into motion and said, "Let's see if there's water down there."

Cal lagged behind as Pru rode up the rise. She turned toward him when she reached the crest and shouted, "There's water there, all right!"

Riding beside her as they neared the water hole, Cal reached over and drew back on Pru's reins. He said, "Let me check it first."

"Why?"

"It's a water hole, not a free-running stream."

"So?"

"I need to be sure the water's drinkable."

Kneeling at the water's edge moments later, Cal scooped up a handful of water. He smelled it, tasted it, then walked to Pru's mount, swung her down from the saddle and said, "It's fine."

"Yahoo!"

Cal smiled at Pru's unexpected jubilation and watched as she crouched at the water's edge, splashed some water on her face and neck, then cupped a handful and drank it down. She glanced at the horses as they waded into the water hole beside her, then laughed and said, "If anybody had told me a year ago that I'd be sharing my drinking water with a horse, I would've said they were crazy."

Her smile fading when she stood up, Pru said, "Thank you, Cal. Thanks for everything."

"Don't thank me yet. We've got a ways to go before we get where we're going."

"I told you, I'm not worried about it." Pru walked

closer. Her delicate features were soberly composed, her gaze intent when she said, "I know you'll do everything possible to get that herd to the railhead. I can't ask for more than that."

She was so close he could see the dark specks of color in her light eyes, the flush of her cheeks, and the moisture on her lips. He could see the small pulse throbbing in her temple as she whispered, "I . . . I haven't been easy to get along with. I know that. I also know I wouldn't be in a position even close to making it on the Rocky W if it wasn't for you and the men you hired, and—"

"Pru—"

"No, don't stop me. I've been wanting to say this, and there's no better time than now. I've been wrong, Cal, holding off from you when I've been wanting the same thing you do. I want you to know it doesn't make any difference to me why you came back to Lowell, or how long you're going to stay. You said to me once that I'm not a widow anymore, that I have a right to have someone love me, that you wanted that man to be you. If you still mean what you said . . . if you still want me—"

"If I still want you . . . ?"

"If you do . . ."

Rigorously controlling his passion, Cal whispered, "You know what you just said, don't you, Pru?"

Pru nodded.

"Are you sure? You're not going to change your mind again tomorrow after we reach the railhead, or the next day when you hear something about me in town that you don't like, or maybe afterward if things don't go the way they should?"

"I'm done with being 'the widow,' Cal, and I'm done with thinking the way I used to."

Cal responded softly, "Then let me show you what I'm thinking."

He drew her into his arms. She uttered a soft sound the moment before his mouth closed over hers, and he swallowed it and made it his own. His kiss pressed deeper; his arms crushed her closer; the heat inside him grew to an explosive force.

Sweeping her up into his arms, Cal carried Pru to a shaded bower. He crouched beside her as he laid her there. His heart pounding, he forced himself to say, "This is your last chance, Pru. If this isn't what you meant to say . . . if you need to think things over to be sure—"

"I'm sure."

With those words reverberating inside him, Cal lay beside her and again took her into his arms. His heart thundered in his chest as he crushed her mouth with his, as he separated her lips to relish her more fully. His kisses deepened, his caresses grew more fervent, the need within him grew to an overwhelming swell. He wanted to tell her that while she lay in his arms, the past faded and the painful memories dimmed. He ached to whisper that when he held her close, he was free of the dark moment in time that marked him. He hungered to say that she had become necessary to him in so many ways—that the same qualities that had angered him at first now filled him with pride; and the sweet body that had stirred to life under his hands now gave him new life. He wanted to respond, yes, he wanted her—that he needed her, that she had become as essential to him as breathing.

But he did not. Incapable of speaking the words, he expressed his feelings with the kisses he rained on her brow, her eyelids, the curve of her cheek. He spoke them with his trembling hands as they pushed aside her shirtwaist and bared her breasts to his loving. He proved it with his kiss as he suckled the firm mounds with growing ardor, and Pru clasped him tight against their burgeoning crests.

The demanding urge within him deepening, he loosened Pru's split skirt and pushed it down from her hips. He followed its descent with the caress of his lips. He felt Pru go still when he paused at the warm delta between her thighs. He heard her sudden intake of breath when he tasted the honeyed moistness gently, then slid his tongue fully into her intimate heat.

Stirred to new heights of passion, Cal cupped her rounded buttocks with his palms. He lifted her to him and indulged himself fully, sweeping, drawing, taking her moist response inside him with silent wonder.

He felt the moment nearing. Her whispered words were broken gasps. Her body was shuddering. She was writhing with the sheer power of her emotions, and he pressed his ministrations with growing fervor.

He heard her gasp at culmination, and tasted her body's sweet homage. He accepted it fully, cherishing it, encouraging her throbbing response until her body stilled.

Her eyes were closed, her breathing still strained, when he stood up and stripped away his clothes. She caught her breath when their naked flesh met. Her eyes opened to his impassioned gaze, then flickered closed when he slipped himself inside her.

He whispered, "Open your eyes, Pru."

Satisfied only when her gaze met his fully, Cal rasped, "I want you to see who's claiming you, Pru. I want to hear you say my name."

Pru swallowed. She gasped through trembling lips, "It's you, Cal—only you."

Culmination came then in a few sharp thrusts—stealing his breath, quaking through him as Pru's liquid heat bathed him with pulsating promise.

Their bodies were slick from the heat of their passion when Cal raised himself to look down into Pru's still face at last. He brushed her mouth with his, then teased the curling tendrils at her hairline with his lips. He waited until her eyes opened again before he whispered with unsmiling solemnity, "There's no going back now, Pru. Because . . . you're mine."

Where in hell were they?

Derek scanned the herd with his spyglass from the safety of a nearby rise. He felt the weight of his men's stares as they waited behind him, and he scanned the herd again.

"Well, how does it look?"

Derek replied cautiously, "Something's wrong."

Harry's bearded face grew dark. "There's nothing wrong down there."

"That herd's moving slow . . . too slow, and Star and the widow ain't there."

"So what?"

"So what?" Derek growled, "So where are they? What are they doing? Are they hiding out somewhere where they can get a bead on anybody who tries taking the herd?"

"That don't make sense."

"Neither does the fact that they're nowhere to be seen."

"Maybe Star took the widow back," Lefty interjected. "She's as green as they come. Maybe she was causing him trouble because she couldn't keep up."

"Not that skinny witch." Jack sneered. "She'd die before she'd admit she couldn't do what she started out to do."

"Everything looks fine to me." Clearly impatient, Lefty pressed, "This was your idea, remember? So, we're here now and there's only three wranglers with that herd. We got them outnumbered. We need to hit them now. A few lucky shots, and we can have that herd running our way without any trouble."

"It's too easy. Something's wrong."

Lefty snapped, "The only thing that's wrong is that Star and the widow ain't where you can put a bullet in them to make your woman happy."

"I'd watch what you say if I was you."

"But you ain't me, and I'm saying we take that herd now, while we can."

"Lefty's right."

"I think so, too."

That last coming from Jack snapped Derek toward him as he said, "I thought you had something else you needed to accomplish here."

"Hell, I can get that Star fella and the widow anytime I want, but there's never going to be a better time than now to get that herd down there. And a little money in my pocket wouldn't hurt me one bit."

Harry nodded, "That goes for me too."

Derek remained silent. They were right. They'd been watching the herd for more than an hour and Star hadn't shown up. They'd never have a better chance to take the herd, no matter what Celeste had to say about it.

He didn't care, anyway, because however mad she got, she needed him.

He nodded abruptly. "Let's do it!"

Cal glanced at Pru where she rode beside him. She avoided his gaze, but he knew she felt no regret about their lovemaking. She wouldn't look at him for the simple reason that she knew how little it would take for him to pull her down from her horse and make love to her again, then and there.

The truth was, they had stretched their time together at the water hole to the limit and had been making their way back to the herd for more than a half hour. They'd be meeting up with the others soon, yet Pru's scent was still in his nostrils, and her taste sweet in his mouth. His realization that with one whispered word Pru could completely erase all thought of responsibility from his mind was somehow unsettling.

But she felt so good in his arms. It was only afterward, when reality intruded, that he—

Cal tensed at the bark of gunshots in the distance. Within moments, the pounding of heavy hooves shook the ground.

Turning sharply toward Pru, Cal ordered, "Get over into that stand of trees and wait for me there. I'll come back for you."

Pru's expression was stricken. "Is it rustlers?"

"Get going!"

"No, I'm coming with you."

"Do what I said, damn it! I don't want you in the way."

Pru's jaw locked tight, but she turned toward the treeline. Waiting only until she reached it, Cal turned his horse toward the sounds of continuing gunshots.

Arriving within minutes at a wild scene of stampeding cattle, clouds of dust, and sporadic gunfire, Cal turned his mount into the fray. He saw Larry attempting to head off the stampede at the head of the herd, then saw him sway when gunfire barked again. He raced toward him, uncertain if he would fall, then drew back and changed direction when Larry regained stability and continued on. Leaning low over the saddle to avoid being hit, Cal saw a horseman materialize suddenly out of the grainy mist, his gun aimed in Larry's direction. Cal fired, and the rider disappeared under the pounding hooves.

Riding alongside the frenzied herd, Cal saw another unfamiliar rider, then another, both with guns raised. He fired again and again, hardly reacting when one of the rustlers went down. A sudden barrage of bullets snapped around him, and he crouched lower over his saddle. He was attempting to locate the source of the gunfire when Pru rode into view in the distance. He called out for her to go back, his heart seeming to stop when he realized she couldn't hear him.

Panicking as Pru rode closer, Cal scanned the racing herd again. Through a break in the dust, he saw a rider raise his gun in Pru's direction. Cal fired, saw the man sway, then regain his seat before turning his horse out of the stampede.

Pru continued her approach. Her gun was drawn, and she was firing. He didn't realize until he nearly reached her side that she was firing into the ground in an attempt to clear her way.

Sweeping Pru onto his saddle the moment he reached her, he galloped out of the fray and lowered her to the ground. He snapped, "Stay here, damn it! And don't move."

Startled, he saw her raise her gun toward him. He didn't have time to react before she fired—and he turned to see an unknown horseman within the stampeding cattle slip from view.

Her gun still in hand, Pru stared at him in stunned silence. Suddenly aware that the gunfire had stopped, Cal ordered again, "Stay here!"

He then turned his mount back toward the racing beeves.

Still covered with gritty residue from the stampede, Cal assessed the milling herd cautiously. They had driven the cattle directly to the water hole after bringing them under control. He had ordered that the herd be given room to spread out there, aware that the uneasy cattle would need ample room to lie down and rest when they were done—the key to preventing a recurrence of the near disaster they had suffered.

Satisfied that all was well, Cal turned back to the men grouped around the campfire as Josh responded, "To tell you the truth, Cal, I don't know how it started. All of a sudden there were gunshots, and the herd started running." He looked at the freckled wrangler who sat nearby, clutching his bandaged arm, then continued, "Larry was out in front trying to turn the herd. I saw him get hit, but I couldn't get near him. Then I realized somebody was shooting at me, too."

"Did you see who they were?"

Josh shook his head. "No, and there's no way to tell who those two were who went down after they got trampled by the herd. There was hardly enough left of them to bury."

Pru made an indistinguishable sound, and Cal

shot her a concerned glance. He turned back toward Winston when the big man added, "It's funny, but I had the feeling somebody was watching us for a while before it happened. I don't know why they'd do that except to pick us off one at a time—and even that don't make sense—especially since they always seemed to make sure they hit a herd when the hands were somewhere else—like they didn't have no interest in fighting. It wasn't until you came home that things started getting dangerous. Anyway, those fellas didn't show themselves until the herd panicked and started running, which probably saved us, because with the dust being so thick, they had trouble seeing what they were aiming at."

Cal pressed, "Did you see how many of them there were?"

"I'm thinking there were four of them, because two were still firing after the other two went down. One of them got hit, though." Winston smiled at Pru, who remained silent nearby. "The boss lady got him, and he took off. The other fella must've figured it was all over then, and he lit out after him."

Cal glanced at Pru, remembering how she had looked when he went back for her after the herd was brought under control. She was waiting where he had left her, and she hardly said a word when he took her into his arms. She hadn't said much since. She had just leaned back against him and closed her eyes when he lifted her up onto his saddle.

He studied her more closely. It wasn't like her to

be so quiet. He knew the men had the same thought when Josh said tentatively, "It's been a hard day, ma'am. If you was wanting to wash yourself up a bit, me and the boys would be glad to hang a blanket for you so you'd have some privacy."

"No . . . no, that's all right." Pru took a breath and stood up. Her legs wobbled, and Cal grasped her arm.

"I'm all right."

But she was so pale that she looked like she wouldn't make it as far as her bedroll.

Cal slipped his arm around her and curved her against his side as he drew her away to speak more privately. Unmindful of the men's knowing glances, he said, "You're better than all right, Pru. You're damned fine. And you're a better shot than I gave you credit for. If it wasn't for you, I wouldn't be standing here now."

"That was a lucky shot, and you know it." Pru took a ragged breath. "I don't know how I hit that rustler. I just saw him aiming at you, and I pointed my gun and fired."

"Lucky for me."

Tears suddenly welling, Pru rasped, "Lucky for me, too."

His throat suddenly tight, Cal brushed her mouth with his, then said, "You'd better get some sleep. I'm not going to take any more chances. We're going to get those beeves to the railhead tomorrow, even if we have to drive them until dark."

Cal watched as Pru spread her bedroll and

slipped inside. He then walked to the other side of the campfire, picked up his own bedroll, and laid it down next to hers. When he looked up, Pru said, "The men will think—"

"Do you care what they think?"

Motionless for a long moment, she then shook her head.

Cal lay beside her, wishing he could hold Pru in his arms, and knowing he couldn't.

Pru lay beside him, wishing Cal could take her into his arms, and knowing he wouldn't.

Their eyes met, and Pru repeated softly, "Lucky for me, too."

Chapter Twelve

A tally string in his hand, Cal counted the cattle as they filed into the railhead pens. He glanced at the stock buyer, who was holding a similar string, then heaved a silent sigh of relief when the last steer was enclosed. They matched strings, came to a mutually agreeable price, and settled their business as Pru looked on silently and the men waited nearby.

"It's good doing business with you, Cal." Rob Ryland was a dark, barrel-chested man whom Cal remembered from the days when he had helped run Texas Star cattle. The fellow was pleasant and honest, and Cal liked him.

Cal leaned back against the fence as Rob continued, "It's kinda like the old days. I figured you and your brother would be running your pa's cattle one of these days. I'm glad to see you're back. Are you expecting your brother at any time?"

"Taylor went into another line of work, from what

I hear." Cal shifted his broad frame, "I don't expect to see him back here any time soon."

"Too bad. Seems like them rustlers who've been hitting the ranches in your part of the woods have been doing a lot of damage—especially to the Texas Star and the Rocky W." Rob shook his head. "From what I hear, they've been concentrating on the Rocky W since you got back."

"You heard that, did you?"

"You know how it is, Cal; wranglers come here from all over this part of the state. There isn't much I don't hear about." With a polite nod in Pru's direction, Rob continued, "No disrespect to you, ma'am, but talk was that maybe you'd made a mistake hiring this big fella here, with what's been going on at your ranch since he came."

Cal frowned. "What are you talking about?"

"I mean that this lady's house was wrecked only a little while after she hired you."

"How'd you know about that?"

Rob smiled and continued, "Then them rustlers came out in the open and went after the cattle you had just put together, like maybe they was watching what you was doing on the Rocky W. It seems funny to me, especially since they tried again for the same herd, knowing you was probably watching out for trouble." He shrugged. "It looks to me like it might be something personal."

"Whatever it was, Rob, we don't have to worry about them rustlers anymore," Winston said. "Only two of them are left. One has a bullet hole in him, and the other is running hard."

"I'm hoping you're right. It would help my business if you was." Extending his hand to Cal, Rob added, "I'll be seeing you here again, I'm assuming?"

Cal shook his hand without responding, then took Pru's arm as they headed toward the bank. He was frowning.

Pru studied his expression for a moment, then asked, "What's the matter, Cal?"

Cal shook his head.

"Cal?"

"It's time we got back." Cal's response was terse. "There are things I've got to do."

"Don't touch me!" Celeste shuddered with barely controlled ire as Derek faced her boldly in the deserted cabin. She spat, "You failed again, damn you!"

"Two more of my men were killed, and Jack came away with a bullet in him! Don't that mean nothing to you?"

"Two more or ten more—what difference does it make?"

"It makes a difference to me."

"That's what you said the last time . . . the last time, when you told me you were going to make sure Cal Star paid for what he did. Either that was all talk or Cal Star proved he's a better man than you are."

Derek took a threatening step toward her. "You're so damned smart."

Unwilling to back down, Celeste continued, "That's right, I'm smart—smart enough to see you're no match for Cal Star."

"He's lucky, that's all. He should've been traveling with that herd so I could've picked him off like I planned. Instead, he was off somewhere with that widow, and he didn't come back until that herd was running and the dust was so thick I could barely see in front of me."

"Cal Star seemed to be able to see well enough. He killed two of your men."

"He was lucky, I told you!"

"What's that supposed to mean, Derek? That you've been depending on luck all these months while you've been telling me how great you are? How there's nobody who can stop you when you set your mind to something like you set your mind to getting me?"

"You got that the wrong way around, don't you, darlin'?" His tone caustic, Derek continued, "It wasn't me who put us together. It was you."

"Me?" Celeste gave a hard laugh. "Well, maybe I did . . . because it suited me at the time to find someone who could amuse me in bed while he was taking care of business. But you're not taking care of business anymore."

"What's that supposed to mean?"

"You know what it means."

Derek took a threatening step, and Celeste whipped

a gun from her reticule with a flash that left Derek gaping. She snapped, "Try it and you'll discover your luck's run out."

"Wait a minute, Celeste—"

"I'm tired of waiting!"

"Pull that trigger and you'll be making the biggest mistake of your life."

"You think so?"

"You got a yen for what I can give you, and you know it."

"You give yourself too much credit."

"Maybe . . . but that ain't all I was meaning." Derek added without taking a breath, "I'm going to get Cal Star."

Celeste studied his malevolent stare.

"I'm still alive and I'm going to finish what I started."

Celeste frowned. "He's not going to get scared off."

"I ain't intending to scare him."

"I don't want you running off half-cocked!"

"I ain't intending to do that, neither."

Celeste's voice dropped a note softer. She slowly lowered her gun. "I haven't forgotten everything we've accomplished together, Derek. I'd like us to see this through to the end."

"That's not going to happen with you pulling a gun on me."

Hesitating only a moment, Celeste slid her gun back into her reticule and faced him boldly. "You're right . . . pulling that trigger would've been the biggest mistake I ever made."

"Until the next time."

"Let's be honest here, Derek." Celeste took a step closer. "You're my best ally, in more ways than one. Until Cal Star came back, everything was going fine. It'll go fine again as soon as we get rid of him, even though getting rid of him's not going to be as easy as I thought."

"One rifle shot—"

"No, not that way! I told you, we have to be careful."

"*You* have to be careful—"

"We're in this together."

Derek eyed her coldly. "I thought we was. Now I ain't so sure."

Celeste paused, then said, "We've made a lot of money, Derek, and we've had a good time along the way. It can be that way again."

"Maybe."

"Maybe? You know damned well you've never had a woman better than I am. And I'm telling you now that I've saved the best for last."

Derek did not reply.

"Maybe we need to seal our bargain again . . ."

"I thought you said you didn't want me to touch you."

"Maybe I changed my mind."

"Maybe I did, too."

"Really?" Celeste began unbuttoning the buttons on her bodice. Derek made no sound as she slipped her dress off her shoulders, then lowered her chemise to expose her perfect breasts. She could see his chest begin a slow heaving as she said, "It's all yours, if you want it."

When he still resisted, she cupped a breast with her palm and whispered, "I'm waiting . . ."

His mouth was hot and wet when it clamped over the rounded mound, and Celeste gasped aloud. He clamped his teeth onto the erect crest and bit her, and she cried out with passion at the pain. In a sudden erotic frenzy, she urged him on, groaning, "Harder . . . harder!"

Passion and pain . . . and her delirium grew.

She was as naked as he when he threw her on the bed and jammed himself cruelly inside her. Her lust grew in a libidinous swell and she groaned loudly.

A harsh shout escaped her lips as Derek ejaculated inside her, and she rode the swell with uninhibited fervor.

Lying motionless beside him moments later, Celeste felt the brush of his hairy skin and breathed the fetid odor of his exertion.

She smiled.

Brutish . . . animalistic . . . yes, but he'd do . . . until she found someone better.

Cal approached the Texas Star branding corral slowly. He saw Mitch look up, then signal Randy and Big John with a glance before they turned their horses and rode off toward the herd.

Buck looked up from the branding fire, then

straightened as Cal rode nearer. Cal felt the harsh intensity of his father's gaze as he drew up alongside him and dismounted.

He was prepared when Buck spat, "I thought I said you weren't welcome here."

He responded levelly, "I want to talk to you, Pa."

"I don't want to talk to you."

"There are some things I need to get straight with you—some things that need to be said."

"I've done all the talking with you that I need to do."

"All right, then, don't talk. Just listen." Cal searched his father's face as memories of better times flashed across his mind. He remembered a time when there had been warmth in those eyes now looking at him so coldly, and a smile on the lips now compressed into a harsh line. The ache inside him expanded as he began, "I suppose you heard what happened when the boys and I drove the Rocky W herd to the railhead a few days ago."

Buck did not reply, and Cal continued, "I figure you heard about all the problems the Rocky W's been having since I signed on there, too." He paused again, then pressed, "It's got people talking, and it's got me thinking maybe there's something to what they're saying."

Buck's lined face tightened as he snapped, "So, what're they saying besides you're some kind of a hero all of a sudden because you brought down four of them rustlers when nobody else's been able to lay a hand on them?"

"A hero . . ." Cal gave a hard laugh. "That's a joke."

"You don't need to tell me that."

"No, but I do need some answers." Cal took a breath. "I need to know once and for all. Did you send me that letter . . . the one about Bonnie?"

Color flushed Buck's face a deep red. "I told you not to speak your sister's name to me!"

"Somebody sent it."

"I told you once, and I'm telling you for the last time—if you got a letter, it didn't come from me."

"*If* I got a letter?"

"That's what I said."

His own ire rising, Cal snapped, "I got the letter, all right, and that's why I'm here. So if you didn't send it, who did?"

"How would I know?"

"And why would somebody send me a letter that would make me come home—then try to drive me out?"

"You're not making any sense."

Cal pressed on sharply, "Celeste doesn't want me here, does she?"

"Oh, so that's where you're heading!" Buck's face flamed. "You actually had me thinking for a few minutes that maybe you did come back to make up for the past, but I'll be damned if Celeste wasn't right all along."

"What do you mean?"

"She said you was jealous of her!"

"Jealous!"

"She said you came back thinking you could step

right back into the spot you left behind, but when you couldn't, you were jealous that she took your place and you wanted her out."

"That isn't true."

"She said you'd try something like this."

"Pa . . ."

Buck took a threatening step. His thin frame quaking, he rasped, "Just to set you straight once and for all, Celeste is the best thing that ever could've happened to me. She's wonderful . . . generous, loving, sincere. She got a bad bargain when she married me, but that doesn't mean anything to her. She understands me better than anybody. There's nothing she wouldn't do for me . . . and there's nothing I wouldn't do for her."

"Listen, Pa—"

"No, you listen to me, because I'm telling you for the last time. Don't try putting a wedge between Celeste and me, because it won't work. I love her, do you hear? And she loves me. And that's the way it's going to stay."

"I'm just trying to say—"

"I know what you're trying to say!"

"Pa—"

"Get out of here—off Texas Star land. You turned your back on this ranch years ago. As far as I'm concerned, you don't belong here."

Cal did not respond.

"Do you hear me? Git, and don't come back!"

Cal remained silent at Buck's harsh words. He watched as his father turned back to the fire in final dismissal. He remounted his horse with the thought that maybe his father was right; maybe it was too late—for everything.

Buck rode back toward the Texas Star ranch house. His throat was tight and his stomach in knots. He couldn't forget the way Cal had looked as he approached the branding fire. The thought had struck him that under different circumstances, a man would be proud to have a son like Cal.

Under different circumstances.

Cal had been right about one thing. He'd heard all about what had happened when Cal drove the Rocky W herd to the railhead. Randy had made sure he heard it, and he'd been unable to suppress a reluctant pride in Cal for what he'd accomplished against all odds. But it was the moment when Cal had stood face to face with him and had looked at him with those eyes so much like Emma's that his heart had almost stopped; and when Cal's mouth had ticked with tension just as Emma's had always done when she was upset, he'd felt a pang of regret so deep that he had been almost unable to speak.

But then Cal started talking, and everything changed.

Someone had sent Cal a letter about Bonnie? He didn't want to believe it was true. He couldn't go over that ground again. He wasn't up to it.

And townsfolk were talking about all the things that had happened at the Rocky W since Cal hired on there? No, Cal was making that up. He was trying to turn him against Celeste, who was beautiful and loving, who wanted only the best for him, who had stood beside him through all his trials, who *lived* for him—and whom he loved in return.

He'd never turn against her, no matter what Cal said. He owed her too much.

Buck sighed as the ranch house came into view. His exchange with Cal had somehow taken the wind out of him. He'd had nothing left after Cal disappeared from sight and the men returned to the branding fire. He had reluctantly called it a day, despite the early hour.

Buck frowned as he drew closer to the house. The buckboard was tied up at the hitching post, and the horse was lathered as if she had ridden home in a rush. Celeste had obviously just returned from town. Strange; she hadn't mentioned she was intending to go. He hoped nothing was wrong.

Concerned, Buck nudged his mount to a faster pace.

"You are a fool, Celeste! You should not have allowed that man to mark your flesh!"

Madalane's words reverberated in Celeste's ears as she looked down at her naked breasts, at the teeth marks blemishing the white skin. She scowled at the realization that even observing the bruises heated her blood, even though she had come home feeling battered and bruised by Derek's rough handling.

Her scowl darkened when she glimpsed the teeth

marks at her waist—similar to bruises which she was certain marked other sensitive areas of her anatomy that she could not see as well.

"Fool! How will you hide these foul disfigurements from your husband?"

"Be quiet, Madalane!" Celeste took the cloth and bathed her skin carefully. "I'll find an excuse to keep my husband at a distance. He—"

Halting at the unexpected sound of hoofbeats approaching the house, Celeste looked at the handsome Negress and rasped, "That can't be Buck already! It's too early for him to return." She spat, "Did you give him another dose of your tonic without telling me?"

"I did not!" Madalane glanced toward the porch where Buck's footsteps echoed. She handed Celeste her robe and ordered, "Cover yourself. Pretend to be ill."

Madalane reached the bedroom doorway as Celeste tied her robe and Buck's footfalls sounded in the hallway. She stood blocking his path as he attempted to enter and said, "Celeste is feeling unwell. She has just finished bathing and is intending to sleep for a while."

"She's sick?" Buck attempted to get past her, but Madalane stood fast.

"Celeste wishes to sleep."

"Get out of my way, Madalane."

"Celeste is unwell."

"Let my husband in, Madalane." Celeste's voice was weak. "Seeing him will make me feel better."

Celeste lowered herself slowly onto the edge of the bed as Buck entered the room. She raised a delicate hand to her forehead and whispered wanly, "I'm glad you're home, Buck."

"What's wrong, dear?" Buck's thin face drew into lines of concern.

"I don't really know." Celeste feigned a shaky smile. "I was on my way back from town with Madalane when I suddenly felt ill."

"I'll get Doc Maggie."

"No!"

"But—"

"It's nothing. I'll be fine in a day or so, I'm sure."

"Doc Maggie will be glad to come out."

"Buck, please . . ." Celeste heaved a sigh. "I'm certain it's just that I'm upset."

"Upset?"

"All this talk in town about Cal."

"What talk is that?"

"About what's been happening since he came back."

"I don't understand."

"About the rustlers and all."

"What are you talking about?"

Celeste covered her face with a trembling hand.

Buck stiffened noticeably. "Tell me, Celeste."

She gasped, "I don't want to upset you."

"Tell me."

Celeste looked up at him, her eyes moist. "Some people are saying that . . . that perhaps Cal is involved with the rustlers."

"That's crazy! Four of those fellas are dead because of Cal."

"That's what has some people talking. They're saying nobody could put a hand on the rustlers before he came; then he showed up and brought two of them into town dead, and left another two dead and buried on a trail drive."

"That doesn't make any sense."

"I know! That's what I said, but some people are saying Cal was a part of the rustling gang, that he double-crossed them so he could look like a hero and get back in your good graces."

"Who's spreading this talk?"

Celeste turned her head.

"Celeste—"

"Please Buck, I don't want to see you agitated."

"Tell me!"

"I don't know who started it! And I know nobody will have the nerve to repeat it to you—just like nobody would have said anything to me if I hadn't overheard two fellas talking about it outside the mercantile store."

"What two fellas?"

"I don't know who they were. I never saw them before."

"Saddle bums and troublemakers, probably. Nobody else would believe a word of that story, much less dare repeat it."

"You don't believe it, do you, Buck?"

"Not a word." Celeste watched as Buck's jaw hardened and he spat, "My son may be many things, but he's not a rustler, and he wouldn't kill four men to get back in my good graces."

"I know that's true." Celeste looked up at him with a delicate plea. "You aren't angry with me for repeating what I heard, are you?"

"Of course not. And I don't want you to upset yourself. I'll see to it that the talk stops."

"No, I don't want you to get involved!"

"I *am* involved, Celeste. Cal's my son."

"But you hardly know him anymore."

"He's still carries the Star name."

"That doesn't mean anything! You don't really know anything about him. He's practically a stranger to you now. No one can blame you for what he does."

"No one . . . but me."

"I don't care!" Her voice rising a hysterical note higher, Celeste pressed, "You're just beginning to recuperate from your illness. I don't want you having a relapse."

"I'm fine."

"You're not!"

"Celeste—"

"Please, Buck . . . promise me you'll stay out of this."

"Lie down. Rest for a while, Celeste."

"Not unless you promise you'll stay out of this."

"I can't make you that promise."

"Then I won't lie down!" Celeste stood up abruptly. She clutched her head and staggered.

Jack grasped her arm to steady her. "Celeste, please try to rest."

"I can't. I won't, unless you promise."

Buck's light eyes held hers. "There's no one in this world more important to me than you. You know that, don't you?"

"No, I don't."

"Celeste!"

"I don't know if that's true anymore." Celeste continued in a rush, "Ever since Cal came home, you've been a different man. I want the man I married back—the man I love and who loved me."

"I'm still that man, darling."

"Then prove it to me! Tell me you won't get mixed up in Cal's problems."

"But—"

"I knew it!" Celeste sobbed and covered her eyes.

"All right, I promise." Buck drew her hand away from her face and said, "Stop crying. You have my word."

A small hiccuping sob escaped Celeste's lips as she leaned toward him and whispered, "I just need to know you'll be safe."

"I know. Rest now, darling."

Celeste nodded, then lay back on the bed. She brushed the tears from her eyes as Buck drew the coverlet up over her and said, "I love you, Celeste. You know that, don't you?"

"Yes, I do . . . now."

Keeping the loving expression on her face as Buck kissed her lips, Celeste whispered, "I'll sleep, and I'll be fine when I wake up. You'll see."

She closed her eyes.

The bedroom door was shut tight behind Buck. Celeste listened as his step faded down the hallway. The sound of the porch door closing signaled he had left the house, and Celeste opened her eyes angrily. She glared at Madalane as the Negress entered the room and declared, "Your husband is slipping away from you."

Celeste responded to Madalane's statement with cold silence.

But Madalane was right. It was time for drastic measures.

"It's perfect. It'll work, I tell you!"

Derek stared at Celeste in the solitude of the leafy glade. He had seen her signal in the window and had appeared on the trail and halted her horse midway as he'd done once before, knowing he couldn't afford the disadvantage of another session in the cabin with his crafty henchwoman. She had driven him nearly crazy the last time they had lain together, and he had wanted to put some distance between them.

He was now glad that he had.

Face to face with her on the silent trail, he shook his head with growing incredulity and said, "You don't let no grass grow under your feet, do you?"

"I know what needs to be done."

"But you want *me* to do it."

"You want Cal Star dead as much as I do."

"Thanks to you."

"It's the perfect plan, I tell you!"

Scowling, Derek said, "Tell it to me again."

Celeste took an impatient breath. Derek's limited intelligence oftentimes frustrated her, and this was one of those times. She began slowly, "You want Cal Star dead and so do I. The only difference is that I can't let any suspicion fall in my direction."

"You've told me that a hundred times."

"We'll need to get the widow first."

"Why?"

"Everybody knows how Jack feels about the widow—that he said he's going to get what she owes him one way or another. Everybody knows he's the one who trashed her house, even though no one can prove it; and everybody knows he hates that woman even more now that Cal made a fool of him in public because of her."

"So?"

"He told you himself that he's going to get even with Cal Star, too, for bringing him down in front of the town. *Everybody* knows it. What they don't know is that he's probably more determined than ever to take his revenge since he got shot."

"The bullet only creased him. He'll be as good as new in a couple of days."

"That won't change anything about the way he feels!" Celeste continued irritably, "From what I understand, the widow is alone at the ranch house while the men are working because her son usually rides out with the hands. That's the perfect opportunity for him, and you can make sure he knows it."

"All right, so that takes care of the widow, but it don't do nothing about getting rid of Cal Star like you want."

Her impatience building, Celeste grated, "You've heard what's going on between the widow and Cal. How do you think he'll feel when he comes back to the ranch and finds her dead? He'll figure it's Jack and he'll go out looking for him. When you kill him, everyone will think Jack did it, and no suspicion will fall my way when Buck *dies unexpectedly* a few months later."

"Yeah, that might work."

"What do you mean, it might work?" Celeste was livid. "It *will* work. Especially since you'll take care of Jack, too."

"What?"

"Jack's a liability to both of us, Derek. He knows Lowell too well. If he's left alive, he'll figure out about you and me, and he's not the kind to keep quiet about things if somebody gets their hands on him."

Celeste's words halted as Derek's gaze shifted away from hers. Realization came in a flash, and she snapped, "He knows about you and me already, doesn't he?"

There was no need for Derek to reply.

"How did that happen? No one was supposed to know about our association."

"My boys wasn't as dumb as you thought they

was. They figured it out a long time ago, and Jack heard it from them."

Celeste shuddered with fury. "Fool! You're a fool!"

"Don't go calling me names! You were so sure Cal Star would run off at the first sign of trouble, but he didn't—so you ain't no smarter than me!"

Celeste struggled to bring her anger under control. She took a few stabilizing breaths, then said, "We'll make it all come out right if you'll do what I'm telling you now."

"A foolproof plan—just like your others, huh?"

"Don't underestimate me, Derek!"

Derek eyed her coldly. "No, I'd never do that."

Celeste's gaze pinned him as she said, "This plan will work, and the best part is that it will appear to be a natural progression of events. Jack will take care of the widow, and everybody will know he did it. When Cal goes after Jack, you'll take care of both of them at the same time, and everybody will think they killed each other. You'll have your revenge on Cal Star like you wanted, with nobody the wiser, and I'll still be the patient, long-suffering wife of ailing Buck Star."

"Everything just how you want it."

"Exactly."

Derek's gaze lingered. "You got me wondering, Celeste, about when it'll be *my* turn."

"You don't have to worry about that." Smiling for the first time, Celeste replied, "I already told you. You're my best ally. We *need* each other to get what we want."

"Yeah." Derek's gaze slipped hotly down her body.

Annoyed at the responsive heat that ignited inside her, Celeste said, "There'll be plenty of time for that later, when we're on safe ground again. Just make sure everything goes the way it should."

"I'm thinking Jack's got the first step here."

"Just see that he gets it done." Celeste paused, then added, ". . . and gets it done right."

"Something's wrong about what's been happening here, Doc. I can feel it."

Doc Maggie frowned as she returned Cal's stare. Her office was empty and silent at this early morning hour. She had enjoyed Jeremy's company while Cal and Pru were on the trail, and she believed the boy had enjoyed hers, but there had been no mistaking Jeremy's happiness when his mother finally walked back through the doorway to claim him a few days earlier. What had surprised Doc, however, was that the boy seemed almost as glad to see Cal as he was to see his mother.

She had known with just one glance at Cal and Pru, however, that all had not gone smoothly on the trail. The account of the Rocky W's clash with the rustlers made its rounds quickly after their return, and the town was jubilant. The rustler gang had been all but annihilated—but her own reaction to the story was mixed. Cal had proved himself again by saving Pru's herd—but two of the rustlers had gotten away. That worried her.

She had been unprepared for the questions Cal had raised when he walked into her office a few moments earlier—issues that obviously lay heavily on his mind.

Doc responded, "You really think there might be something personal in the attacks on the Rocky W?"

"I don't know, but Rob Ryland's comments are making more and more sense to me. That letter I received about Bonnie . . ."

"What about it?"

"I talked to Pa again yesterday, just to make sure he didn't send it."

Doc said hopefully, "You talked to your pa?"

Cal shook his head. "It was a waste of time. Nothing's changed. All I know for sure is that he didn't send the letter, and neither did you. So, who wrote it . . . and why? I'm thinking maybe it wasn't sent with good intentions in mind."

"What are you saying?"

Cal's scowl deepened. "I thought maybe Celeste—"

"You didn't say anything to your pa about Celeste?"

"I did."

"That was a mistake."

"I know that now. Pa ran me off the ranch because of it."

"I told you, your pa thinks the sun rises and sets on Celeste. He won't listen to a word against her."

"I need some answers, Doc. I need to know who

sent that letter. I don't expect I'll understand what's really going on until I do."

"I can't help you there, Cal. I wish—"

Cal halted her statement with a glance as Pru's step sounded outside the doorway. Doc saw the spark that flashed between them as Pru entered the office, as well as the new tone in Cal's voice when he said, "Are you ready to go back to the ranch now, Pru?"

Jeremy grinned as he stepped into view from behind his mother. As if reading Doc's mind, he said, "Mama and Cal don't hate each other anymore, Doc. They like each other now. I like it better this way."

Surprisingly, the boy's comment brought a frown to Cal's brow. Choosing to ignore it, Doc responded, "I like it better this way, too."

But she was uncertain as the door closed behind them. It was obvious that Cal hadn't confided the depth of his concerns to Pru—a sure sign of a potential problem in the future.

That thought plagued Doc as she stepped to her window and followed their progress down the street.

Jack's sweaty face drew into malevolent lines. He unconsciously rubbed his wounded arm as he rasped, "I'm going to show that widow once and for all that having Cal Star prancing around her don't scare me off."

Derek assessed Jack cautiously as his henchman sat on the cot he had occupied in their hideout since their return from the Rocky W trail drive disaster several days earlier. Jack's wound had been no more than a painful scratch, and it was almost healed, but his anger had obviously festered until it was now an open sore that could be cured in only one way.

Derek smiled at the ease with which Jack was falling in with Celeste's plans.

"And you don't need to worry about me," Jack added. "I know what I'm after and how to get it. That widow's going to learn I meant every word when I said I'd get what she owed me one way or another."

Derek responded cautiously, "I don't blame you, but you need to be careful and make sure the time is right. After all, killing a woman—"

"I ain't going to kill her." Jack sneered. "I'm just going to make her wish she was dead."

Derek hesitated. This wasn't exactly what Celeste wanted, but the outcome would be the same. Star would go after Jack, especially after the widow identified her attacker, and Star would end up dead anyway.

Derek ventured, "You know that'll bring Star down on your back."

Jack's expression grew rabid. "I'm not afraid of him!"

"No, but you won't want to be watching over your shoulder for the rest of your life, neither."

"I'll see to it that Star gets what he has coming, too."

"Maybe you'd like some help with that."

A slow smile curved Jack's lips. "Yeah, that sounds like a good plan. First the widow, though. I want to take my time with her."

"That sounds all right to me. When are you planning on visiting her?"

Jack stood up, glanced at the morning sun shining outside the window, and said, "Right now looks like a good time to me. Are you coming?"

A clipped laugh was Derek's response as he followed Jack out the door.

"Do you think we'll find any more calves that need to be branded?" Jeremy's small face was creased with the concern of a budding cowman as he turned to Winston in the sunny pasture. "I'm thinking there're a lot of other things that need doing on this ranch before it'll be in the shape it should be."

"You've been thinking about that, have you?" Winston withheld a smile and glanced at Cal as he approached. "I suppose you should ask the boss about that," he said.

"Ask the boss about what?" Cal's expression was sober as he halted beside them.

"Jeremy wants to know how many more calves need to be branded. He's worried about all the work that needs to be done on the ranch."

Cal surveyed the surrounding landscape with a squinting gaze. He remained silent until Winston prompted, "The boy's waiting for your answer, Cal."

"I don't know, Jeremy." Cal's expression remained solemn. "I figure on taking a look around tomorrow while the boys finish up here. You can come along if you want."

"Can I?" Jeremy's expression brightened. "That would be fine. Mama's feeling better about things now that she paid a few bills in town, but I can tell she's still worrying. I figure she's thinking about all the things that need to be done on the ranch."

Cal looked at him without responding.

"I can tell when she's worrying, you know." Jeremy continued, "Because she hasn't been hearing me when I talk sometimes these last few days—especially this morning. She acted the same way when she was worrying about where we'd go next, before we came here."

Cal nodded. He knew it was true. The only thing was, he figured Pru was preoccupied for an entirely different reason. He had gone into the house the previous night after the men had retired to the bunkhouse. His intention had been to check some figures in the ledger he had left behind. He supposed nothing would've happened if Pru hadn't walked out of her bedroom at that moment, with her dark hair loosened from its braid so that it spilled over the shoulders of her demure nightclothes. She had stopped still with surprise at seeing him there, and he remembered she had looked so beautiful, he had ached at the sight of her.

He had asked simply, "Is Jeremy asleep?"

At her nod, he had swept her into his arms.

He remembered the breathless gasps and moments of pure ecstasy that followed as they lay together in her narrow bed—the tender loving that moved him still in remembrance. But he remembered even more clearly that when the loving was done and Pru lay quiet in his arms, her eyes had been filled with tears.

He hadn't needed to ask the reason for those tears when she stood up and quickly dressed, then urged him back to the bunkhouse, hoping the men hadn't started to wonder.

He had shown her love in so many ways, but he had never said the words.

He now wondered if he ever could.

Pru had avoided his gaze at breakfast that morning, but she had raised her mouth to his when he deliberately lingered behind Jeremy and the men and took her into his arms.

It had been hard to let her go.

But the truth was, he might be forced to, in the end.

That difficult thought lingered as Cal said gruffly, "All right, fellas, let's get back to work."

Jack ordered, "You wait here. I can take care of the widow by myself."

Derek glared at Jack's turned back. He didn't like taking orders from anybody, much less from a man like Jack, who wasn't half as smart as he thought he was.

They had arrived at a vantage point overlooking the ranch house a few minutes earlier and had spent the time canvassing the surrounding countryside as the hot Texas sun beat down on their backs. Derek could see the widow moving back and forth past the kitchen window, and it appeared to be just as Celeste had said. Star, the boy, and the ranch hands were gone for the day, and the widow was alone in the house. Derek had briefly indulged the thought that he'd join Jack in taking his pleasure with the widow, but it was obvious Jack had something special in mind for her, and he wasn't invited. He didn't like being shut out, but he supposed it was all right this time. Jack might as well enjoy himself—while he still could.

"Keep an eye out while I'm down there. I don't want nobody sneaking up on me."

More orders.

Derek forced a smile. Yes, Jack's time was definitely limited.

"The widow's been known to keep a shotgun close by," Derek offered, "so I'd watch out if I was you."

"I know. I ain't worried about it."

Derek nodded. He didn't want anything to go wrong. Despite his original protests, he figured Celeste's plan to get the widow, Star, *and* Jack out of the way once and for all was pretty good. Once that was done, Celeste and he could go on like they had before. Celeste would wait only a few months after Cal Star was taken care of before she made sure that the old man she was married to *died unexpectedly*, but a few months more of the kind of heat she stirred in him sounded pretty good right now. He might even consider following Celeste back to New Orleans when she left. It could be fun for a while.

Derek remained hidden as Jack rode his horse toward the ranch house. He watched as Jack dismounted a safe distance from it, then continued his approach on foot.

Pru paused and stared at the containers lining the kitchen shelf. They were dented and marked from the merciless trashing of the house weeks earlier, but she had determinedly refilled them with her baking supplies, and had told herself when she was done that she was even more organized than before. For the life of her, however, even with the beginnings of an apple cobbler lying on the table behind her, she couldn't remember what she had been looking for when she'd turned to the shelf a few minutes previously.

She hadn't been able to complete a single thought all morning.

Pru blinked back tears. She was only fooling herself. She knew what the problem was. Simply, it was harder than she ever dreamed it could be to hold back the words *I love you*. Those words had risen to her lips so many times while she had lain in Cal's arms the previous night. She had wanted to say them, speak them aloud, but she had known instinctively she should not.

Strangely enough, she could see the love in Cal's eyes whenever he looked at her. She could hear it in his voice, could feel it in his touch, could sense it rising in an overwhelming swell when they lay flesh to flesh. There was more between them than just physical passion. Cal wanted *her*. The need to hold her intimately close was as strong in him as it was in her—she knew that without a doubt.

But the words remained unspoken.

Those important words.

Pru took a shuddering breath. She had asked herself why. The answer was heartbreakingly hard to accept, but distinctly clear. Cal had never deceived her. He had told her he had returned to Lowell to settle the past, but that his stay was temporary. He had told her she deserved to be loved, that he wanted to be the man who would love her, but as sincere as she had known those words to be, they had spoken only of a present that was impermanent at best. She had finally accepted those terms because she had no choice—*because she loved him.*

It was a mystery to her how or when the initial animosity between them had made such a sudden reversal. She just knew that it had. Yet she had not realized how difficult it would be to love someone without—

A sudden brush of movement behind her interrupted Pru's thoughts. A second too late to escape the hand that slipped cruelly over her mouth, she struggled fiercely to free herself from the arm that pulled her back painfully tight against a hard, male form. Her heart pounded as the smell of perspiration and unwashed flesh met her nostrils, and a terrifyingly familiar voice rasped in her ear, "Nice to see you again, boss lady. You and me have a debt to settle."

Jack.

Pru glanced toward the living room, and Jack snickered knowingly. "Your shotgun ain't going to do you no good out there in the parlor. You should always keep it close by when you're alone. Didn't your boyfriend tell you that?"

Pru twisted and squirmed, fighting him with all her might, and Jack laughed aloud. She felt herself breaking free, but then his arms clamped even tighter as he laughed more loudly.

He was playing with her, enjoying her panic. She knew it, yet she could not seem to stop the frantic struggling that gave him so much pleasure.

She felt it then—the moment he lost his grip—and she propelled herself forward. She heard the table topple behind her as she staggered toward the doorway, only to be caught by her braid and dragged backwards again. She screamed in panic as he turned her toward him. She swung her fist with all her might, landing a blow to the side of Jack's head. She saw anger flash in his eyes the moment before his fist crashed against her jaw, and darkness abruptly enclosed her.

She did not remember falling. Her first sensation was the pain of being dragged roughly across the floor toward her bedroom; the second, her frightening inability to coordinate her reeling senses. Momentarily helpless as she was pulled up onto her feet, she stared into Jack's sneer as he thrust her backwards.

She came alive the moment her back touched the bed. She scrambled across the narrow bed and jumped off the other side, darting this way and that with the bed between them, holding him off.

Increasingly agitated, Jack bellowed, "Stay still, damn you! Stay still, or you'll pay for every minute you make me waste!"

Pru was unaware that tears were streaming down her cheeks as she made a quick rush for the door, only to be caught again. She heard the rending of her dress as Jack's hand closed on the cotton fabric. She felt the rush of cool air against her back as Jack dragged her relentlessly backwards. She fought him desperately as he twisted his hands in her hair and forced her around toward him, then crushed her mouth under his.

Gagging at the sour taste of his mouth, almost retching as he thrust his tongue down her throat, she pushed with one hard thrust. Free of his grip, she turned again toward the door, only to feel his hand clamp on her shoulder. She was unprepared when his fist crashed against her ear, and she staggered to the floor.

"Stubborn witch! I'll show you who's boss!"

He hit her again, once . . . twice . . . a third time.

The world spun around her. It did not steady until she was lying with her bared back against the bed. Her blurred vision cleared to reveal Jack looming over her the moment before he ripped open the buttons on her dress.

His voice rasping with new heat, he said, "Damn . . . look at what you was hiding under them widow's rags."

She tried to stand up, only to be felled again by Jack's fist crashing against her cheek.

The acrid taste of blood filled her mouth as darkness consumed her once more.

Cal rode resolutely back toward the ranch house. He had left Jeremy with the men after making a lame excuse to return—simply because he could no longer bear the image of Pru's tormented expression when he'd left her that morning.

He needed to explain to her what he had left unsaid, that it made no difference how he felt when he held her in his arms, how much he longed to openly claim her, or how much she returned the emotion that tore at his heart. He was a marked man—marked by the words that had brought him home.

Have you forgotten Bonnie?

Those words were burned into his heart. They affected his past, his present, his future.

Troubling him even more was his suspicion that Rob Ryland had been right, that the new frequency of attacks on the Rocky W were due to his presence on the ranch—that he was putting Pru and Jeremy at risk simply by his association with them.

A hard decision loomed before him as the ranch house came into sight.

Derek went still as the familiar rider appeared on the sunlit terrain. His heart began beating a rapid tattoo. There he was, Cal Star, in clear sight—*a perfect target.*

Derek turned toward the rifle on his saddle, then stopped. He looked back at the rider, his brow furrowed with contemplation as Star continued his steady approach toward the ranch house. Celeste's plan was good, but this was working out even better now that Star was coming up on Jack while he was having his way with the widow. Hell, blood was sure to be spilled, either Jack's or Star's—or maybe both! In any case, he'd wait until the fighting was done, and he'd finish off whoever was left standing. Nobody would know the difference. They'd just think nobody survived the shootout.

Celeste would be real happy with him for working it out so easy, too . . . and he'd make sure she showed her appreciation in the way that mattered most.

A broad smile spread across Derek's face. He waited. This was going to be better than he'd expected.

"All right, boss lady, are you ready for me?"

Jack stared down at her as Pru struggled to clear her mind. She was lying on her bed and Jack was leering down at her—yet she was strangely unable to move. Her head was pounding, her jaw ached, and her arms felt leaden, too heavy to lift.

What was wrong with her?

"What's the matter? Can't put your thoughts together? That's something new for you, ain't it? You, with all them orders you was always spouting, and with all that talk about the way I looked. You know something? You don't look so fine right now, either. Hell, your dress is ripped, and your face is all swollen."

Jack's voice rang hollowly in Pru's mind as he leaned over her and whispered menacingly, "And I sure like what you was hiding from me all them days while I worked for you."

Pru flailed weakly when he reached for her and said, "Don't get anxious now. I won't make you wait much longer." He snickered. "I've got big plans for us this afternoon, and before I leave, you're going to know what it's like to be with a *real* man, not some puffed-up cowboy who trades on his family name—a yellow coward who sneaks up on a man so he can put him down in front of the town and make him a laughingstock."

Pru gasped, "Cal . . . Cal didn't do that!"

"How would you know? Just because he's been taking care of you the way you want, that don't make him a man. Hell, if I'd known what you wanted when I was here—"

"G . . . get out of here!"

"That ain't hospitable, boss lady."

Pru struggled to rise, only to be struck down by another stinging blow.

"Stay still!" Jack snapped, "I ain't even started with you yet."

Pru struggled to focus as Jack took his time rolling a cigarette, then struck a match to it. Still disoriented, she was strangely mesmerized by the flare of the flame and the puff of smoke that rose slowly toward the ceiling.

"Like I said," Jack said, "I got big plans for us today, but first I'm going to make sure you remember our little get-together. I figure there's no better way than to leave my brand behind."

Pru blinked. Her vision was slowly clearing and life was returning to her limbs. The word echoed.

Brand . . .

She gasped when Jack abruptly straddled her with his knees, pinning her to the bed. He leaned closer, his fetid breath washing over her face as he whispered, "That's right, I'm going to *mark* you, boss lady, just like all them cattle your boyfriend just branded. You're going to be wearing my initials on your hide, so every time that cowboy looks at you, he'll remember me."

Pru stared as Jack put the cigarette to his lips and drew deeply. With the lit end blazing bright, Jack lowered it slowly toward her.

"No!" Pru gulped. She shrank back against the bed as the cigarette neared her skin. She struggled for breath and gasped, "Don't . . . Cal will—"

"That's what I want to see—what Cal will do after I brand you."

A maniacal gleam in his eyes, Jack pressed the cigarette against her breast.

Pru screamed aloud at the pain, but Jack held it fast.

Her pain was so intense that she did not hear the hoofbeats racing into the yard, the heavy footfalls that raced across the porch.

Hardly conscious, she saw only that Jack turned toward the bedroom doorway, his expression startled. She saw him draw the gun at his hip and aim it at the opening. She saw his finger clenching on the trigger.

Gasping, she lifted her arm with a supreme effort and knocked the gun from his hand.

In a flash of movement too quick for Pru's comprehension, Cal burst through the doorway, lifted Jack physically from the bed, and tossed him against the wall. He leaned over her, his mouth tight as he drew her dress together to cover her and rasped, "Pru . . . darlin' . . . are you all right?"

Pru did not have time to respond before Cal turned to grasp Jack by the back of the neck as he attempted to race past. She heard the crack of Cal's fist against Jack's jaw and saw Jack topple backward, then saw Jack's rabid expression as he staggered to his feet and lunged at Cal.

Pru forced herself to her feet, clutching her dress closed as the two men tumbled across the floor to the sound of pounding fists.

They were still fighting viciously as Pru made her way painfully to the parlor and picked up the shotgun leaning against the wall. She turned back toward the bedroom.

Cal was a moment too late to escape the chair Jack swung at his head. Dazed, he was momentarily unable to react as Jack dove for the gun Pru had knocked from his hand. Cal's eyes widened as Jack pointed the gun in his direction, then turned it unexpectedly toward the bedroom doorway—the second before two barks of gunfire rang out almost simultaneously.

He saw the gun drop from Jack's hand, a bloody spot appearing above his belt as he fell to the floor. He gasped aloud when he looked at the doorway and saw Pru lying there.

Her eyes were closed as Cal carried her to the bed. He could see the slow pounding of the pulse in her temple as he covered the bloody wound in her chest and rasped, "Pru, darlin', open your eyes. Look at me."

He heard the thudding of hoofbeats a few moments before Winston appeared in the doorway. He heard Winston grate, "What's happened here?"

"Get Doc Maggie. Hurry up." Cal's voice was a hoarse rasp. He turned back to Pru, hardly conscious of the sound of Winston's departure as her eyelids moved, then slowly lifted. He whispered, "You're going to be all right, darlin'."

She rasped, "Jack . . ."

Cal glanced at the lifeless figure lying a few feet

away and said, "You don't have to worry about him anymore."

"He . . . he burned me."

"Don't talk, darlin'. Save your strength."

A deadening ache grew inside Cal as she whispered again, "He said he'd brand me, like my cattle."

He swore under his breath.

Pru's eyelids fluttered. The pulse in her temple slowed.

Panicking at the sight of Pru slipping away, Cal urged, "Pru, darlin' . . ."

Her lips formed words he could not hear, and Cal lowered his ear toward her in an attempt to discern them. He snapped back up as her halting words became clear.

He stared at Pru, his throat tight as her lips stilled, and her eyelids slowly closed.

Gasping an incredulous protest, Cal folded Pru into his arms and clutched her tight against him. Tears streaked his cheeks as the words she had rasped resounded over and over again in his mind.

They were precious words . . . haunting words.

Because she had said *I love you*.

Chapter Thirteen

"I should've known better than to think you could do anything right!" Celeste's exquisite features were drawn into furious lines as she stepped down from her buckboard outside the dilapidated rendezvous cabin Derek and she had used countless times before. Turning toward her scowling henchman, she continued hotly, "Cal Star is still alive, and you managed to ruin everything!"

"Seems to me you got it all wrong." Tired of Celeste's criticisms, Derek snapped, "It was *your plan* that didn't work."

"My plan was simple—flawless."

"Not if it didn't work."

"I depended on you, Derek, and you let me down again."

"What's that supposed to mean?"

"It means I'm getting tired of your inadequacies."

"I ain't 'inadequate' where it counts most."

Celeste's reply was frigid. "Whether you know it

or not, where it counts most is getting results, and there you're sadly lacking."

"I done plenty for you, and you damned well know it! You wanted Jack dead, and he's dead. He won't go telling anybody what he knew about you and me."

"You didn't kill him. That widow did!"

"I'll get Cal Star the minute he's in my sights, don't worry."

"No, damn it! I don't want you to—not now! There's too much been happening connected to him. We're going to need some time for things to settle down a bit. I told you, I don't want—"

"—any suspicion falling on you. Yeah, I know."

Celeste stared at Derek's sweaty face. He was unshaven. His hair was separated into greasy strands, he needed a bath, and she suspected he'd been wearing the same clothes for more time than she cared to consider. She had hoped she'd soon be rid of him and be back in a comfortable New Orleans suite where she would live the life to which she had been born, where she'd have her choice of lovers, and of the many ways they would please her. Instead, she would be tied to this degenerate scum who brought out the basest part of her nature for more endless months until the last torturous details of her final vengeance were completed.

It was almost more than she could bear.

She declared resolutely, "I want Cal Star *dead*—but I want him dead on *my* terms."

"It seems to me everything's always been on your

terms, and it ain't worked out so great for me, so far. It's about time I do things my way for a change." Derek's thick features drew into a malicious sneer. "Star won't even see the bullet coming."

"No!"

"I ain't listening to you no more! And don't you try working your wiles on me, neither. I could've put a bullet into Star when he rode up on the Rocky W ranch house when Jack was in there, but I didn't because you didn't want it that way. I would've sneaked up and put a bullet into Star right afterwards, too, without anybody being the wiser if that big cowhand hadn't come racing up and seen that Jack was already dead inside that house. So Star got out of it all alive because of *you*, not *me*, and don't you forget it!"

"Excuses—"

Gasping when Derek grabbed her arm roughly, Celeste shook herself free and grated, "Let me go, you idiot! The bruises have finally faded from the last time we were together. I don't intend dodging my husband's attentions forever because of you!"

"Are you saying you're starting to like having that old man lying on top of you?"

"Don't be ridiculous! I despise him, but I need to please him a little while longer."

"Like I please you?"

"Get away from me!"

Derek sneered. "We'll see how long that lasts."

Rabid, Celeste spat, "It'll last as long as it takes for you to do something right again!"

"Don't worry about it . . ." Derek advanced threateningly on Celeste. "I'm going to get Cal Star, all right."

"And you're going to do it right this time."

Derek's stare was deadly.

"But we need to wait."

"Wait, hell!"

"We're going to wait, Derek . . . a few more months." Celeste added, "Do it right, and I'll make the waiting worthwhile for you when my husband's estate is settled."

"What's supposed to keep me happy in the meantime?"

"We'll work something out."

Derek took another step toward her.

"Not now!" Celeste continued, "Everything will have to rest for a while . . . to let things settle. But the next time we go after Cal Star, we won't miss."

Satisfied that Derek's silence signaled his compliance, Celeste turned toward her buckboard.

Perched on the seat with reins in hand, she turned to look back at him. She repeated coldly, "Next time, Derek, we won't miss."

"She's going to be fine now. Don't worry."

"You're sure?"

"Cal . . . have I ever lied to you?"

Doc Maggie's words lingered in his mind as Cal stood staring down at Pru. She lay in her bed, bruised, silent, and still, much as she had since Jack's attack a few days earlier. Cal had searched

Doc's expression for any reservations, hardly daring to believe that the uncertainty of the past few days was over. He had gone directly to Pru's bedside while Doc went to Jeremy's room to take a short nap during the boy's absence.

His throat tight, Cal crouched beside Pru's bed. He remembered that Pru had been hardly breathing by the time Doc raced her buckboard into the ranch yard; that he had been holding Pru in his arms, willing life into her, refusing to let her slip away. He had since marveled at the turn of fate that had brought Winston back to the ranch for bales of wire, making the big cowboy available to go for Doc Maggie without delay.

In the time since, he had reassured Jeremy that his mother would soon be well, and had finally talked the frantic child into going off to work with the men for a few hours that morning.

Cal unconsciously reached out to stroke a straying wisp of hair from Pru's cheek. The bruising was fading and the swelling had almost disappeared, but the memory of Pru's battered face was still strong in his mind. It raised a ferocious heat inside him, and he knew that if Jack hadn't already been occupying a spot on Boot Hill beside others of his ilk, he would've been driven to put him there.

Strangely, he had learned so much during the dark days while he remained silently watchful beside Pru's bed. He hoped—

Cal's thoughts stopped abruptly as Pru's eyelids began fluttering. He held his breath as they lifted weakly. His heart pounded as her gaze touched his, and she rasped, "Cal, is Jack—"

"Jack won't bother you anymore." Cal's throat was tight. He had needed to reassure her of that several times during her semiconsciousness of the past few days.

"Jeremy?"

"He's fine. I talked him into leaving your bedside for a few hours to 'help the hands.' "

Pru's weak gaze clung as Cal continued, "I wanted to have you to myself for a while, darlin'." He continued softly, "Maybe that was selfish, but there are things I need to say to you, things I need to explain, whether you're ready to hear them or not."

Pru's gaze held his as he began hesitantly, "I hardly know where to begin, Pru . . . how to explain. There was so much darkness in my past when I came back to Lowell, shadows I couldn't seem to overcome no matter how hard I tried. They followed me, affecting everything I touched. I was aware of that when I accepted the job on the Rocky W, but I told myself I wouldn't be staying long enough to get involved in the problems of a bossy widow who didn't know how much trouble her ranch was really in. I never suspected for an instant that I'd want you the first moment I touched you, or that the feeling would refuse to let go until I made love to you. After I made love to you, after I realized that loving you meant more to me than I had ever dreamed it could, I told myself it was a love to enjoy now, with no thought for more. But I was fooled again. When just loving you wasn't enough, I told myself life was too hard, too cruel to think past the present, that it was *safer* that way—for both of us."

"Cal—"

"Let me finish, darlin'." His voice hoarse with emotion, Cal continued, "Then bad things started happening again, and I began wondering; but it was when I saw your life threatened in that stampede, and after, Rob Ryland brought his suspicions out into the open, that I started to convince myself that *I* was the biggest threat to your future. I was on my way back to the ranch to tell you that, and to say I was leaving, when I heard you scream."

Pru took a shaky breath. A tear slipped out of the corner of her eye, and Cal slid his arms around her. Holding her so close that his lips brushed hers as he spoke, he whispered, "In that single moment, I knew I was wrong. In that single moment, I knew that no matter how great my fears, the thought of losing you struck greater terror in my heart than an uncertain future ever could."

Tears were streaming from Pru's eyes, and Cal wiped them away gently with his palm as he rasped, "Maybe I should still play it safe for you and me. Maybe I should leave Lowell and all the memories, both good and bad, behind me. Pru . . . darlin' "—Cal's voice dropped to a husky whisper—"I just can't do that—not anymore. It took that single moment to make clear to me that no matter how hard I tried to reason away my love for you, it was forever a part of me."

Cal took a deep breath. "I love you, Pru. I love you now, and I'll love you the rest of my life. I don't have much to offer you except my heart, and a determination to keep you safe from whatever threatens you—just as long as I can keep you forever in my arms."

Appearing uncertain for the first time, the burning gold of his gaze intent on hers, Cal rasped, "Tell me . . . I need to know, is that good enough for you, Pru?"

Pru's lips quivered. She whispered, "I love you, Cal." His heart pounding with the realization that the hopes and dreams of a future he had never dared contemplate lay in her response, Cal pressed, "I need to know the rest, Pru."

He felt her shuddering. He saw her struggling to restrain her tears as weakness began overwhelming her. He felt his throat choke as Pru strained to respond, although consciousness waned.

She uttered a single word as her eyes fluttered closed, and his heart leaped with joy.

Because she had said, "Forever."

A bright afternoon sun shone on the familiar knoll as Cal drew the buckboard to a halt. He stepped down and swung Pru to the ground beside him, then slipped his arm around her waist—more to comfort himself than to assure Pru safe footing on the uneven ground.

Almost two months had passed, and Pru's wound was nearly healed. She was thinner, more fragile in appearance than she had been before, but the dark hair she presently wore swept softly to the top of her head gleamed with health, her light eyes were bright and clear, and the blush on her cheeks bespoke a recuperation that was almost complete.

She was beautiful.

A beautiful bride.

Cal drew Pru closer against his side as they approached the small, fenced-in plot of ground. She leaned subtly against him, the hem of her simple white wedding gown sweeping the ground as they walked. He had insisted they be married as soon as they could, and the ceremony had taken place in the parlor of the Rocky W ranch house only an hour earlier, with Lowell's Reverend Aims officiating and wellwishers attending. He had insisted that she wear white, despite Pru's uncertainty as to the color—because to him, the event deserved no lesser color; because they had come so close to losing each other before their lives together had even begun; because this day was the first day of the many upon many they would share; and because . . . because he loved her.

The wedding had been small, the guest list limited to Doc Maggie, who attended with an outlandish grin; Larry, Josh, and Winston, who afforded the occasion all the spit and polish they could manage; Mitch, Big John, and Randy, from the Texas Star ranch, who were rather solemn; and a few locals from town, including a beaming Agnes Bower and her husband Harvey.

Jeremy had stood proudly in a place of honor beside his mother, his suit pressed, his hair slicked back for the occasion, and his face wreathed in smiles.

Notably absent from the festivities were Taylor Star, Cal's only brother, for whom he knew no address, and Buck and Celeste Star, who had chosen to ignore his invitation.

Cal and Pru had left the reception Doc Maggie had arranged at the ranch house in order to make an important visit that Cal felt could not be overlooked. Now, as Pru and he looked at the two headstones standing side by side on the Texas Star knoll, he took a deep breath and strove for control of the emotions rising within him.

His strong features tenuously composed, Cal said aloud to the images so vivid in his mind, "Ma . . . Bonnie . . . I want you to meet my wife, Pru. I needed to come here today so I could share the day with you and let you both know that Pru's made me happier than I ever thought I could be again." He paused as his voice thickened, then added, "I wanted you to know, too, that whatever the future holds, I'll never forget you."

Cal swallowed past the lump in his throat as Pru drew away from his side unexpectedly and placed her small bridal bouquet of wildflowers between the stones. Her eyes were bright with unshed tears when she turned back to him and said, "I need to say something to your mother and sister, too, Cal; but, if you don't mind, I'll speak the words directly to you."

Emotion filled Pru's voice as she said, "I want these two people you love to understand that they needn't worry about you anymore. I want them to hear my promise to live with you, work beside you, and love you all the days of my life. I want them to know that your happiness is my happiness, and whatever darknesses face us, we'll overcome them together. Together, Cal, for the rest of our lives."

Pru heard Cal's whispered words of love as he clutched her close, and she breathed them in joyfully. They had come so far from that first day when she raised her shotgun against the big stranger who glowered down at her from horseback.

In truth, she hadn't expected for a moment that she'd end up in his arms.

Their love was a gift.

Pru raised her mouth for Cal's tender kiss.

She accepted the gift gladly.

Oh, yes—with all her heart—she surely did.

Standing unseen in a forested glade nearby, Buck watched the bridal couple as they drew back from each other's arms at last. They paused a moment longer beside the solitary graves before turning toward their buckboard.

Buck maintained his silence as Cal swung his bride up onto the seat, took his place beside her, and snapped the conveyance into motion.

He waited only until the buckboard had slipped

from sight before walking to the spot where the couple had lingered. He stared down at the bouquet lying between the twin gravestones.

His expression unchanged, he finally turned and walked away.

Epilogue

Have you forgotten Bonnie?
It is time to go home.

The fading rays of sunset shone on the sheet of paper where the two lines of cold reproach were once again transcribed. The ink was barely dry when the paper was folded, then stuffed into an envelope and appropriately addressed.

The question was harshly posed.

The writer knew it would bring about the desired results in time.

. . . And that patience had its own rewards.

Water for Elephants

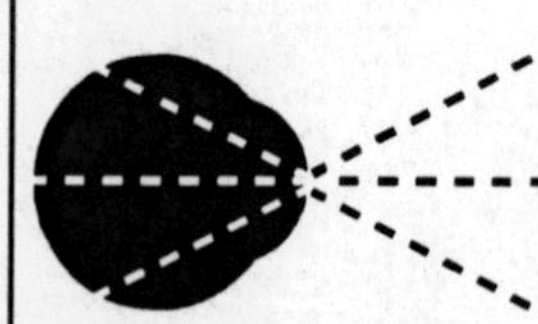

This Large Print Book carries the Seal of Approval of N.A.V.H.